Frankie and the Secret

Also by Thomas L. Tedrow

Missouri Homestead
Children of Promise
Good Neighbors
Home to the Prairie
The World's Fair
Mountain Miracle
The Great Debate
Land of Promise
The Younguns of Mansfield
Frankie and the Secret
The Circus Escape
The Legend of the Missouri Mud Monster
Long Road Back
Up and Over the Rainbow
Mountain Ark
Hills of Gold

Dorothy—Return to Oz
Grizzly Adams & Kodiak Jack

The Younguns/Book Two

Frankie and the Secret

Thomas L. Tedrow

THOMAS NELSON PUBLISHERS
Nashville • Atlanta • London • Vancouver

Published in Nashville, Tennessee, by Thomas Nelson, Inc., Publishers, and distributed in Canada by Word Communications, Ltd., Richmond, British Columbia, and in the United Kingdom by Word (UK), Ltd., Milton Keynes, England.

While this book is fiction, it retains the historical integrity and general history of turn-of-the-century America. Any references to specific events, real people, or real places are intended only to give the fiction a setting in historical reality. Names, characters, and incidents are either the product of the author's imagination or are used fictitiously, and their resemblance, if any, to real-life counterparts is purely coincidental.

Library of Congress Cataloging-in-Publication Data

Tedrow, Thomas L.
     Frankie and the secret / Thomas L. Tedrow.
          p.   cm. — (The Younguns ; bk. 2)
     Summary: Frankie, a retarded twenty-five-year-old, knows who's been burning barns in Mansfield, Missouri, during the summer of 1907, but he was sworn to secrecy.
     ISBN 0-8407-4133-2 (pb)
     [1. Secrets—Fiction. 2. Child abuse—Fiction. 3. Father and child—Fiction. 4. Mentally handicapped—Fiction.] I. Title. II. Series: Tedrow, Thomas L. Younguns ; bk. 2.
PZ7.T227Fr   1996
[Fic]—dc20   95-20461
                                                                                      CIP
                                                                                       AC

Printed in the United States of America

1 2 3 4 5 6 7 - 02 01 00 99 98 97 96

To my family. Yesterday, today, forever.

Contents

1

Ghosts of the Past

❖

Rev. Thomas Youngun, the middle-aged, underpaid, Methodist minister of Mansfield, stood on his front porch watching the heat lightning explode like fireworks over the darkening Ozarks. The planks creaked under his weight.

A hot, humid blanket of warm June air hung over the late afternoon sky. Thunder boomed in the distance. The summer of 1907 had descended on Mansfield, Missouri, with a vengeance.

A thunderclap, so loud that it shook the rafters, broke overhead. Rev. Youngun grabbed onto the porch railing to steady himself.

Ratz, the stray cat the Youngun children had adopted, got so scared that he coughed up a hair ball. The cat meowed and moved forward to rub against Rev. Youngun's leg.

He looked down and saw the twin green eyes shining up at him. He started to reach down and stroke the purring cat, then saw the hair ball.

"Oh, Ratz," Rev. Youngun said, kicking the mess over the side of the porch. The cat looked up, meowed, then walked slowly into the house.

Inside, Beezer the parrot squawked, "Bad cat! Bad cat!"

Why did I let them keep so many pets? he wondered. *They've got Dangit, Ratz, Crab Apple the mule, Bashful the fainting goat, T.R. the turkey, Bessie the pig . . .* Thunder boomed overhead, breaking his concentration.

Where are *those kids?* he thought, looking toward the barn.

"Larry, Terry, Sherry. Time for supper," he shouted. No one answered.

All he heard was silence. *Wish the kids would come just once on time,* he thought.

He called out their names again, but didn't get an answer. *I guess they're down at that fort they built.*

He took a deep breath and let it out slowly, then shivered for no reason at all as a bolt of lightning struck the tip of Devil's Ridge. *Wish they hadn't named that ridge Devil's Ridge. Always makes me think bad things are coming.*

Then he thought about the fort where the children seemed to spend all their waking hours. *Don't like where they built the fort. Don't like it one bit at all,* he thought, going back into the kitchen to check on the dinner.

Raising three children by himself had been no easy task. Disciplining their wild streak made the task even harder. But being a widower, life had left him with no choice in the matter.

When his wife, Norma, had died from the fever five years before, Rev. Youngun thought that his life had ended. But looking at the faces of his three children, he knew that he had to carry on.

He stopped in the parlor and looked at the picture of Norma that sat on the table next to his rickety reading chair. *It's been five years, Norma. Five years. I wish you were here. You always had everything under control.*

On the wall behind the chair was the picture of Larry, Terry, and Sherry taken at Easter. *Norma, you'd be proud of our children. Larry's a handsome ten-year-old boy. And Terry, why he's a seven-year-old redheaded bundle of energy and . . .* he paused, looking at the picture of Sherry.

And Sherry, she's the spitting image of you, Norma. Only five years old, and she's already a little lady. She's got your charm and stubbornness. I see you in her more every day.

He sniffed at the liver cooking in the kitchen and then heard a knock at the back kitchen door. "Rev. Youngun, you home?"

Rev. Youngun smiled and walked toward the kitchen. "Yes I am, Eulla Mae," he called out, recognizing the voice of his neighbor.

The screen door creaked open as she entered. "Got some fresh carrots for you." She smiled, sniffing the air. She sniffed again, a grin breaking across her face. "They'll go good with that liver you're cookin'."

Rev. Youngun looked at the big, muscular woman and shook his head. "You're always doing too much for this family," he said.

Eulla Mae peeked at the liver in the frying pan. "I just get to worryin' 'bout those three kids not havin' a momma to make sure they're eatin' right and . . ."

Rev. Youngun smiled. "And with you watching over them, they're going to be all right."

Eulla Mae smiled, shaking her head. Her ebony cheeks showed the hint of a blush. She put the carrots next to the sink-tub and began pumping the water.

"Just wash these carrots and peel 'em. Then slice 'em and boil 'em. They're good for the kids, and I know they'll love 'em."

"I hope you're right." He smiled hopefully, knowing how much he had hated cooked carrots when he was little.

"Believe me," Eulla Mae said, "all kids will eat carrots if you just tell them how good they're for you."

"And since I know *that's* not true, I just hope they eat the liver." He sighed.

She laughed. "Out of these carrots will come miracles."

"Amen." He followed Eulla Mae's pointing finger to the wall clock.

"Where are them rascals anyway?" she asked.

Rev. Youngun peeked out through the small half-curtain above the sink-tub. "They've built themselves a fort and have been practically living over there."

"A fort?" she asked, pulling off the green stalks from the carrots.

Rev. Youngun nodded. "They call it Fort Mansfield."

Eulla Mae chuckled. "Them kids sure have good imaginations."

Thunder boomed in the distance. "I just wish they'd built it closer to home," he said, looking out the window again.

"Where'd they build it?" she asked.

"Up on the old Sutherland homestead."

Eulla Mae put the carrots down and looked Rev. Youngun in the eyes. She thought of the two upright headstones which marked the remains of Jack Sutherland and his wife. All she could do was shake her head and exclaim, "Where the fire monster lived? You shouldn't let them kids play around up there!"

She paused, then mumbled something, turning away.

"What did you say?" he asked.

"Hope the Lord stays by their side up there."

"They'll be all right," he said, trying to reassure her.

But Eulla Mae was a constant worrier. "Bad things might happen to them," she said, holding onto his gaze. Pounding thunder echoed behind her last word, as if to drive the point home.

He waited until the thunder had died out. "I didn't find out where they'd built it until it was too late. Sheriff said it was all right since Michael Sutherland's never gonna get out of prison and . . ."

She shook her head. "It ain't safe to be playin' games when that crazy barn burner's ghost is probably still walking the hills and . . ."

"Eulla Mae," he said, shaking his head, "what am I going to do with you?"

She continued as if she hadn't heard. "Sometimes kids don't come back from the woods. Some say they get lost, but I think . . ."

He interrupted her. "And I think you're getting carried away."

"I can feel the Lord telling me that they shouldn't be up there."

"Oh Eulla Mae," he said, wanting to drop the subject.

"I wouldn't let my kids build a fort where a crazy man and his crazy son once lived."

"But that's all in the past," Rev. Youngun said.

Lightning cracked over the ravine behind the house. Eulla Mae looked out the rectangular window at the flashing sky.

"The past is never far behind," she said, shivering. "It's always just a memory away from comin' back again." Rev. Youngun laughed but she waved him off. "It's true! It was a summer like this five years ago when that Jamie Johnson got burned up in her father's barn."

For a moment, Rev. Youngun considered the tragic story. Eulla Mae continued, "I know Norma wouldn't have let them kids play 'round up there. Mommas know better than poppas 'bout such things."

"Oh Eulla Mae. They're just kids having fun and . . ."

"You might be a man of the cloth, but that don't mean you're always right." She dried her hands and stood at the back door. Rev. Youngun was silent.

"Well," she said, wiping off her hands, "I got to get back and fix Maurice his dinner. He's probably pickin' clean the chicken I got simmering."

Glad to change the subject, Rev. Youngun asked, "When are you leavin' for that vacation Maurice keeps talkin' about?"

Eulla Mae shook her head. "Lord knows that man's gonna wear out that vacation he's talkin' 'bout so much."

Rev. Youngun grinned. "From what he told me, it sounds like that cabin you're going to is heaven on Earth."

"I hope so." She sighed, opening the door.

"Thanks for the carrots," Rev. Youngun said. "I'm sure the kids will love them."

Eulla Mae closed her eyes, praying silently for a moment. "I'll tell Maurice to go get the kids," she said with a serious look on her face when she opened her eyes. "If you're not worried 'bout them, I am."

"I don't want to impose on Maurice."

"The old Sutherland place is up our way. Maurice won't mind."

Rev. Youngun looked out the window. "I'll just go call them again. It's getting dark."

"They won't hear you. They're too far away. Let Maurice call them for you."

Suddenly, a long, jagged bolt of lightning cracked across the sky, catching them both off guard. Eulla Mae wrapped her arms around her waist trying to ward off a chill. "Bet that Michael Sutherland's sittin' in jail right now, thinkin' 'bout the night he burned that Johnson girl," she said quietly.

"Terrible thing that was," Rev. Youngun said. "Just terrible."

"I think I'd rather be dead than burned up like that," she said, feeling goose bumps crawl up her arm.

"Don't say that, Eulla Mae," he said, but understanding why she'd said it. *In a way Jamie's life did end the day of that fire,* he thought.

A moment passed before they spoke again. Then Eulla Mae looked toward Devil's Ridge and said, "Can't help but worryin' 'bout that man."

"Who?"

"Michael Sutherland!" she exclaimed.

"But he's in jail."

Eulla Mae looked at Rev. Youngun. When she spoke, her words were carefully chosen. "But his thoughts are here . . . I can feel it in my bones. In my bones," she said, closing the door behind her.

After Eulla Mae had left, Dangit the dog came up to the back door whining for food. "Go get the kids," Rev. Youngun said, but the dog just sat there, wagging his tail.

From the frying pan Rev. Youngun cut off a small piece of liver and left it on a napkin to cool. "I'll give you this treat if you take this to the children," he said, writing out "Come home now," on a piece of paper.

Dangit sat up and yipped agreement. Rev. Youngun gave him the liver, then rolled up the note and put it under his collar. "Go give that to Larry. Hurry up now," he said.

Dangit jumped off the porch and headed toward Devil's Ridge. He knew where the children were and raced to beat the darkness that was coming on fast.

2

Fort Mansfield

❖

Larry, Terry, and Sherry Youngun had lost track of the day and were still playing at their fort. Drenched with sweat from running up and down the ridges, they'd raced up the dried-up streambed and were now reconnoitering back at the fort.

They had found the perfect place behind Devil's Ridge on the old Sutherland homestead. Even though on one side there was a burned-out home where only a chimney stood, and the graves of Jack and Caroline Sutherland were on the other side, to the Younguns it was the perfect place. It was like a kids' kingdom in the middle of the forest, awash with honeysuckle, wild blackberries, cherries, and Indian legends. The trees took on wild shapes in their imagination, and the curved rocks in the ravines became dinosaur ribs and bones.

They called it Fort Mansfield and convinced themselves that they were battling on ground that no human foot had ever walked on, overlooking the cans and bottles left by hunters. It was a place without parents, without teachers. A place where kids ruled and made the rules. Where they weren't told to act their age or to grow up. They were what they wanted to be when they wanted to be it.

Except for Sherry, they wore long pants to protect their legs from the thorns and snakes. They arrived at the fort each day like pioneers who'd just made it through a primeval forest. They always brought with them something to add to the fort, sometimes a stick or log that they'd found along the trail to add to the walls. The dirt, brush, and wood makeshift structure was something they worked on every day after chores. It was better than any real fort could ever have been because they'd built it themselves. And for a short moment in time, they were soldiers.

They called themselves Confederate soldiers and refought the Civil War every afternoon, taking the names of the South's famous generals. Larry was the leader by age and size. But Terry contested him each step of the way, with Sherry usually siding with Larry against her redheaded brother.

Their battles were fought according to strict time schedules, with victory declared each evening before supper. But tonight they were running late, and Terry Younggun leaned against the dirt and brush wall of the fort as he waited for the return of scouts Cubby George and Frankie Frank.

The sun's dying rays highlighted his auburn hair, which the gnats were swarming around. Terry swatted them away. *Wish I knew why these stupid bugs were attracted to ears and eyeballs.*

He dug three dead ones out of one ear and four out of the other. Usually by the late afternoon when the air cooled off, the gnats faded away, but for some reason today they were still going strong.

He marched around trying to shake the bugs off. "Wish I was home suckin' on a lollipop," Terry grumbled as he sat down.

Though he was supposed to be looking out for Yankee troops, all he could think about was candy. *Wish I had a pocketful of sweets,* he sighed, upset that his candy stash was empty.

He could feel a sugar fit coming on and tried to block out the thought. But it didn't do any good.

Everywhere he looked, he saw sweets. The dying red sun looked like a gumdrop. The clouds looked like cotton candy. The trees looked like licorice sticks, and Devil's Ridge looked like a giant cookie. Even the hooting owl in the distance seemed to be calling out the word *cookie.*

Wish I had me a cookie, he thought, licking his lips. Sherry walked by carrying one of their wounded soldiers. "That dolly dead yet?"

"Nope, I'm gonna save him." She grinned.

"Got any candy?"

"Left my gumdrops at home."

"See anything?" Larry called from the other side of the fort.

Terry groaned and looked around. "Naw, nothin' out this way." *Wish she woulda brought 'em. I need gumdrops bad.*

As hard as he tried, he couldn't concentrate on soldiering. All he could think about was the candy in Bedal's General Store. There was everything a kid could want. The only problem was that Terry didn't have any money. *Wish we were attacking Bedal's candy counter. That'd be a battle worth fightin'.*

In his mind he saw himself rushing in with his stick rifle shouting, "Give me all your candy, you Yankee."

I'd just sit there and stuff my mouth with chocolate until it oozed out. Then I'd carry fifty pounds of gumdrops to my room and eat a pound every night 'fore I went to sleep.

"Keep an eye out. Yankees always attack at dusk," Larry said, swatting a firefly and gnats from his thick, blond hair.

Terry shook his head. "Tomorrow, let's play share-the-allowance and go down and buy some candy."

"I told you not to spend all your money," Larry said. "Always save a penny for a rainy day."

"Penny this," Terry mumbled.

"What did you say?" Larry shouted.

"Penny for your thoughts," Terry said, not wanting to upset his brother.

"Watch out for sneaky Yankees—that's what I'm thinkin' 'bout."

The fragrance of wild cherries floated across the fort. Terry started to talk about candy again but stopped when his gaze rested on the two heavily mottled headstones. Someone had knocked a chunk off the top of Jack Sutherland's tablet, which gave it an odd, notched looked.

"Dead men don't tell tales . . . do they, Larry?" he asked.

Larry looked at the graves and felt delicious creeps run up his arms. "Depends if you believe in ghosts or not."

All Terry could do was shiver and turn away, wishing the graves weren't so close to the fort. He tried to shrug off the goose bumps that raced up his spine, but couldn't.

3

Son of a Barn Burner

❖

Michael Sutherland, the last person to live in the Sutherland house before it was burned down, was thinking about Mansfield, about his old house, not knowing that the Younguns had built a fort on his property.

The lightning and thunder that cracked and boomed over the Missouri State Prison seemed to call out to him to remember that summer past when another fire had changed his life.

It's nearing the Fourth of July—the fifth anniversary of the fire. The fire that took my girl Jamie from me.

Listening to the crack and crackle of the thunder over the birch and pine trees from his cell, he could almost feel the tingle of the lightning rods, could feel how his house used to shake with the thunderclaps. In his mind he remembered the lightning fires that used to catch in the pines. How they prayed for rain to follow the lightning so the woods would not burn up.

Then he thought about his father, Jack Sutherland, the notorious barn burner who had ignited a path of death and destruction through the Ozarks. *He went crazy after Momma died. He wanted to blame everyone for her dying.*

Though his father had been captured and hanged a decade ago, he still seemed to have a hold on his son's soul. Like a moth's attraction to flame, Michael Sutherland was drawn to thoughts of his father. It was as if his father's memory stalked his every step. A memory that always seemed to spring to life at the sound of lightning and thunder.

Auntie Gee said lightning was an omen. Said it was like my daddy's calling card. Said that like a night moth that flies during the day, it's always an omen of bad things to come.

For a brief moment Michael Sutherland thought about the woman who'd reluctantly taken him in after his father was hanged for being a barn burner. He remembered her favorite saying: The ways of the Lord are mysterious.

Said she saw my father in me every day. Would never explain. Just kept her distance. Treated me like I was some wharf rat who might bite her.

Thinking about his father's sister, who seemed old beyond her years, made him sad. She'd never liked him.

She treated me just like the rest of the town did. Like an outcast. Like a stray dog who's messin' up your trash. They all called me "son of a barn burner" and just left me to fend for myself. Sutherland shook his head, thinking about the odd jobs he had worked to survive. How he kept to himself, trying not to cause any problems. *That's why I moved back to my family's house as soon as I was old enough to be on my own.*

But Jamie changed my life . . . she sure did. The memory of meeting the new girl in town made him gulp. Thinking about her always did.

Though she wasn't a beauty, to Michael Sutherland Jamie was the most beautiful person in the world. She accepted him as a person and didn't care what others said about him or what his father had done.

I just couldn't stay away from her. Wanted to be by her side every waking moment. Just couldn't stop touchin' on her . . . holdin' her hand . . . couldn't wait to touch her lips.

He looked at the wall like he was seeing into the past. *And we were going to get married. Have children. Jamie and me. We were going to be together until death do us part.*

His body tensed. With a slow, deliberate motion, Sutherland began rocking back and forth, clenching his fists.

I didn't burn her. I didn't set the fire. Her daddy lied, but no one would believe the son of a barn burner. They sent me to jail for life for somethin' I didn't do.

He hit his fist into his palm over and over. *I told 'em I was innocent, but they all wanted to see me hang. They listened to Jamie's daddy lie on the stand. Called him a hero for saving her life.*

He spit into the corner. *Hero! When I came back she was already burned up. He claimed he pulled her from the fire, but he didn't have no burn marks on him hardly at all.*

Jamie. If she hadn't been knocked unconscious by the falling beam, she'd have told what really happened. I wasn't even there when the fire started.

His eyes rimmed with tears. *I wish I could see her. I wish I could hold her again. Don't care what her face looks like.*

He had heard that she'd become a recluse after the fire. That she sat in her rocker in the dark house, waiting out the daylight for darkness because she didn't want her face to be seen.

Her beauty's in her soul. I always told her that. She wasn't the prettiest girl in the town, but Lord, she had beauty inside her that no one else could match.

While the lightning and thunder battled overhead, Sutherland was back in Mansfield in his mind. Back to the days before the trial. When he was happy for the first time in his life.

I gotta get back there. Got to prove I didn't burn her. Got to make the town see that I'm not like my daddy.

The people of Mansfield wanted to forget about Michael Sutherland. When they sent him to prison, most of them did just that.

But Mansfield never left Sutherland's mind. He was determined to get back there . . . any way he could.

4

Enemy Soldier Comin'

❖

Something moved in the bushes behind the burned-out Sutherland house. Larry peered into the last light of day, trying to find it again.

"Did you see anythin'?" he asked his brother.

Terry shook his head. "Nothin' but nothin' out there."

Larry wasn't sure and had a thought that was strong enough to worry the warts off a frog. *I hope it's not Missouri Poole sneakin' up again,* he thought. *I don't want her jumpin' on me again.*

Missouri, the pretty hill girl who had a crush on Larry, had vowed to kiss him before the summer was out. Said she had itchy lips which only Larry could scratch. And Larry knew she was bulldog stubborn.

Ever since she'd jumped out at him when he was walking in town, putting her arms around him and trying to kiss his lips, he'd been afraid of her.

If I see Missouri comin' out, I might just have to shoot, he thought, shaking his head at the chilly thought. *Ain't gonna let no girl kiss me if I don't wanna.*

He couldn't understand why he got the chills thinking about it or why he felt attracted to her. *Why'd God have to give girls itchy lips anyhow?*

"General Jackson," Terry called out, using his brother's soldier name, "I think I see some cookies are out there."

Larry turned with a questioning look. "Some what?"

Terry coughed. "Er, I think I see . . ." He peered out again. "Enemy soldier comin'!"

Larry looked over the dirt embankment they'd put up near the ruins of the Sutherland homestead, trying to see what his brother was pointing to in the twilight.

"I don't see nothin'," he said.

"Right there," Terry pointed. "Where them gumdrop lookin' rocks are."

"Use soldier talk," Larry said, disgusted.

Then Larry saw the shape in the bushes. Something was definitely there. "You're right, General Stuart," Larry answered, using Terry's soldier name. "Sound the battle cry."

Terry let out his best rebel yell, then shouted, "Yankees attackin'!"

Larry tapped his stick rifle on top of the fort's hospital. "General Barton," he shouted to his sister, "blow out the candle and come grab a weapon!"

Sherry crawled out from the pine bough lean-to they'd made for their headquarters. "What's wrong?" she cried, nervously clutching her dolly as thunder boomed.

Sherry was Fort Mansfield's chief nurse and only nurse. She went by the war name General Clara Barton after the famous nurse. Her dollies served as the battle wounded.

Terry pointed over the dirt wall as thunder pounded overhead. "Enemy. Hear their cannon?" he asked. "They're hidin' out there in them bushes waitin' to drop mortar shells on us."

"Where?" she whispered, looking over the wall with one eye closed.

"Twenty yards that away," Terry nodded.

"Up where?"

"Up near the Yankee graves," he said, pointing toward the graves of Jack and Caroline Sutherland.

"Can they get through?" Sherry asked, worried more about the graves than about the imaginary Yankee troops they were always fighting.

"Naw," Terry said, shaking his head. "We've built enough traps, holes, and trip ropes to stop the entire durn Yankee army."

Sherry looked out again, feeling better. "No Yankee will get in here," she said to herself.

"And even if they do," Terry said, puffing his chest, "any Johnny Reb worth his salt can stand blindfolded and hog-tied and still lick ten Yankees." He patted the walls that he'd help build. "Fort Mansfield is what the Confederates needed. Had this and they'd have won the war."

"What war?" Sherry asked.

"The Civil War, you dummy."

"What was the war about?" Sherry wondered.

"How the heck should I know? War is just war." Terry shrugged. "Don't ask so many dumb questions. It's just a game."

"Yoo-hoo," came a familiar girl's voice from the woods.

"Halt!" Terry shouted.

Larry ducked and crawled over to Terry. "Is that Missouri?"

Terry smiled. "Got you a girlfriend, don't ya?"

"Yoo-hoo, sugar face, are you there?" Missouri Poole called.

"Sugar face?" Terry snickered.

"Hush," Larry whispered. "Don't tell her I'm here."

"Larry, are you there?" Missouri shouted.

Terry looked at his brother. "You want me to lie?"

"No," Larry said, feeling like a trapped rabbit, "just tell her that you don't see me around."

"But I do," Terry said.

"And now you don't," Larry whispered, crawling into one of the tunnels they'd dug out.

Missouri came through the bushes. "Terry Youngun, is your brother here or not?"

Terry looked around. "Nope, don't see him."

Missouri eyed him. "Are you telling me a fib?"

Terry shook his head. "I said, I don't see him." Missouri started forward, but Terry raised his stick rifle. "Don't come no further."

Missouri stopped. "You're mighty brave for a little squirrel."

"This is Fort Mansfield and no girls allowed."

Sherry stood up from the makeshift hospital lean-to. "I'm a girl!"

Terry gave her a disgusted look. "You're just my sister."

Missouri took three steps forward. "I'm comin' in."

Terry saw where she was standing. "Take one more step, and you'll fall into the deepest hole you've ever seen."

Missouri stepped back, looking down at the branches which did seem to be covering something. "How do I get in?"

"You don't," Terry said, raising his stick rifle. "Step in that hole, and you'll come out in China. Take two steps thataway, and you'll land in a pit full of girl-eatin' snakes."

"You're pullin' my leg," she said, looking around.

"No. And we got ourselves a trapped Skunk Ape over yonder that'll do more than pull your foot."

"A Skunk Ape?" she exclaimed.

Larry growled from his hiding place. "Hear that?" Terry asked. "Sounds like it wants to eat you."

Missouri waved to Sherry and asked, "Sherry, is Larry around there?"

Sherry looked around, then shook her head. "He was here a little while ago."

Missouri said, "It's gettin' dark and I gotta go. You tell that brother of yours that I walked all the way up here from town to get me a kiss."

"You give me a penny if I go find him?" Terry asked.

Larry whispered to Terry from the tunnel, "Don't tell. I'll give you a nickel."

Missouri reached into her pocket and pulled out a shiny penny. "Here's your penny. Now tell me where he is."

Terry shook his head. "Price just went up to a dime."

Missouri shrugged. "All I got is a penny."

"Well," Terry said, "looks like you'll just have to go on home without a kiss."

"You tell Larry that I'm gonna kiss him before the summer's out."

Terry smiled. "Ever thought 'bout kissin' a cat or a dog or somethin' worth kissin'?"

"Terry Youngun," Missouri said, "you ever thought that I might pay my sister Georgia to come kiss you till you suffocate?"

Terry's eyes went wide. *Georgia looks like a cross between a weasel and a warthog.*

He shivered thinking about how weird Georgia was. *Be like the kiss of death. I'd have to burn off my lips . . . heck, cut 'em off and bury 'em.*

"You hear me, Terry Youngun?" she asked loudly. "You want me to have Georgia come hunting you down?"

Terry was shocked with horror. He didn't like girls much anyway, and he sure didn't like Georgia Poole. *Be like havin' a dead cat tryin' to smooch you.*

He thought about the spider he'd tried to stick down Georgia's dress on the last day of school and how hard she'd hit him. For the rest of the day she used his head as a target for her spitballs.

I don't want to get her mad at me. He still worried about closing his eyes in church since she had lately been sitting behind him.

"I asked you a question," Missouri shouted. "You want me to get Georgia on you?"

"Please don't do that, Missouri."

"I'll protect you," Larry whispered.

"You and who else?" Terry answered from the side of his mouth.

"Guess I'll go home to get Georgia then," Missouri said.

"No don't," Terry pleaded. His heart was pounding. He could feel his skin crawl.

"I swear I'll keep you safe," Larry whispered.

"Right as rain," Terry said sarcastically. He kicked some dirt into the tunnel to shut his brother up.

Missouri took two steps then stopped. "Just don't ever lie to me, or Georgia will be comin' 'round to kiss on your face." She paused for emphasis. "You understand?"

"Yup, no problem. If I see my brother, you'll be the first to know. Just tell your sister to stay home."

Missouri looked at Terry, then grinned broadly. "Might be fun to have a double weddin'. You and Georgia and me and Larry."

"And it might be fun to jump off a cliff," Terry mumbled.

He watched Missouri take the path back toward town, then looked into the tunnel where his brother was hiding. "Give me the nickel."

"Don't got it with me," Larry said, crawling out. He stood up and dusted the dirt from his knees. Terry started up over the embankment. "Where you goin'?" Larry asked.

"I'm goin' to find Missouri and tell her the truth. Least she'll pay me a dime for findin' my cheapskate brother."

Larry grabbed Terry's shirt. "And I'll have to tell Georgia that you love her." He smiled deviously. "Then she could kiss your lips."

"That'd be like havin' a couple of stinky slugs crawl 'cross my face."

"I'll tell her, I swear," Larry said.

Terry stopped, then shook his head. "You owe me then."

Larry smiled. "I'll give you a nickel's worth of protection from Georgia. Now back to our positions."

"I wanna go home," Sherry said.

"We'll leave after Cubby and Frankie get back," Larry said.

Terry thought he saw something moving out in the woods.

"General Barton," Larry said to Sherry, "grab a weapon and protect the wounded."

Sherry nodded and grabbed a wood-wedge pistol from the pile they'd made. "One of them's real bad sick," she said, saluting her brother.

Larry glanced at the doll in her arms. "Let me know if we need a burial detail," he said, looking out over the wall.

The darkening sky and the two solitary Sutherland graves that stood watch over their fort gave him a quick shot of the willies. Larry tried to remember what his father had told him about Jack Sutherland, the barn burner, and his son, Michael, who'd been sent to prison.

Lightning broke across the sky, highlighted by the last rays of the sun. Larry looked at the remains of the Sutherland house and then at the graves. *Hope Cubby gets back here quick,* he thought.

Love Letters

❖

Clicking his tongue, Sutherland counted to thirty, trying to time his heartbeats. He'd found two ways of detaching himself from the horrors of prison. To escape what was bothering him.

One was through reading. He'd spent his time learning to read and write and used books as an escape. The other was through counting his heartbeats, taking his pulse and measuring his emotions as a way of getting inside his mind.

A single candle burned in the corner of his cell, lighting up what had become a personal shrine to Jamie Johnson. He'd put up drawings he made from memory of her face as it had been and the happy times they'd had together.

Sutherland looked over the letter he'd written to Jamie. Though he'd written her every week for five years without getting an answer, he had never given up hope that one day she'd understand that he hadn't harmed her.

Then he'd finally gotten a letter from her. He read it again, tears swelling his eyes:

I'm writing to ask you to never write me again. I am going to be married soon and don't want to think about the person who burned my face.

I hate you and hope you rot in jail as you deserve. My father was right about barn burners' sons: they are like their fathers.

I have destroyed all your letters and will never open another. Do not write again. I am finally happy with someone who loves me, no matter what my face looks like.

Jamie Johnson

Oh Jamie, he thought, *I never did nothin' to hurt you. I wish it was me that was burned, not you.*

Sutherland looked over the letter he was sending to her in response. He'd worked on the ending of the letter over and over and read it again by the light of the flickering candle:

> I got your letter about you getting married. Even though you asked me to never write you again, I have to send you one more, even if it turns out to be the last one you ever read from me.
>
> I'm happy that you found someone who loves you. I hope you are happy with the man you are going to marry. He is very lucky.
>
> I never did nothing to hurt you. I didn't set the fire. Your father lied. I have told you that in every letter, but I guess you won't believe me.
>
> I wish I could come back there and tell you all of this. That it never mattered what your face looks or looked like. I loved you for you, and you loved me for me.
>
> I will always love you with all my heart, and you are the only person who ever loved me.
>
> Michael

Thunder broke his concentration. Sutherland sealed the letter and tossed it toward the letter box outside his cell. He stretched, touching the low ceiling, then sat on the edge of his bunk, moving his feet in circles. Counting his heartbeats, he watched the lightning.

Memories of the springs, caves, rivers, and hollows flooded over him. Sounds of the woods filled his ears. He thought of Jamie.

It was a summer night just like this. I'd been out sittin' on the bluff, watchin' the lightning, when I went to see Jamie. His throat got dry at the memory. *I just wanted to talk sense into her father. Tell him we wanted to get married. Show him the locket.*

But her father was drinking again. Didn't like me comin' round. Kept tryin' to keep me from his daughter.

She loved me for me. She knew the hurts inside me and made me feel like my brains were okay. That was somethin' that nobody else ever did.

Sutherland squeezed his eyes shut to block out the thunder that was disturbing his memories. *Lost my girl because of who my daddy was.*

Sutherland slowly pounded his head against the cell wall. *Don't want to think about Daddy. Don't want to think about him. Want to think about the locket. Need to sit in my Secret Tree. Need to touch Jamie's locket again.*

His cell-mate sat up. "You tryin' to kill yourself?" he asked. "Tomorrow, I'm goin' to get the warden to move me out of this nut cell."

With a glare at Sutherland, the convict pulled the folded dirty towel he used for a pillow over his head, grunting something about wackos. Sutherland waited until he'd fallen back asleep before he slipped back into the forests of the Ozarks in his mind.

He was back watching his father burn barns and homes. Running and hiding from the law. His father's hand clamped over his mouth so he wouldn't shout out. It all came back to haunt him again.

The bad memories of his father's capture, his trial, and watching him being marched to the gallows were worse than the prison walls that held him.

Thoughts about his Auntie Gee who'd reluctantly taken him in. About the lectures of being the bad seed of a bad seed and how he was cursed. Of moving back to his father's house when he got old enough because it was his only real home—bad as it was. Of hiding Jamie's locket in the secret hole in the fireplace, just in time, before he was arrested for setting the barn fire.

It all made his head throb. Sutherland watched the lightning break up the night sky, wishing it would break down the prison walls. He sat perfectly still, in a cool, detached way.

For Michael Sutherland, prison was just another page in his unhappy life. Though shunned as the son of Jack Sutherland, the real torment had been the abuse he'd suffered as a child. It was the secret pain that could have twisted his mind but instead had driven him into his own private world where he could escape.

It was the isolation of the Ozarks that had kept secret the pains of Michael's youth, and the isolation that kept Jack Sutherland from the law while he burned valuable property. He knew the woods and invisible trails by which he escaped and then returned to burn again and again.

But the Ozarks were also what had kept Michael Sutherland alive. The woods seemed to hold out invisible arms which had soothed the hurt and pain of the young boy. It was the only comfort the boy could find.

He thought about it now in his prison cell. He thought about how he'd run from his father's abuse, down the secret paths that even his father didn't know. Under the logs where he'd burrowed hollows like a rabbit. Inside caves he clung to the walls like a bat, always hoping that his father wouldn't find him.

If he was lucky, he'd escape his father's wrath, then make his way to his Secret Tree. The place where he could curl up and protect himself. He'd once hidden there for three days, until his father calmed down.

After his father died, it was the place where Michael still went to think and make big decisions. Like the night he decided to go back and tell Jamie's father they were going to get married.

Need to sit in my Secret Tree, he thought, rocking back and forth on the edge of the prison bunk. *Need to find a way to stop Jamie from marryin' some other man.*

Jamie was the only person he'd ever told about what had been done to him. She made him feel good about himself like no one had ever done before.

I got to get back and see her . . . I got to tell her that I didn't do nothing to hurt her . . . got to stop her from marryin' someone else. We told each other till death do us part . . . till death do us part.

6

Jamie Johnson

❖

Jamie Johnson sat in the dark of her small house outside of Mansfield, rocking slowly, listening to the cicadas sing. She was waiting for night to come on. No one but her father had seen her face since the fire.

She looked at the letter she'd written to Michael Sutherland and wondered why he'd never answered any of her others. *He's got to know that I still love him. He's got to know that I still care,* she thought, rocking slowly back and forth.

She looked out toward the dying sun, knowing that her father would soon be coming in from the fields. They lived together, but it felt like they lived apart.

Though he'd stopped drinking and found religion after the fire, Jamie suspected it was all from a guilty conscience. She still remembered the havoc that his drinking had brought to their lives. How it was like a monster crawling out from under his skin every time liquor went down his throat.

He moved us from town to town. From every problem his drinking had caused.

Momma said Daddy claimed to have a disagreement with the lumber boss or the farm boss ... always something other than what it really was. It was always something to blame besides his drinking. Kept moving us from town to town like tumbleweeds. Always the new girl in town who couldn't have anybody around because Daddy was always drunk in his chair.

She shook her head at the memories. Of having to tell her friends that her daddy had "bad spells." That he had different illnesses.

Her jaw tensed as she tried to block out the hurts from the past that flooded over her. Not wanting to remember what she'd learned to live with. The horrible nightmare that could spring out from inside him any time he gave in to the urge to drink. Then he'd go to sleep and wouldn't wake up for a day.

We had to hide the truth. Say he was sick. Always telling his employers that he'd hurt his back or wasn't feeling well when he was too hungover to get up. Having to make excuses for why he couldn't come to the door or go to church.

And now he's religious, she thought, shaking her head. *Can't even look me in the face while he's praying. Can't even talk about what happened that night without looking down.*

The creaking rocker was the only sound in the room. *I never had any boyfriends. People didn't want their boys going with a drunk's daughter.*

Then I met Michael. Oh, Michael, why'd you have to go and get so mad? I told you we'd elope, but you wanted to do things right and ask Daddy. But he was drunk again . . .

She thought the liquor was responsible for everything that had happened to her because it had been in control at the worst of times . . . including the night the fire took her looks away.

She touched the scars on her face that the fire had left. It was the only way she could visualize what had happened because she never looked in mirrors since that one time when the bandages were removed.

I look like a monster, she thought, feeling the tears come again, even after all these years. Jamie laughed out loud. "Mirror, mirror on the wall, who's the ugliest girl of all?"

She broke down crying. *I have to think of happy times.*

Jamie closed her eyes, and for a brief moment she was free of her body. Free of the dark memories that seemed always to surround her.

She was back in the woods behind her house, kissing Michael. They had only moved to Mansfield a month before, but she and Michael Sutherland had been drawn together instantly.

She called it love at first sight. Michael called it God's miracle. But her father said they were like two moths drawn to a flame and did his best to keep them apart. He said that Michael Sutherland wasn't good enough for his daughter.

She knew about Jack Sutherland, but she couldn't condemn Michael for being his son. Jamie didn't care about the whispers in town or the drunken ravings of her father who claimed that Michael was nothing but a barn burner's son. She had her own rumors and stigma to live with.

They'd proclaimed their love for one another and shared the pain of their upbringing as if they were gifts of trust and confidence. Each helped the other. He understood the pain that her father's drinking caused, and she helped soothe the little boy inside him who'd been so hurt by his father.

The night they planned to get married was the last happy memory of her life. She always floated back to that night when she wanted to escape the scars of her face. The sticky, summer heat tonight took her back to that evening five years before, when everything seemed so wonderful . . .

She was in the barn, waiting for the horse to drop the new foal. Michael wasn't supposed to be in there alone with her, but he was.

"I love you," he whispered to her.

"I want to have lots of babies." She smiled. "Let's get married." The horse whinnied behind her.

For Michael, it was the first time in his life he'd ever felt loved. He felt wanted and needed. It was the most wonderful feeling he'd ever experienced.

"I want to do it proper, and ask your father," he said, picking up the lantern.

Jamie shook her head and took the lantern from his hand. She put it down on the stool next to the stall.

"He's not feeling well," she said, which was her way of saying that he'd already drunk too much.

"But I don't want to lose you and . . ."

She hushed him with the tip of her finger on his lips. "I'll always be yours," she whispered. "And don't you ever forget it."

"I've got a memory like an elephant," he said.

She reached behind her neck. "Here, I want you to have this."

She took off her gold locket and handed it to him. Inside the locket was the picture they had paid the photographer to take.

"Till death do us part," Jamie whispered.

"Till death do us part," he whispered back, kissing her cheek.

"I do," she smiled, pretending they were exchanging vows.

"But we're not married yet," Michael whispered.

"It's only a matter of time." She smiled, kissing his lips lightly.

"Jamie, come here," her father called out from the house. His words sounded slurred.

"You've got to go, Michael. Before he comes out to the barn," she said, squeezing his hand. The mare stepped uncomfortably from side to side.

"But your locket," he said, holding it out for her.

"You keep it. It's my way of promising that we'll get married," she said.

"But I want to take you to the fireworks in town."

Jamie looked down. "I don't think Father will let me go tonight."

"I'm gonna walk with you to the house and try to reason with him. Then I'm gonna ask him—no tell him—that we're goin' to get married."

Jamie shook her head. "Not tonight, Michael. There's a new foal coming, and with Father not feeling well, I'll have to stay and help the birthing."

"You can't save him from himself," Michael said. "And his drinkin's gonna be the ruin of us if we let it."

"Just wait until tomorrow, Michael. It'll be a better day." Her father called for her again. "You better go."

"But I want to talk to him tonight."

"Not tonight," Jamie repeated. "Do it tomorrow."

She watched as he walked toward the woods. The light from the lantern reflected off the gold chain that hung from his fingers.

As Jamie sat in the darkness of her house, she tried not to think of the fire that followed.

7

Jack's List

❖

Sherry crawled back into the fort's hospital lean-to and sat in front of her "wounded" dollies. She'd gotten used to having them hurt in every imaginary attack.

The candlelight flickered, sending dancing shadows across the faces of her dolls. "Don't die," she warned, "or Larry will bury you with the ghosts out there."

Building the fort near the burned-out ruins of the Sutherland home had been a natural thing. The burned rafters and remains of the house had been like a magnet to the local kids, drawing the Younguns and their friends. They'd picked through the remains, finding treasures that they'd taken home and hidden in their rooms. But there was one treasure that they hadn't taken home.

While poking around the stone fireplace they'd found a metal box. Inside were things they knew belonged to the Sutherlands. Things that adults would take away from them if they found out.

So the Younguns and Cubby and Frankie had made a pact not to tell anyone. The box would remain the secret of Fort Mansfield. But inside were things that they all liked to touch—especially Sherry.

Making sure no one was looking, Sherry pulled the box from under the doll blanket. Placing it next to the candle, she carefully opened it.

She lifted out the pictures of the Sutherland family. Even in the family portrait, the evil eyes of Jack Sutherland shined through.

Next, she took out the envelope that was sealed with red wax. "Wish we could open it," she whispered, holding it up to the candlelight.

There was a letter inside that she was curious about, but Larry had said that they shouldn't open it. Now Sherry moved the envelope around in the light, until she couldn't stand it anymore.

Looking around, she carefully opened the envelope. The letter inside didn't make much sense to Sherry because she could hardly read a word yet. The hastily scrawled ink on the yellowed paper was fading.

I swear by the flame of my soul that these people will burn:

Doctor
Sheriff
Undertaker
Frankie
Rev. Youngun

It was signed, "Jack Sutherland." Beside his signature was the unsteady signature of a child. Sherry had no idea that it was the name Michael Sutherland.

She looked at the list again, feeling let down. "Wonder why this was sealed?" She shrugged. She dropped the list to the ground and put the envelope back in the box.

At the bottom of the box was what she was looking for. Sherry was fascinated by the gold locket that was wrapped in oilcloth. The locket had a picture of a young man and a girl inside.

Taking it out, she put it on for a moment. It was the prettiest thing she'd ever seen. "Wish this were all mine," she whispered, feeling a tingle as she held the locket to her skin.

She popped the clasp and looked at the picture of the young man and woman. Michael Sutherland and Jamie Johnson stared back at her, frozen in time.

"I wonder who they are?" she whispered, then snapped it closed. *I'm gonna keep it. No one will ever know.* She slipped the locket under her dress.

8

Cubby and Frankie

❖

Cubby George, son of the town's doctor, saw Fort Mansfield through the trees. He turned and shouted over his shoulder, "Frankie, I'm runnin' ahead. You bring the supplies on in."

Frankie Frank, the twenty-five-year-old man-boy with the mind of a four-year-old, shouted, "Frankie's comin'."

He had a strange way of talking about himself as if he were talking about someone else. But it was all part of his slow-motioned ways.

Just four feet, eleven inches, with stubby fingers and oversized hands, Frankie was like any other kid his mental age. Only his eyes gave the impression that his mind was slower than his body.

"Watch out for the sticker bushes. They're bad up here," Cubby called. His plum-black skin glistened in the last remaining light of day.

"Okie-dokie," Frankie shouted. Then he looked around. "Frankie's scared of the dark."

"Just come on," Cubby said, tired of having to take care of his clumsy friend.

"Frankie wants to light a candle."

"No, I told you," Cubby said, stopping and staring back. "Lightin' a candle in these dry woods is dangerous."

"Frankie don't play with matches," Frankie said, mimicking his grandmother's instructions.

"That's right. And you give me those matches in your pocket when we get to the fort."

Frankie made a face that Cubby couldn't see. *Found these matches myself,* he thought. *Not playin' with 'em, just keepin' 'em.*

Cubby headed through a stand of birch trees then pushed through the bushes. He broke into the clearing around the fort. The ragged rebel flag hung limp from the makeshift pole.

"Comin' in," he shouted to the guard on duty.

Terry was thinking about Tootsie Rolls and didn't recognize Cubby in the twilight. "Halt, gumdrop."

"Gumdrop?" Cubby asked, moving forward. "What kind of soldier talk is that?"

"Er, halt, Yankee."

"Don't shoot," Cubby said. "It's me. I'm a Johnny Reb."

"Friendlies comin' in," Terry announced.

Larry opened the brush gate they'd made. Cubby ran in, wiping sweat from his face. "Where's my sword?" he asked, looking around frantically.

Larry closed the gate. "Here it is, General Lee," he said, using Cubby's soldier name. He handed him his barrel-stave sword with the carved-notch handle.

Cubby waved it in the air. "I'm ready to fight them Yankees! No one beats us Rebs."

Cubby and the Younguns really knew nothing about slavery or why the Civil War had been fought. They'd just seen the old daguerreotype photos of the Rebel leaders at the library and decided that they'd all be Confederates.

The summer before it had been cowboys and Indians, and the year before that they'd been Teddy Roosevelt's Rough Riders fighting the Spanish.

So when they'd found an old Rebel flag in the church box it made sense to become gray warriors fighting General Grant and his blue troops that summer.

"Where's General Frankie?" Larry asked.

"He's bringing in the supplies." Cubby smiled.

The dwarf-sized man-boy loped through the woods. He heard an owl hoot. "Frankie's comin'!" he shouted to the brown bird with the big eyes.

Frankie wanted to light a match because it was getting dark. He looked around nervously when he heard a low rumble of thunder. "Frankie don't play with matches," he repeated, over and over.

Frank's head was bigger than normal, but it was something that the children were used to. It was a fluke of nature that had left Frankie in a perpetual twilight world of childhood. But there was something about Frankie that everyone liked, and he was watched over carefully by all the people of Mansfield. They had even elected him honorary mayor.

Clumsily running through the small pocket prairie, Frankie waded knee-deep through the thick grass and yellow tickseed flowers, his eyes blinking faster than normal. Then he noticed that his shirt and pants were covered with burrs, briars, and seeds.

"Oh no," he moaned, looking down, "Grammie will be mad at Frankie."

He pulled at the stickers as he walked and didn't watch where he was going. Pretty soon he walked into a large prickly pear plant. "Ouch," he cried, "Frankie hurts bad."

His right hand was covered with small thorns from the cactus pads. "Frankie hates those things," he muttered, pulling them out with his stubby fingers.

Careful not to blunder into any more painful obstacles in the dying light of day, Frankie made his way along the edge of the glade. He blinked like a firefly, trying to see in the diminishing light.

In front of him, red cedar trees were quickly reclaiming the abandoned Sutherland homestead as their own. He knew that just beyond them were the two graves and his Secret Tree.

Thinking about the graves always gave Frankie the shivers. He covered his eyes, slowing down his breath as his grandmother had taught him.

"Feel better," he said, picking up a branch and swinging it around. He knocked off a load of the pungent ice blue berries from the red cedars.

Frankie came to the big hollow tree that was his secret place. *Michael said this was his Secret Tree,* Frankie thought.

From the fort he heard his name, "General Frankie, hurry up with the supplies."

"Frankie's comin'," he shouted.

Looking around to see if anyone was watching, he put the cherry branch down and edged into the narrow opening of the hollow tree. There wasn't enough light to see.

Frankie took out one of the wooden matches he had been saving. It was the only thing he'd ever hidden from his grandmother, and now he wished he hadn't told Cubby about them.

"Frankie don't play with matches," he mumbled, trying to strike the match against the inner bark of the tree. He dragged the head three times, but it still wouldn't light.

"Frankie don't play with matches," he said, looking at the match, wondering why it wouldn't light like it did for the man in town who'd dropped them.

Then he put his finger on his nose and pinched his nostrils, trying to remember the way the man had done it. Holding his breath, he concentrated as hard as he could, his eyes blinking faster and faster.

When the thought came to him, he expelled the air loudly and steadied himself on one foot, using his hand against the tree to keep from falling over. He struck the match against the bottom of his shoe and it flamed to life.

Carefully holding the match in the air, Frankie looked at what he had come to see in the secret place that Michael Sutherland had showed him. The match threw off just enough light to see the words that were carved into the inner bark:

Don't Tell Secrets

He was in the secret place that Michael had shown to Frankie and then had made him swear not to tell anyone. It was the place where Frankie had learned about keeping secrets.

"Don't show my Secret Tree to nobody," Michael had told him. "It's my secret place. It's where I used to hide from Daddy."

Frankie didn't know what to say. But something inside him made him understand the pain that Michael Sutherland felt because once Frankie had hidden in the bushes and watched Michael being beaten by his father.

Thinking of it now made him upset. Frankie felt a tremble coming on, so he worked to control his breathing.

"Frankie don't want to think 'bout bad things," he mumbled.

The match in his hand burned down to his fingertips. "Ouch!" he cried, dropping it to the ground. For a moment, the red ember tip smoldered in the leaves, then it died out.

Frankie's chest pounded and his heart raced. "Breathe one . . . breathe two . . ." Frankie repeated from memory until he calmed down.

"Frankie, hurry up! It's gettin' dark!" Cubby shouted from the fort.

Frankie slowly squeezed back out of the Secret Tree.

With the cherry branch over his arm, he marched like a soldier toward the fort. It was getting darker. He knew his grandmother would be worried about him.

"Where are you, Frankie?" Cubby shouted.

"Frankie's comin'!" he shouted back. He heard the thunder and wished he was inside with his grammie.

"You still got them matches?"

"Frankie's got matches. Don't play with matches," he answered.

9

Missouri Poole

❖

Missouri Poole ran to keep up with the last light of day. The thunder and lightning seemed to spur her on.

She was disappointed that she hadn't seen Larry, but she had the whole summer to track him down. "I know he was up there," she said, jumping over a log on the path.

Cutting through Salamander Ravine and up and over Justin's Point, she saw her farmhouse down below and slowed down her pace. A smile broke across her face.

"Can't wait till Larry and I get married." She laughed.

Though she was only ten years old, Missouri knew that Larry was the one for her. She'd known it since she first saw him at school. Sitting behind him in class, she spent the year drawing pictures of the two of them holding hands, kissing, and getting married.

All the kids had thought she was crazy when she announced it on the playground, but Missouri had the faith of the ages behind her.

"Faith will see me through," she declared.

At the large rock at the turn in the path, she stopped and climbed on top of it. She looked around, watching the darkening sky.

"Wonder if he'll carry me over the threshold?" She grinned, then frowned.

What threshold? Where we gonna live? She concentrated on the problem as she climbed down off the rock and continued toward her house. Then she came up with the answer.

"He can just move into my house," she said out loud. A bird chirped in response. "My momma can cook for the both of us, while Larry helps my daddy on the farm."

She walked on, engrossed in the thought. "We can live in my room until the first babies come, then we can build us an addition on to Daddy's house."

By the time Missouri got home, she had everything worked out except for the date. She figured that they'd get married before they turned twelve and live happily ever after.

Her sister, Georgia, was sitting on the front steps, chewing on a piece of straw. The thick glasses perched on her nose seemed to weigh her face down. Kudzo, the old hound dog, was fast asleep beside her.

"You're late," Georgia said. "Pa's mad."

"Couldn't help it," Missouri said. "I was out tryin' to find my husband to be."

Georgia shook her head. "If he's hard to find now it'll be worse later. Remember Auntie Peaches said to never marry a man who gets itchy feet at sundown."

Missouri smiled. "My Larry don't have itchy feet, but I sure do have itchy lips for him."

"Is Missouri home yet?" the voice of her father boomed out.

"I'm here, Pa," Missouri answered.

"Come on in and set the table. We've still got to have a family sing before prayers."

"Yes, Pa," Missouri said.

"Why you like boys so much?" Georgia asked, adjusting her glasses.

"One day you will too," Missouri said, "and I got a redheaded one that you can marry. We'll keep it all in the family."

Georgia shook her head. "If you're talkin' 'bout that Terry Youngun, I'd rather marry a monkey than that squirrel head," she said, watching the lightning break in the distance. "All he likes to do is pull pigtails and eat candy."

"He's not that bad." Missouri shrugged. "At least you'd have yourself a husband."

Georgia patted Kudzo. "I'd rather marry this ol' dog than that troublemaker. Last time I saw him he tried to stick a spider down my dress."

"Least it weren't a snake. Guess that means he loves you." Missouri smiled, always a believer in true love.

From inside, the big bass voice of her father that boomed like a bullfrog raised in song. "Swing low, sweet chariot, coming for to carry me home . . . come on in and sing, girls. We're going to sing our way to heaven!" he commanded.

The two girls went inside and joined in the song. "I looked over Jordan and what did I see, coming for to carry me home . . ."

"Sing louder," their father commanded. "We're almost up to heaven with our voices."

Missouri nodded, but in her mind all she could see was Larry's face. That was heaven enough for her.

10

Maurice's Dream Vacation

On the outskirts of Mansfield, Maurice Springer stood on the front porch of his house, watching the lightning. The odd-sized patch of land he'd cleared by hand was fading into the night.

Below him Sausage, his roly-poly dog that he'd saved from the animal pound, slept at his feet. The only movement the dog liked was eating, and even that tired him.

Maurice had gotten a letter from his cousin Speedy a few days ago that seemed to be the answer to his dreams. Unable to collect the ten dollars that he'd lent Speedy on his last visit to St. Louis, Maurice had written to say he'd accept a week at the Ozark cabin Speedy had bragged about instead.

Speedy had agreed for the week beginning after Independence Day. Maurice looked at the letter describing Speedy's mountain place.

"Gotta read it once more." He chuckled, lighting the lantern that hung from the ceiling. "I need that vacation."

It was all Maurice had thought about for the past few days. "Imagine, me takin' a fishin' vacation."

The smile that broke across his smooth brown face was filled with more happiness than he'd felt in a long time.

Dear Cousin Maurice:
    Some people say I'm payin' you back too much by tradin' you use of my Ozark Hollows cabin in exchange for the IOU you got of mine. It bein' all stocked with food and all. Some folks say you should give me back the ten dollar IOU and ten more!

But I feel gen-er-us and with you bein' cousins and all, I gess it's only right.

So rip up my IOU and here's the key to my Ozark cabin in heaven. The place is as pretty as a pick-ture, sittin' on Norfolk Lake that's filled with catfish and trout and cold 'nough to keep milk cold.

Just be careful and don't mess up the place. You wood not believe the use I get out of this cabin.

My regards to Eulla Mae.

Speedy Springer

Maurice held up the key and smiled. *Gonna be back to bein' a pioneer for me. I'm gonna be like Daniel Boone. Catchin' fish. Huntin'. Lyin' in the sun. Eatin' wild berries.* He chuckled again. *I bet Speedy's got a pantry full of food and smoked hams hangin' in the attic.*

Be like dyin' and goin' to heaven, he thought, picturing the cabin in his mind. *Yes sir, I probably should have paid Speedy for what he's offerin' me. That IOU's nothin' compared to what he's givin' me.*

Fireflies blinked the front yard alive. Like tiny sailors' beacons, they flew around Maurice and landed on his shirt, but he didn't seem to notice. All he was thinking about was the first real vacation of his life.

The reality of sunup to sundown work for Maurice and the rest of the Ozark farmers didn't include much time off, except for going to church and funerals. The Springer family cemetery plot, on the hill above the African Methodist Episcopal Church, bore mute testimony to the hard work that had been passed down in their family.

But Maurice had decided that if Speedy couldn't pay his debt, he'd accept the offer of using the cabin as payment. It was a chance to take a vacation with Eulla Mae, and the men from church offered to look after his farm.

Speedy said his cabin was better than eatin' corn on the cob with a lot of salt and butter. Said that the fish just jump on the hook, and everywhere you step, you're steppin' on wild berries.

Maurice licked his lips. "Berry pie. I could eat a hot piece right now," he said, rubbing his hands together.

Sausage looked up and barked. Maurice waved his hand, trying to quiet the dog. "Quiet." Sausage barked again, wiggling around. "I ain't got no food for you. All I'm talkin' 'bout is dream food."

Sausage snapped at a firefly in front of his nose. "You must think that's a flyin' piece of meat with a candle on it." Maurice chuckled.

He saw a figure come over the hill from the Younguns'. He squinted his eyes. "Eulla Mae, I thought you were inside cookin' dinner," he shouted, taking the lantern and walking out to greet her.

"Wanted to take Rev. Youngun some garden carrots. Those kids need vegetables."

Maurice shook his head. "Don't think you'll get much thanks from them kids for carrots." He kissed her cheek and gave her a hug. "I'm powerful hungry, Eulla Me."

"I got a whole chicken simmering."

"Let's eat," he said, pulling her by the hand.

Thunder and lightning hit at the same time up over Devil's Ridge. Eulla Mae shivered. "Those kids still hadn't come home yet."

Maurice shrugged. "They'll get home. They ain't gonna stay out long with all this lightning."

"That's what I'm worried 'bout," she said. "They've built some fort where they've been playin'."

"Kids do those things. They'll be all right," he said.

"But they built it up at the Sutherland place," she said, looking into his eyes. "You best go on up there and hurry them home."

Maurice let out a long sigh. "Here it's my dinnertime, and you want me to go runnin' up in the dark woods and . . ."

Eulla Mae stopped him by shaking her head. "Go on and do it. I'm worried 'bout them bein' up there after dark."

Maurice coughed, cleared his throat, then said, "You wanna come with me? We can walk and talk and . . ."

"Maurice Springer! You just hurry along up there," she said, taking the lantern from his hand.

"But I need the lantern to see, sugar bee."

"What for? You know these fields like the nose on your face."

Maurice looked around, feeling a sudden chill. "But I was born with my nose and . . ."

"And you've been tellin' me what a Daniel Boone woodsman you are," she said.

"But it's gettin' kind of dark and . . ."

Eulla Mae shook her head. "Sooner you go the sooner you'll get back."

He started forward, then stopped. "Kind of gives me the creeps, goin' up to that burned-out old place."

"Oh go on, you big ol' scaredy-cat," she said, pushing him.

"Why don't Rev. Youngun go up there himself?"

"'Cause I said you'd do it for him."

Maurice looked at Eulla Mae, then at the woods. "Them kids are always causin' me problems."

She smiled, then walked on to the house, saying over her shoulder, "Hurry up 'fore it gets totally dark. Never know what's out there."

Maurice shivered. He took two steps, then began whistling. *Wish I were down at Speedy's cabin right this instant.*

11

Speedy Springer

❖

While Maurice was thinking about Speedy, Speedy was thinking about his wallet.

Speedy looked around the card room in the back of his juke joint in
St. Louis and caught his own image in the floor-to-ceiling mirror to his
left. *What you gonna do now, Speedy my man?* he asked himself.

The gamekeeper called out the time. "Would you keep it down?"
Speedy said.

"Just doin' my job," the old man said. The gamekeeper ran his fingers
through his slicked back hair. He knew Speedy was in a tight spot, and
he was enjoying it.

Speedy looked at the man's wide, confident grin and shook his head.
Should have fired him long ago, he thought.

The heavy red-flocked wallpaper, that was intended to give off a rich,
settled look, suddenly bothered Speedy. *Looks cheap. Got to think 'bout
changin' that.*

The piano player in the next room ran up and down the keys. "Are
you playin' or foldin', Speedy?" the judge asked.

"I'm playin', I'm playin'," Speedy said.

The judge shook his head. "Then let's get on down with the game."

Speedy smiled for a moment. Then his smile evaporated.

He was faced with a good hand of cards, but no money. Even though
he dressed like a gentleman, owned the juke joint, and liked to flash cash,
Speedy was perpetually broke. Everything he had was borrowed,
hocked, or on loan. Everything, that is, except for his mountain cabin.

But Speedy was a quick thinker. He had not become the owner of a card club by having a chicken heart. His brain worked best under pressure, and when his back was to the wall he had the nerve of a bank robber and the wits of a traveling salesman.

His was a good poker hand—three queens and a pair of nines—and Speedy looked through the cigar smoke at Judge Parker and Captain Amos of the St. Louis police department, who had a big, heavy body and wide, square shoulders that gave the impression of abnormal strength. *Bet he scares the heck out of crooks,* Speedy thought absently. He looked back at his cards. *I'll win hands down,* he thought, *but I can't if I got to ante up. Wonder if I can bluff 'em this time?*

"You gonna fold, Speedy?" the judge asked, getting irritated at the wait. The judge had taken his shoes and socks off and was scratching his feet against the table leg.

Speedy looked at the cards again and put on his best poker face. *I'm down to nothin'. Not even trolley fare to get home. Guess it's time for the old cabin trick.*

"Heaven help me." He sighed. He looked at the judge and shrugged. "Guess you'll probably beat me again, Judge, but I'm just stubborn." Speedy reached into his pockets with exaggerated motions, trying to find some money.

Captain Amos shook his head. "Speedy, looks like you're out of money. How you gonna raise the pot?"

"Only God knows," Speedy said, turning his pockets inside out. He took out his handkerchief and patted his forehead, wiping the sweat from his smooth, dark face.

"You worried 'bout somethin'?" The police captain laughed.

Speedy nodded, then pulled out the deed to his Ozark Hollows mountain cabin.

"Guess I could risk my pride and joy . . . my little piece of paradise." He sighed, showing the document.

Judge Parker looked at the deed. "I've heard a lot about that place. Is it as pretty as everyone says?"

Speedy paused, wanting to answer the judge just right. He'd told so many tales about the cabin he'd never actually seen that he wondered what the judge had heard.

"It's prettier." Speedy smiled.

"And when you row out onto the lake, catfish and trout jump into your boat?" Captain Amos asked, raising his eyebrows questioningly.

Speedy laughed, remembering when he told that whopper. "Not just into the boat. All you got to do is take a hot fryin' pan down to the lake and they'll jump in there!"

"Before you clean them?" the judge asked, making a sour face.

"Judge," Speedy explained, "the fish from the lake not only jump out clean, they even bring along their own fish sauce to dip theyselves in."

The captain and the judge laughed uproariously and accepted the deed instead of cash. But their moods changed when Speedy laid down his cards and won the pot.

"You always win, don't you?" Captain Amos said, shaking his head.

"Just lucky, that's all." Speedy shrugged.

"You must have the fattest mattress in town with all the money you've got stuffed in it," the judge said.

Speedy laughed. "Money? You politicians got all our money. Me, why I'm just a hardworkin' man with nothin' to hide."

"I'm sure." The judge laughed as he put on his shoes.

After they'd left, Speedy folded up the cabin deed and kissed it before putting it into his pocket. "You're my Ozark Hollows ace in the hole." Then he heard the knock on the door.

"Judge," Speedy stuttered, "what are you doin' back?"

The judge pulled out a wad of bills. "Just had a campaign donation. I want another shot at that cabin of yours."

The look on Speedy's face was a study in wary frustration. "It's your money," he said, sitting back down to the table.

12

Time to Go Home

❖

Up at the fort, Terry closed his eyes, wishing he had just a stick of gum. *I'd even settle for some ABC gum*, he thought, then changed his mind. *I'm not that hungry*, I guess. He made a face at the thought of putting already-been-chewed gum in his mouth.

"Let's go home," he said to his brother. "It's gettin' too dark to play soldiers."

"Frankie's comin', then we'll leave," Larry answered.

Terry looked at the first star in the evening sky and thought that it looked like maple sugar candy. "Wish I had me some," he mumbled. *I need some money*, he thought. *I need to get to Bedal's General Store and fill up my candy stash.*

The problem was that Terry had spent all his savings and had already borrowed against a month's chore money.

He squinted in the descending darkness, trying to make out who or what was out there. "A big Sugar Baby's comin' in," Terry shouted, recognizing Frankie as he came out of the bushes.

"Will you stop talkin' 'bout candy," Larry said.

"Okay. Friendly, comin' in," Terry said.

They'd lit several candles inside the fort walls, and in the flickering light their images danced throughout the fort. Cubby put away the lucky stones he'd taken out to look at. "Bring in the food. I'm powerful hungry," he said, forgetting to ask Frankie about the matches.

"Hey, Terry, you want some sweet cherries?" Cubby asked.

"I'll take a piece of cherry pie."

"Beggars can't be choosers," Larry said.

"Frankie's got cherries," Frankie said proudly, holding out the branch heavy with ripe fruit as he entered through the brush gate.

Larry smiled. "Are they good enough to eat?" he asked, pushing the gate back behind him. "Bring them over to the candle."

"Frankie ate 'em," he said, proudly, putting one into his mouth. He blinked fifteen times without speaking, then smiled. "Tummy good food. That's what Grammie says."

"That's good," Larry said, patting Frankie's head. "Do you know where to find more when we need them tomorrow?" he asked, pulling off a plump cherry for himself.

Frankie thought for a moment. He stopped and touched his nose, then pinched his nostrils, trying to bring the thought to mind. "Yes!" he exclaimed. "But Frankie wants to go home."

"We're leavin' in a moment," Larry said.

Thunder boomed in the distance. Frankie jumped and shivered, blinking like a cornered rabbit.

"It's okay," Larry said, trying to calm his friend down, "enemy won't get over these walls."

Frankie breathed deeply, slowing his blinking down in the process. Then he grabbed the stick rifle and skipped away between the candles.

Cubby shook his head. "Sometimes he stands there, pinchin' his nose, tryin' to get his brain workin' and he goes purple in the face, eyes blinkin' like he's tryin' to fly."

Larry shrugged. "Frankie's in a world of his own. That's just the way he was born."

Frankie skipped over to Terry who was looking at a broad-headed skink that he'd found in the creek. Frankie jumped on Terry's back shouting, "Gotcha!"

The lizard jumped from Terry's hand. He pushed Frankie off in disgust. "Every time you say that stupid word, you lose me somethin'!" Then he looked at Frankie. "Say, you got any candy on you?"

Frankie smiled. "Grammie gave Frankie a gumdrop."

"Where is it?"

Frankie rubbed his stomach. "In here."

"That doesn't do me much good," Terry grumbled.

Near the fort's entrance, Cubby peered out into the woods. "Where's the enemy?"

Larry stood behind him. "Did you see a Yank?"

Cubby nodded and pointed into the darkness. "I think I see one," he whispered.

"Where?" Larry asked.

"There," Cubby said. Larry peered over the embankment. "Was right out that away," Cubby said, pointing toward the nearest bushes.

Dangit jumped out from the bushes, wagging his tail. "It's just Dangit," Larry groaned.

The dog bounded over the wall and jumped up against Terry. "He's got somethin' stuck under his collar."

Larry took out the piece of paper. It was the note from their father. "Pa says to come home."

"Frankie says go home too," the man-boy said.

"Let's pack up," Larry stated.

Cubby stood up. "How come you're givin' the orders today?"

Larry shrugged. "'Cause today's my day to be head general."

Thunder boomed in the distance. Frankie pointed his stick rifle at the dog. "Bang, bang," he said.

Lighting cracked overhead. Cubby looked at the remains of the Sutherland home. "I'd hate to see Jack Sutherland comin' at me in the dark," he said, picking the candle up so he could see better.

"What'd he look like?" Larry asked, feeling a shiver coming on.

Cubby nodded his head. "My pa said he was the devil hisself."

Frankie was tired and wanted to go home. "Frankie's hungry," he said, rubbing his tummy and smiling like a big teddy bear.

"We're all hungry," Terry said, picking up the stick weapons around him. "I could eat a rock candy mountain myself right now."

"Grammie wants Frankie home before dark."

"Well you're in trouble now, 'cause it's already dark. Grammie's gonna whup your behind."

"Grammie's gonna be mad at Frankie."

Terry looked at Frankie. "I bet you know where your Grammie hides her candy." He looked into the man-boy's face. Frankie turned away.

"Come on, Frankie," Terry pressed, "tell me if you know. 'Cause I want you to run home and get me some candy."

"Can't," Frankie said. "Frankie don't tell secrets."

"You can tell me," Terry said, feeling his aggravation rising. "I won't tell anyone. Cross my heart and hope to die, stick a red-hot needle into my eye."

"Frankie can't tell."

"Quit talkin' 'bout yourself like you're someone else."

"Frankie can't tell a secret. Can't."

"Candy shouldn't be a secret," Terry snapped. Dealing with Frankie was like trying to crack a safe with a constantly changing combination.

Larry came up with a candle. "Leave him alone. We gotta go."

"I want to know one of his secrets," Terry said, disgusted.

Larry shook his head. "You know that Frankie never tells a secret."

"Never to anyone," Frankie said, shaking his head. "Frankie's hungry," he said again in his odd way.

"We're goin'," Larry said.

"What time is it?" Cubby asked.

Terry pulled out his cracked, broken pocket watch. "It's candy time."

"That's what your watch always says," Cubby said in frustration. "Why don't you get it fixed?"

"'Cause it's always candy time to me," Terry smiled.

"That's 'cause you can't tell time," Cubby said.

"Don't need to tell time. I can eat candy any time. I even eat it when I'm sleepin'."

Larry knew by the dark sky that they were late. "Uh-oh. We got to skedaddle. It's way past supper time."

13

In the Dark

❖

Leonard Johnson finished up the evening chores and walked down the path toward the small house that he shared with Jamie. *Wish she'd just try to live life again,* he thought when he saw the tightly pulled curtains.

Jamie never came out during the day. No matter how hard he tried to persuade her, she didn't want to expose her face to the light of day.

I have faith, don't I, God? he wondered to himself. It seemed that he relived the tragic fire that had disfigured his daughter every day of his life. *Please give me strength and show me the way to open Jamie's eyes.*

Though he'd given up drinking five years before, there wasn't a day that went by when he didn't feel an urge to drink. As was his habit, he tried to remember the day he'd been baptized. The day he seemed to go into the trance of glory.

He'd stood there, basking in the glow of faith and the way the town had treated him like a hero for saving Jamie from the fire and for capturing Michael Sutherland.

Feeling the urge for a drink growing, he tried to concentrate on the moment he'd been saved. In his mind he was walking among the spectators who had come to have their infirmities cured. He remembered walking past a child with crippled hands and a paralyzed woman on a stretcher. *Then the preacher called me forward and pushed me under the water. Preacher said, "I now baptize you to look upon the glory of God so you can harken to His call."*

But he still felt the urge, gritting his teeth at the frustration.

God don't fail me. God set me free from the demon in the bottle.

He stopped before opening the door, trying to compose himself and at the same time come up with a prayer for strength. But none came to him.

Would the truth set me free? he wondered. But he dismissed the thought quickly, knowing how it would shatter the fragile link between him and Jamie that he was trying to build upon. *I've got to let what happened that night stay in the past.*

Opening the door slowly, he asked, "Want to go for a walk?" He tried to sound cheerful.

"I'll go by myself later," Jamie said, looking away.

Johnson took off his hat. "Looks like the angels are going to light up the sky tonight." Jamie silently moved the rocker back and forth. "You want me to make us a stew for supper?" he asked.

"I'm not really hungry," she said, looking toward the window.

"Jamie, you gotta quit hidin' like this. You can't stay inside forever. God's made a great world for us all out there."

"I can stay inside if I want," she said quietly. "It's my life."

Johnson went about his business, washing his hands and putting on a clean shirt. He started singing the first verse of "Amazing Grace," then stopped. "There's gonna be a church sing this Sunday. Why don't you come?"

She turned to face him. Even the filtered twilight did not hide the hideous scars. "You think anybody would want to sing with me around?" She laughed bitterly. "They might run and hide, but not sing for joy."

"People understand, Jamie. They're always askin' 'bout you, wonderin' why you don't never come to town and . . ."

"And I think it's obvious, don't you?" she said, staring at his eyes. Then she turned and looked back out the window. "I just can't understand why he hasn't written me back."

Johnson didn't say anything.

"You'd think he'd have written once in the past five years. To at least explain what he did . . . why he did it."

Johnson walked over to the door. "Guess I'll just go feed the horses," he said.

"Would you put this in the postbox?" she asked, holding out a letter. It was addressed to Michael Sutherland.

"Oh, Jamie," Johnson said, "you got to stop hurtin' yourself. He ain't never gonna write you back."

"I'll write till I get an answer," she said, handing him the letter.

Johnson put it into his pocket. "One day you'll listen to me." He sighed. "I warned you about him then, and I'm tellin' you now. He'll never write you back 'cause he knows what he did to you."

Jamie didn't respond for a moment, then continued rocking. "Will you put it in the postbox?" she asked quietly.

"I'll do it. Just like I done with all the rest of your letters. I'll send them to where he is." Jamie just nodded.

Johnson walked up the path toward the burned shell of a barn still humming "Amazing Grace." He stopped and looked at the letter.

"I'll send this where I sent all the others," he mumbled. He knelt down behind the half-wall that still stood, took the letter from his pocket, opened it, and read it like he'd done with the others. Then he burned it.

When all that remained was a curled, black ash, he ground it with his boot on the spot where he'd burned every letter she had addressed to Sutherland . . . and every one that had come from him. *Got to protect my Jamie,* he thought.

"He's not good enough for her," he said, adjusting his hat. *That's why I sent him that letter from Jamie that I wrote. To get him to quit writin' my daughter. I'm sick of thinkin' 'bout him. He's nothin' but a barn burner's son.*

Holding Hands

❖

With their play weapons put away, everyone was ready to leave. The only problem was who would take Frankie home. It wasn't that he couldn't get home by himself, because he got around town on his own all the time. But they'd promised Frankie's grammie that they'd always try to have someone walk him home from the fort.

The Younguns were late for supper. Larry looked at Cubby. *I gotta get Cubby to do it.* "Remember those boys from Mountain Grove who tried to beat up on Frankie last week?" he asked.

Cubby nodded. He didn't want to take Frankie home, but he didn't want anything bad to happen to him. "Yeah, I remember," he said, thinking about how he and Larry had defended Frankie against the boys who were calling him names and making fun of him.

"Frankie don't want to fight bad boys," Frankie said, shaking his head.

"You got nothin' to worry 'bout," Larry said. "Those boys won't mess with you again."

"Then why do I got to take him?" Cubby asked.

"It's on your way," Larry said, trying to catch Cubby's eye so he'd understand.

Frankie held up his hand. "Grammie wants Frankie home. Grammie wants Frankie home."

"I'll take him partway, then he can make it to his house on his own," Cubby said.

A long, slow, crackling bolt of lightning made them all jump. Larry looked at Cubby. "Take him all the way home. It's on your way."

Cubby made a face at Larry and groaned. "All right. I'll take him."

It thundered again. Frankie started to shiver. "Come on, General Frankie," Cubby said, shaking his head, "we better get home 'fore the rain comes."

"That's just heat lightning," Larry said. "Pa said we need rain but none's comin'."

Frankie skipped around. "Rain, rain, go today, come again another away."

Terry started to correct him, but Larry leaned over and whispered, "He don't know no better."

"Sounded ignorant. That's all," Terry said.

Larry held up a candle and looked at his sister. "Sherry, you take the secret box and hide it in the secret tunnel."

Sherry slipped back inside the lean-to, careful not to burn herself on the candle. She picked up the metal strongbox. She took the locket off and looked at it, then put it back into the box and began to crawl out.

"That locket should be mine," she whispered, stopping at the entrance. "I'm the only girl here."

Looking to see if anyone was watching, she went back and opened the box and took the locket out. Slipping it back around her neck, she shivered at the feel of the gold on her chest.

Got to keep this a secret, she thought, fixing her dress to hide the locket. Then she blew out the candle and crawled out. She picked up the other candle in front of the hospital hut and walked along the maze of paths to the pile of brush and opened the brush entrance to the crawl space they'd made in the dirt mound. Sherry inched her way in and placed the box in the back, holding the candle at her side.

Frankie took Cubby's hand happily. "Hold hands and skip home, okie-dokie?" He smiled, blinking rapidly.

"No okie-dokie," Cubby said.

Frankie squeezed his hand and pulled him forward. Cubby blushed. "We don't got to hold hands. We're boys."

"But Frankie likes to hold hands."

"Then hold your own," Cubby said, pushing him away. Frankie's face went from glad to sad. "Don't cry," Cubby said.

Larry came up and put his arm around Frankie. "Frankie, you just be good and walk next to Cubby. He'll get you home."

Thunder boomed overhead and Frankie shivered.

"We all better get home fast," said Larry. He looked at Cubby. "Be careful with the candle."

Dangit yipped impatiently. "We're comin'!" Terry laughed and picked up a candle.

"See ya'," Cubby waved to Sherry.

"Bye, Cubby, bye, Frankie," she said.

"Goin' home with Cubby to my Grammie," Frankie said proudly, grabbing onto Cubby's hand.

"I ain't holdin' hands with no boy," Cubby said, shaking free.

"But Frankie's your friend."

"Yeah, yeah, yeah," Cubby said, clearly embarrassed.

"Then be friends," Frankie said, "and hold hands like Grammie." He grabbed Cubby's hand again and skipped forward.

"We ain't *that* good friends," Cubby said, pulling his hand loose.

As they passed Jack Sutherland's grave, Cubby looked at the tombstone: "Here Lies Jack Sutherland Hanged for Being a Barn Burner."

"What's it say?" Frankie asked.

Cubby held the candle up and read it. On the last word, thunder boomed overhead. "Lord, bless me," Cubby whispered.

"Bad man," Frankie said, pointing to the grave.

Cubby shivered, feeling goose bumps form up and down his arms and legs. "Come on," he said, grabbing Frankie's hand, pulling him along. "Let's get home 'fore Sutherland's ghost grabs us."

"Cubby's Frankie's friend," Frankie said.

"Just don't you be tellin' no one 'bout you and me holdin' hands," Cubby said, walking carefully down the trail toward Mansfield.

"It's a secret?"

"Yeah . . . and keep it that way," Cubby said.

"Frankie don't tell secrets." He smiled, squeezing Cubby's hand.

15

Auntie Gee and Grammie

Auntie Gee, Michael Sutherland's only relative, pulled on her pipe until she felt the warm smoke draw into her mouth. She shook the match out, watching the smoke curl up toward the ascending moon.

Not hard to read this weather, she thought, letting the smoke filter through her lips.

A woman in her mid-fifties who looked much older, Gee wore the lines of a lifetime of worry under her eyes. She was eccentric, and she was Jack Sutherland's sister, which made her a loner.

A loud clap of thunder made her blink. *Old-timers say that goin' from a wet May to the dry June is a sign of fury to come. I got a feelin' in my bones that the fury's comin'.*

She looked up at the sky. Her pipe glowed softly, its ember glow making her eyes look bright. *My shame is overpowering,* she thought, gritting her teeth. *The pain I feel for Michael is his pain. I relive his agony night after night.*

Lighting cracked overhead, and for a moment she saw the horrors that Michael had suffered in the Sutherland home. Saw the abuse she had kept secret from the world.

Lord, forgive Michael. It ain't his fault. I shoulda told the sheriff 'bout my brother. I should have told what my brother did to the boy.

Turned him crazy. Made him hear voices. Weren't his fault what happened to that girl.

The thought of Jamie Johnson turned her stomach. *Made her face look like nothin' no one would ever want to look at. Michael's in prison, but she's livin' in purgatory.*

On the other side of town, Frankie's grandmother, June Schmitt, looked out through the curtains of the kitchen window. *Wish Frankie would get home. I don't like him bein' out after dark.*

She felt her breath go short. "Oh Lord," she moaned, clutching her chest.

Propping herself up against the wall, she managed to make her way to the kitchen table. Taking a deep breath, trying to hold back the pain and tears, she slowly closed her eyes.

Her pain was not in her mind. The pain she felt was so strong that at times it seemed to erase the past and future, leaving only the stab, burn, throb, or ache of the moment that seared her insides.

Pain's gettin' worse, she thought, holding her side. *Don't know how much longer I can take it.*

She uncorked the bottle of pills. Taking one out, she swallowed it dry.

Can't hardly afford the medicine I need. Opening her purse, she looked at the envelope that had been left under their door. Inside were two one-dollar bills.

Bet this is Dr. George's doin'. She smiled, shaking her head. *He said that the Lord would provide, but I think the Almighty's got a helper down here.*

She thought about how different life would have been for Frankie and her if they'd lived somewhere else. *The Lord has blessed us with the people of Mansfield. They've been good to us. But what's going to happen to my Frankie if I don't get better? Who'll take care of him?*

These were the worries that had kept her awake since she'd been to see the doctor. The worries of Frankie being left alone or being sent to a state home made her sick to her stomach.

Dr. George was sure she had cancer but sent a report to the big hospital in Springfield to see what they thought, then told her to go home and keep taking the pills. There was nothing Dr. George could say or do to make her worry less.

I'm goin' to God's hands. But whose hands will Frankie go to? He's still got a lot of years left till he gets called home.

Outside, she heard Frankie saying good-bye to Cubby. *Oh thank God, he's here*, she thought, trying to stand up. But the pain was too much, so she stayed at the table until it subsided. She wanted to go to the door to tell Frankie to come inside, but she didn't have the strength. She leaned on the table, not bothering to wipe away the tear that slid erratically down her cheek.

I know it's God's will, but . . . but, God, can't you wait just a little longer? I ain't got everythin' ready for Frankie. Unable to hold it back, racking sobs shuddered through her body. *My Frankie's a good boy, Lord. He's a smart man-child. Give me some more time . . . just a little bit longer.*

16

Losing Hand

S peedy looked at the cards in his hand. The judge was on a winning streak, and Speedy was broke again.

"Don't like losin'," Speedy mumbled.

"Tonight you better get used to it," the judge laughed, adjusting his pince-nez glasses.

But Speedy wasn't happy.

The gamekeeper called out the time. Speedy turned and saw his sly smile and the light reflect off his gold tooth.

"Ante up or drop out," the judge said with a grin. "I'm just warning you. No matter what you got, the pot is mine." He eyed the pile of bills on the table.

Speedy tapped his front teeth. "Here, take my teeth and just end my misery," he said, trying to build up his confidence.

"Might just do that," the judge said.

Should have never agreed to this, Speedy thought. *Should have left well enough alone, but oh no. Speedy's got to get greedy, thinkin' he can come back and take the judge for some more.*

"Speedy," the judge said, "either play and pay or you're out, scout."

"Hold on. I'm considering how much I feel like beatin' you."

The judge chuckled. "Just keep talking that way and puttin' in your money."

Without another nickel in his pocket, Speedy considered his hand again. *Three nines. Should stand me well.* "Either I have to go to see my banker, or you'll have to take my IOU."

The judge gave him a hard stare. "Leave the game and you lose. Those are the rules you set up."

"Then you'll accept my IOU?" Speedy asked.

The judge shook his head. "I don't want your IOU, but I will accept the deed to your cabin."

"My cabin? Why that place in Ozark heaven is worth more than your mansion up the street."

The judge grinned. "You either ante up twenty bucks or fold. I'll accept the deed to your cabin, but I don't want another of your IOU's."

Speedy felt the deed in his pocket. *Lucky cabin, work your magic for ol' Speedy. Just one more time, and I'll never risk you again.*

Carefully taking the deed out and unfolding it on the table, Speedy handed it to the judge. "This is the closest you're ever goin' to get to my place."

"Put it on the pot and show your hand."

Speedy kissed the deed, then laid down his cards. The judge smiled. "You just kissed that cabin good-bye because I just whupped you," he said as he laid down four aces.

Speedy took a deep breath, fluttering air through his lips. He watched the judge rack in the money, look at the deed again, and fold it into his jacket pocket.

"I really do sympathize with you, Speedy," the judge said with the sympathy of an executioner.

"I'm sure you do," Speedy said, wishing he hadn't gotten out of bed that morning.

The judge slapped Speedy on the back. "Come on! After all the money you've taken from me over the years, you probably own a dozen cabins like this one."

"Guess I better make arrangements down in Ozark Hollows for the transfer of ownership and . . ."

The Judge interrupted him. "Don't bother. I've been needin' to get away, so I'll just go down there for the Independence Day holiday and check out my little piece of heaven."

Speedy wasn't paying attention. *I lost my cabin,* he thought, closing his eyes. *What'll I tell Maurice?*

"Did you hear me, Speedy?"

"What?"

"I said I'll go down there and spend the Independence Day holiday fishin' and relaxin' at my new place."

"That's good, Judge . . . that's good," Speedy said absent-mindedly. Then it dawned on him what the judge had said. "Independence Day! Judge, can't you wait until the next weekend?"

The judge shook his head. "When I get a bug to go see somethin', I like to do it while the feelin' is hot."

"But . . . but . . ."

"Speedy, my good man, everything will be okay. I'll send a telegraph to the local sheriff and tell him that the new owner is coming to town." The judge stood up and shook Speedy's hand. "It's been a pleasure doin' business with you."

Speedy watched the judge walk away. *What am I gonna tell Maurice? He and Eulla Mae are plannin' to go down there and . . . I'll think of somethin' . . . give me a few days, and I'll think of somethin'.*

Ghosts

Maurice made his way carefully up across the field toward the woods. "Them Younguns should know better than to be out after dark." He looked around, feeling a sudden, unnatural chill. "That's right. Ain't no reason for kids to be out this late."

A loud boom of thunder exploded overhead, and Maurice almost fell down. "Lord a' Moses," he grumbled, steadying himself. He tried to get his bearings. "I should have left on my vacation this morning. I'd be eatin' catfish and drinkin' berry juice right this moment."

By day he knew the fields he'd plowed and the walk paths he'd made like the back of his hand, but in the lightning-cracked twilight it was as if he'd gone blind.

Carefully making his way through the wildflowers that glorified the edge of his property, Maurice edged toward the dark, foreboding forest ahead.

Then he heard it. "What the devil is that?" he gulped, trying to figure out what was coming toward him.

He tried to see through the moonlight, but all he could see was a dark shape racing toward him. It was dark, long, and running on all fours.

Maurice ran to the tree to his left, but the dark object kept coming at him. "Lord, help me," Maurice prayed. Then the creature jumped up onto his chest.

"Ahhhhh!!" Maurice screamed. "Get off! Get off!" he shouted.

Then he felt a soft, wet tongue licking his face. It was Dangit.

"Whoa, boy, quit lickin'," Maurice said, trying to sit up. Dangit jumped up and knocked him back over. The dog slobbered all over his hands.

"Where are those Younguns?" Maurice asked, pushing the dog away. "Did they put you up to trickin' me?"

Dangit backed away, barked twice, then raced back into the woods. "Guess he wants me to follow him," Maurice grumbled. "Everyone's givin' ol' Maurice orders tonight."

Not too far ahead, the Younguns were walking carefully through the moonlit woods. Terry was grumbling that he wanted candy, and Larry was telling him to hush.

Dangit circled around them, barking at the fireflies that were darting in and out of the bushes. Sherry held on to Larry's hand. "We almost home?" she whispered.

"Not too far, sis," Larry said quietly.

"I ain't afraid," Terry said. Then a bolt of lightning cracked the tree just ahead on their path.

Terry screamed, fell to the ground, and rolled under the bushes. His reaction was so funny that it made both Larry and Sherry laugh.

Terry looked out, then crawled out of the thick branches, glad he hadn't wet his britches. "Thought it was Dracula comin' to take us away."

"You thought it was a ghost." Sherry giggled.

"Come on," Larry said. "We best get home quick before Pa throws a fit."

Maurice came to the break in the woods and saw the three Younguns below him. "Might just scare the beejeebees outta them." He smiled. He stepped into the darkness of the thick pine tree behind him and waited until they came up the hill.

"Ghosts ain't real," Larry said.

"I know that and you know that," Terry said, "but you got to tell my heart that." He felt his chest. "It's beatin' so fast I think it's goin' to jump outta my chest and run home in front of me."

Maurice put his hand over his mouth to hold back his laugh.

Sherry jumped when the thunder boomed again. "How come people say ghosts is real?"

"Are," Larry corrected.

"That's what I thought." Terry nodded. "Now you're tellin' me ghosts are real."

"No, I'm not!" Larry exclaimed. "Why, I'd eat my britches if someone could prove me a ghost."

Maurice saw his chance. He funneled his hands in front of his mouth and started moaning the kind of moan that sends quivers up a backbone. "Ahhhh."

"Start eatin'!" Terry screamed, jumping onto Larry's back.

Sherry grabbed onto Larry's leg. The weight was too much, and he began to wobble.

Maurice groaned again. "Come baaack."

"Let's get outta here," Terry whispered, his jaw tensing. "You can eat your britches at home."

"Come baaack," Maurice moaned.

"Come back where?" Larry asked out loud, his eyes bulging with fear.

Maurice was ready to explode with laughter, but he kept the joke going. "Come back to my hooouse."

Lightning lit up the nose on Devil's Ridge. "I ain't afraid of ghosts," Larry mumbled.

Terry looked around. All the circuits in his brain were exploding with fright. "That's good. You stay here, 'cause I'm afraid of *anythin'* that moans like that."

Maurice let loose with a loud wail. "Heeelp!"

Sherry grasped Larry's forearm. "Who is that, Larry?"

Maurice answered with a moan. "It's Jack Sutherlaaand."

"Oh no," Larry mumbled.

Sherry fingered the locket around her neck, suddenly wishing she hadn't taken it. "He's dead," she whimpered.

"Then he must have undead himself," Terry whispered.

Larry shook his head. "Bet he's mad 'cause we built our fort on his property."

"Don't leave me, Larry," Sherry pleaded. She cocked her ears, listening to the sounds of the night.

"Let's skedaddle!" Terry shouted, taking off toward home.

Maurice stepped out on his path with his arms raised. "Gotcha!"

Terry was so scared that he didn't recognize Maurice and fought like a demon to get away. "Let me go!" he screamed.

Maurice began laughing. "Hold on there, you little redheaded badger! It's me, Maurice."

Terry kicked him in the leg. "Ouch! Dangit!" Maurice shouted. "Stop kickin' me!"

Dangit came racing out from the bushes and grabbed onto Maurice's pant leg. "Get off me, dog!" he said, trying to shake the animal loose.

Larry pulled Dangit away. "He didn't mean no harm," he said, petting the dog. "Dangit, Mr. Springer wasn't usin' your name wrong." The dog cocked his head, then started wagging his tail.

Terry went limp in Maurice's arms. "You scared me."

"Yeah," said Sherry, running up, "we thought you was a ghost."

Larry smiled. "You really got us good."

Maurice glared at the dog. "Here I was playin' a joke, and that fool dog tries to pull my pants off."

"Dangit don't like his name used wrong," Sherry explained.

"I know, I know," Maurice sighed, "but sayin' the word . . ." he stopped and looked at the dog. "Sayin' the word D-A-N-G-I-T," he said, spelling it out, "just comes natural."

"That's okay," Sherry said, "'cause Dangit likes you anyway."

Maurice put his arms around them. "You kids best be gettin' on home. Your daddy's worried, and he's got supper waitin'."

Terry blew a long, fluttering stream of air through his lips. "You scared a powerful hunger into me. Hope Pa's got somethin' good cooked up."

"Eulla Mae said he's got liver and..."

"Liver!" the three kids moaned in disgust.

"Hope there's somethin' else," Terry said, shaking his head.

"Eulla Mae took over something from her garden." Maurice smiled.

"Hope it's a strawberry pie," Terry said. "That's all I'd like for dinner. That and a bowl of sugar for dessert."

"Nope," Maurice smiled, "she took over a fresh batch of carrots."

"Carrots!" Terry exclaimed. "I hate carrots."

"Eulla Mae says they're good for you," Maurice said laughingly.

"Well, I'll give mine back to her," Terry moaned.

"Well, all I know is," Maurice said, looking into their eyes, "last one home gets caught by Sutherland's ghooost!" he shouted, racing off down the hill.

Dangit raced after Maurice with the Younguns close behind.

18

Bestest Friend

Cubby was still standing in front of Frankie's house, trying to shake his hand loose. "Let go, okay?"

Frankie grinned. "We're friends, aren't we?"

Cubby shook his hand back and forth until Frankie let go. "Just don't want no one in town hearin' 'bout us holdin' hands comin' home."

"It's a secret." Frankie grinned.

"You best keep it that way or I'll be mad," Cubby said. Thunder boomed across the town. "Gotta go, Frankie. See ya tomorrow." He ran a few feet then stopped. "Give those matches to your grammie."

"Frankie don't play with matches," he shouted, waving goodbye. Frankie ran around the back of the small house to feed his bunnies. For a brief moment the thought of Jack Sutherland beating Michael flashed through his head, but the thought passed quickly. Frankie had trouble concentrating on anything for very long.

But as he put the food into the bunny cages, he thought about the secret he wished he could have told his grandmother. It was something he'd seen when he'd followed Michael back to Jamie Johnson's barn before Michael went away.

"Gotta keep a secret," he said, scratching the ears of the brown and white bunny in front of him. "Gotta keep secrets from big ears like yours," he said, laughing as the bunny twitched its nose.

He pushed his nose against the bunny cage. "Abraham Rabbit, you be good," he said, pushing one rabbit off another. "St. Peter Rabbit, don't hog the food," he warned, waving his finger at the fat, brown rabbit sitting by the bowl.

"And you, Michael Sutherland Rabbit," he said to the small black rabbit huddled in the corner, "you be nice."

"Frankie, come on in here," his grandmother called out from the kitchen door.

"Okie-dokie, Grammie," he answered in his odd singsong manner, blinking his eyes.

"Come now, Frankie."

Frankie lumbered into the house. His grandmother was pale, but Frankie didn't notice. Grammie was always just Grammie to him.

"Sit down here, and eat this food before it gets cold," she said.

"Gotta wash Frankie's hands first," he said, pumping the water into the sink.

"That's a good boy," she said softly, smoothing his hair.

"Frankie's always a good boy." He grinned and blinked seven times.

After dinner, he put his clothes in the laundry basket and slipped into his long nightshirt. "Gotta say good night to my bunnies," he said as he went into the backyard.

The old woman took short, painful breaths as she cleaned the dishes. Frankie's singing from the back made her smile in spite of the pain. *Even though it's dark and Frankie's in his nightshirt, he's skippin' around like it's the middle of the day.*

Frankie shouted his old friend's name. "Michael Sutherland, why don't you come back? I named a bunny after you!"

The old woman stopped. *Hope folks don't hear him callin' out that name . . . that Sutherland name's not taken kindly to around here.*

She never liked thinking about Michael Sutherland, the troubled boy of Mansfield.

He took a shinin' to Frankie, yes he did. Always comin' 'round and playin' with him when no one else would. Like they was two lost sheep, gettin' along in a secret way that only they understood.

Frankie's loud voice drifted in. "Michael Sutherland Rabbit, you're Frankie's favorite, best rabbit."

Putting the dish towel down, Grammie called through the opened door, "Frankie, don't be shoutin' that name too loud."

"Sorry, Grammie," he answered.

Frankie got down on his hands and knees and hopped like a bunny. "Look," he called out to his rabbits. "Frankie can hop like a bunny. Frankie can do anything you can." He laughed and got up and skipped again. "Frankie can fly, Frankie can run." He giggled, tapping the cage door as he came around the second time.

Grammie got the strength to open the door. "Frankie, come on in now. It's bedtime."

"It's beddie time already?" Frankie called back.

She watched him skip around his bunny cages for a moment, then answered, "Yes, it's beddie time. Hurry up. We've still got to clean your teeth."

"Can I stay up five more minute hours?"

"No, Frankie, come on in."

Frankie raced toward the porch, but stumbled on the second stair. "Missed it again." He grinned sheepishly.

"That's all right," she said softly. "One day you'll make it."

"That's right," he said proudly. "One day Frankie will jump up two stairs and fly to the moon."

"You can do anything, 'cause you're my Frankie," she said, kissing his cheek.

He hugged her waist, then began flapping his arms. "Frankie can fly like a bird, Grammie, can't I?" he asked, pretending to fly around the room.

"You sure can. Now go on and clean your teeth. I'll be right in to say prayers with you."

Frankie stopped and thought for a moment. He put his finger on the end of his nose, then pinched his nose shut. He was trying to remember what Cubby said about giving the matches to Grammie, but the thought wouldn't come.

But the memory of the bad secret came. "Grammie," he said, then stopped.

"Yes, Frankie?"

"Nothing." He shrugged.

A mental image of his bunnies came to him, and another thought followed behind. Exhaling loudly, he proclaimed, "I wish Michael Sutherland would come back and play with me. He was nice to Frankie."

"He was a good friend," she agreed.

Frankie tapped her arm. "Do you think Michael Sutherland knows I named a bunny after him?"

"I don't think he does," she said. "But if he did, he'd be happy."

"Wish I could tell him." Frankie scratched his head for a moment. "Think I could go see him?"

He doesn't understand that Michael Sutherland's in prison for life. "He can't have visitors where he is."

Frankie thought for a moment. "Can't keep God out, *that's* for sure."

"Yes, that's right," she said. "Now you run along."

"Frankie told him that God is Frankie's bestest friend."

"Who?" she asked.

"Michael Sutherland. Frankie told him that God was my bestest friend, and he said Frankie was right."

"Yes, now you better . . ."

Frankie interrupted her by putting his finger to his lips. He looked around to see if anyone was listening.

Grammie knew what he was doing but pretended that it was a surprise. This was the way Frankie liked to play the secret game.

"What are you doing?" she asked.

"Looking to see," he said, looking behind the curtain.

"Looking to see what?" she smiled.

"Grammie, Grammie, I'm lookin' to see if anyone's listenin'." Satisfied that no one was, he put his lips to her ears. "Wanna know a secret?" he whispered.

"Yes," she said.

"God loves you," he smiled, then skipped clumsily off toward his bedroom.

She watched him go, happily bumping against the wall. *God loves you too, Frankie. We all do.*

"Wanna know another secret?" he called out from the room.

"And what's that?" she asked.

"Frankie love you with *alllllll* my heart!" he shouted.

Tears came to her eyes. *I can't tell Frankie my secret. I can't tell Frankie what the doctor suspects.*

A wave of fear came over her. Not fear of dying, but fear of having to leave Frankie to fend for himself in the world. *Who's gonna take him in? Who'd want to take him? I got to get Dr. George to promise me not to let them put Frankie in a state home. It'd kill him . . . he'll die without love. . . .*

She choked back a sob. *If the tests come back bad, who's gonna take care of my Frankie?*

In his bedroom, Frankie took out the matches in his pocket and looked at them. "Frankie don't play with matches," he said quietly, hiding them in a corner of his drawer.

19

Fire Escape

Sutherland stood at the cell's window, staring off in the direction of Mansfield. All he could think about was Jamie. That Jamie was going to marry someone else.

The candle flickered in the corner, lighting up the pictures he'd drawn of their times together. He'd left her letter at the candle's base, where it caught the slow drips of the wax.

He struggled not to think about bad times and counted his heartbeats until the hurt had passed.

Frankie Frank, he thought. *The boy with the secrets. Knows about my Secret Tree. Knows things I told him 'bout Daddy.*

Sutherland hugged himself, feeling an unnatural shiver come over him. *Frankie knew somethin' bad he wouldn't tell me. Came to the jail cell window in Mansfield before I got sent here and said he was sorry. But wouldn't say no more. Said it was a secret.*

Lightning struck a tree outside the prison walls. Sutherland held onto the cell window bars, watching it burn.

Frankie used to spy on me and Jamie. Think he saw us kissin', and it made him curious like a little boy.

The smell of the burning tree drifted in. Sutherland looked at the flimsy bedding and the stack of old newspapers in the corner of his cell. "Fire trap," he said softly.

"Shut up, you dang lunatic," grunted his cellmate, unhappy about being awakened again.

Thunder echoed across the landscape like a drumroll. Lightning darted across the sky in all directions.

Then it happened. Lightning struck the wooden shingle roof of Sutherland's cell block building.

The impact knocked him to the ground. He was too startled to know what had happened, and for a moment he was mesmerized by the fingers of flame that were poking through the ceiling.

His cellmate came awake. "What?" He looked at the fire that Sutherland was just staring at. "You are crazy!" Throwing off his old blanket, he stood up, pounding on the cell bars. "Guard! Guard! Get me out of here. Fire!"

Fire. The word feared by men trapped in cells spread up and down the cell blocks. Sutherland watched as the fire seemed to float from the ceiling to the newspapers to the bedding and to the wooden bed frames.

The fire was racing through the flimsy roof. The rafters had caught fire up and down the cell block.

"Get us out! Help! Help!" screamed the thirty men trapped in their cells.

Sutherland calmly waited, watching the flames feed themselves. He'd been on so many barn burning trips with his father that he wasn't afraid of fire. He took the fire as a sign. As an omen. As an opportunity.

In the rush to free the men, the guards herded them down the hall. Behind them, the fire was building in intensity, jumping from cell to cell.

Panic and confusion were everywhere. Sutherland followed the guards calmly out into the yard.

Bells clanged. Guards and prisoners formed a water bucket line to fight the fire. The gates were opened to let the fire wagon enter.

Sutherland didn't look around. He simply walked away from the prison, heading toward Mansfield. *I got to get to Jamie. Give her back the locket. Tell her I love her. That she shouldn't be marryin' nobody but me . . . 'cause we said till death do us part.*

Behind him the fire was raging in the prison, but Sutherland was unconcerned. *Got to first get the locket, and then I'll know what to do.*

20

Smell the Mountain Air

❖

Thunder pounded in the distance. Maurice looked out over the darkening hills. He watched a shooting star streak blue and gold across the heavens.

He'd come straight home after getting the Younguns safely back to their house. All he could think about was his vacation.

It's gonna be good. Just Eulla Mae and me alone, huggin' up together like we was kids.

A wild streak of lightning hit the trees across the ravine, but Maurice hardly gave it notice.

Speedy says it's like nothin' you've ever seen. Clear water, lots of trout and catfish. He grinned. *Just a place to watch the sun rise and set.*

A clap of thunder sounded overhead, but Maurice didn't even blink. *Just peace and quiet. Take off your shoes, feel the mountain streams with your toes. Just me and Eulla Mae . . . gonna be like the honeymoon we never had.*

The trip was so close that he could almost smell the mountain air and taste the water. He breathed deeply, as if he was right up there in the mountains, drinking it all in.

I bet it's a come-on-in-the-water's fine type of place. I can taste those fish now. Bet each one will be ten pounds. Why, I'll toss 'em back if they're less. I can smell that mountain air.

Eulla Mae came out. "You ready for dinner?"

Maurice nodded. "I'm ready for a vacation," he mumbled. Sausage started to get up, but seeing that Maurice didn't move, he flopped back down.

Eulla Mae shook her head. "You're gonna wear out the vacation before we even take it."

"Can't help it." Maurice smiled. "Just think. Five days of fishin' and livin' off the land."

He raised his arms like he was shooting with a rifle at the moon. "I could have made a good mountain man, you know it?"

Behind his back, Eulla Mae rolled her eyes. "I ain't sayin' nothin'."

She had no such illusions of what Speedy's cabin would be like. Speedy was a fast-talker. Everything he'd ever tried to do for them had ended up a disaster.

Eulla Mae felt in her bones that Maurice was building up to a fall in getting all excited about Speedy's cabin. "Just hope that cabin's got a roof," she grumbled.

"Why you always so negative 'bout Speedy?" Maurice asked.

"Not negative. Just realistic. That's all. He's too flashy."

"What's wrong with havin' a successful Springer in the family?"

Eulla Mae thought of Speedy's shiny shoes. "My poppa said to trust a man in work clothes before a city slicker any day."

"You're just cuttin' your nose off to spite your face. And my poppa said clothes make the man."

"Fine thing for your poppa to say since he didn't own but one suit." She saw she had hurt his feelings. "I'm sorry." She sighed. "Guess I'm just tired, that's all."

"You the one who needs a vacation." He smiled, letting the unintended slight pass by.

"We both do," she said, deciding to hope for the best.

Maurice winked. "Gonna be like a honeymoon for us. Just you and me alone."

Eulla Mae blushed. Maurice turned to look at the lightning that cracked behind him, then looked back at his wife of twenty years. "What you gonna do with yourself, girl, when I'm out rowing Speedy's boat on that mountain lake?"

"I'll be out there rowin' with you," she said.

"Don't be thinkin' that!" he exclaimed. "You'll be in the cabin, cleanin' the mess of fish I just rowed in, feedin' Sausage and . . ."

"You're dreamin'," she said. "I'm not goin' on this trip of yours to be your all-day fish cleaner and dog walker."

"Not all day." He grinned. "I'm just gonna go fishin' when I get up at sunrise. The rest of the day you're gonna be makin' Sausage and me pies from the berries I bring in and a rabbit stew or a venison steak from my huntin'."

Sausage heard the mention of food and began barking wildly.

Eulla Mae frowned. "Sounds like you ought to go hire yourself a maid and bring her along." Sausage was still barking. She looked at the dog and said, "And, dog, you better hope no grizzly bear makes a meal out of you."

Maurice puffed up his chest. "I ain't scared of no bear."

"If a bear came runnin' up, who's gonna drive it away?"

"That's why I'm bringin' you," he joked, ducking her playful swat.

'You better get some sleep, Daniel Boone," she teased. "You've still got work to do tomorrow. The carrot patch needs weedin'."

"Work, work, work. I'm tired of workin' so hard. I'm ready for my vacation," he complained.

"You best be rememberin' the lesson of the ant. The ant works every day, all day long. The ant's always workin'. But from all that work, you know what the ant gets in the end?" she asked.

Maurice grunted. "Gets stepped on."

"No, no. The hardworkin' ant builds up his dream."

Maurice shook his head. "And he never gets a vacation."

Eulla Mae turned to go back inside. "You got farmer work tomorrow. So come on to bed."

Farmer work, he thought shaking his head. *Weedin' a carrot patch. That's old men and kids' work.*

Maurice coughed to clear his throat. *I was born fifty years too late. Should have been a mountain man. I should have been like Davy Crockett and lived down in Ozark County where Speedy's cabin is.*

Not even the lightning and thunder shook him from his dreams. Only the fireflies that twinkled around his head seemed to be tapped into the sparkling vacation dreams that Maurice was thinking about.

In his mind he was on Norfolk Lake, hooking a twenty-pound croaker on one line and a ten-pound catfish on the other. *Speedy's a good man. Gonna be a great vacation. Ain't no place better than a mountain cabin.* He nodded, a peaceful sleep coming on.

21

Eatin' Carrots

Across the hill and over the field, Rev. Youngun had the table set by the time the kids came in from taking their shoes off on the porch. "Did you get my note?" he asked sternly.

Larry nodded. "We came right after we read it," which was close enough to the truth he thought.

Rev. Youngun shook his head. "You kids should have been home long ago," he said, with obvious irritation in his voice.

Larry started to speak, but Terry stepped on his toe and took over. "We had to make sure that Frankie got home safely."

"Did you walk him all the way into town?"

"Naw," said Terry pretending to wash his hands, "Cubby took him most of the way."

Rev. Youngun smiled. "It's nice of you children to play with Frankie."

"Frankie's all right," Larry said.

"Yeah," Terry shrugged, "just 'cause he looks like a big chipmunk and acts goofy, don't mean he can't be a good soldier."

Rev. Youngun looked at Terry's hands. "You need water to clean those hands."

Terry smiled. "I was just pretend washin'."

"Well, stop pretending and put water on them. And make sure you don't use the dishrag to dry them," Rev. Youngun said, going into the pantry.

"Where's the hand towel?" Larry asked.

Terry handed him the dish towel just as his father emerged from the pantry. "Larry," he said sternly, "dry your hands on the hand towel."

"Yes, Pa," Larry said, giving Terry the evil eye. Terry turned his back and snickered into his hands.

Terry sneaked into the pantry and looked at the sugar bowl on the shelf. He tried to calculate how fast he could take the bowl down, lift off the top, grab a pinch of sugar, stick it in his mouth, and then put the bowl back.

He decided that he'd get caught. Giving the sugar bowl one long, lingering look, he went back to the kitchen and peeked at the liver and carrots cooking.

Not fit for a dead man to eat, he thought.

Rev. Youngun put his hand on Larry's shoulder. "Has Frankie had any more problems with those hooligans from Mountain Grove?"

"No, Pa. Guess they knew better than to fool around with a Mansfield boy."

Rev. Youngun sighed. "I'm just so glad that you were able to use Bible principles to teach them the error of their ways."

Terry looked up. *Bible principles?* Larry gave him a look. "Yes, Pa," Larry said, "I showed them the error of their ways."

Terry remembered his brother saying to the biggest boy, "Bible says eye for an eye. So if any of you boys try to hit Frankie, I'm gonna blacken your eye for an eye until you learn."

Rev. Youngun patted Larry on the head. "I'm very, very proud of you."

"So am I, Bible boy," Terry whispered as he walked toward the table, swinging air punches around.

By the time they sat down to supper, the pounding thunder that shook the house had put them all on edge. "Calm down, children. It's time to say the blessing," Rev. Youngun said.

Terry looked at the carrots on his plate. He closed his eyes during the blessing and silently prayed, *Lord, please make these carrots disappear.*

He peeked with one eye, but they were still there. He prayed again. *Please, Lord, turn these horrible carrots into gumdrops.* When he opened his eyes, the carrots were still carrots.

"Eat your vegetables," Sherry taunted.

"You eat 'em," Terry said, making a fist.

"Children, children," Rev. Youngun said, "let's have a nice meal." He took a bite of biscuit. "Now, tell me about Fort Mansfield."

Larry began telling about the afternoon while Terry made kissy lips at him behind his hand. "Pa, make him stop," Larry complained.

Rev. Youngun looked at Terry who shrugged. "Just can't stop thinkin' 'bout havin' itchy lips like Missouri says she has." He looked at his father with an innocent look on his face. "What does itchy lips mean?"

Rev. Youngun began to blush. "Ah, that's when . . ."

Sherry piped up. "Means you got poison ivy on your lips."

"That's one way of looking at it," Rev. Youngun said, relieved.

"What's another way?" Terry asked, making another kissy face at Larry.

"I'm gonna get you," Larry whispered.

Rev. Youngun looked at Larry. "You'll do nothing of the kind. We'll talk about your lips later."

While Sherry talked about her dolls, Terry slowly fed his liver to Dangit, then moved the carrots, one at a time, to the corner of his plate. When no one was looking, he forked them off the table to the dog.

Two fell on his lap, so he stuck them in his napkin and put it into his pocket. *Best way to eat carrots that I know 'bout*, he thought.

"So playing up at the old Sutherland place doesn't bother you?" Rev. Youngun asked.

Larry shrugged. "That old burned house makes it seem like a real battleground."

"I guess so," Rev. Youngun said. He looked over at Terry. "Well, I'm glad to see that you're eating your carrots without a fight. Guess you're getting older." He smiled, patting his redheaded son.

"And smarter too," Terry beamed, patting the carrots in his pocket.

Dangit barked under the table, scratching against Terry's leg for more. Rev. Youngun looked under the table. "Be quiet." Dangit wagged his tail, then let loose a liver burp. A piece of carrot dropped out of his mouth.

Rev. Youngun slowly raised his head. "I've told you before. Don't feed Dangit at the table."

"Sorry, Pa," Terry said, "but he looked hungry."

"Eat the rest of your carrots yourself, young man."

Rev. Youngun stared at Terry, wishing that his late wife were there to help him. *Norma would know how to handle Terry. She'd know what to say.*

"Carrots are for rabbits," Terry mumbled. "Why don't we give them back to Eulla Mae?"

"Can't give them back," Sherry said, "'cause we already cooked 'em."

Terry looked at the round, orange circles like they were bug droppings. He moved them slowly around the plate with his fork.

"Eat another piece," Rev. Youngun said wearily.

Pa don't know I stuck some of the carrots in my pocket. Terry smiled to himself. *I got to get to the privy and drop 'em down the hole.*

"Just eat one more for me," Rev. Youngun said. "Show me you can do it."

Terry looked at the carrots. *Why don't you eat one?* he asked himself.

"Come on, Terry, just one," his father pleaded.

"I don't want to waste 'em," Terry said, putting his most sincere expression on. "I just want you to give 'em to someone else."

"Like who?"

"Give 'em to some poor kid who needs 'em more than me," Terry nodded. "That's the Bible way."

Sherry rolled her eyes.

"But carrots are good for you." Rev. Youngun sighed.

"Kids already call me carrottop. Don't need no more carrot juice inside me," Terry said, pushing the plate away.

"That's silly talk," Larry said.

"No, it's not!" exclaimed Terry. "Next thing you know monster rabbits will start attackin' me thinkin' I'm a walkin' carrot."

Rev. Youngun took Terry's fork and stuck it into a piece of carrot, waving it in front of his son's mouth.

Terry watched the carrot move slowly back and forth on the fork. When the carrot stopped in front of his nose, Terry's eyes were crossed.

"Open up," Rev. Youngun ordered.

Terry looked at the carrot with crossed eyes. "Don't want to get sick," he mumbled through clenched jaws.

Rev. Youngun frowned, looking at Terry's eyes. "I told you, cross your eyes and they'll stay that way."

Terry blinked them straight. "I think I'm sick. I better go lie down."

"He's just sick of carrots," Sherry jeered, happy with her brother's dilemma.

Terry glared at his sister, thinking about how he would get even. *Gonna scare the beejeebees outta her later.*

Rev. Youngun looked Terry in the eye. "When I was a little boy, I ate all my carrots."

Terry said through his fingers, "If I'd known you then I would have given you mine."

Larry chuckled and Sherry giggled.

Rev. Youngun shook his head. "I'm at the end of my rope. Go to your room, young man."

Terry got up from the table and went up the stairs. Thunder boomed overhead, and lightning cracked repeatedly like a whip across the Ozarks.

"Listen," Sherry said, pointing toward the window, "Terry got God upset."

"I didn't do all that," Terry shouted from the second floor. "Someone else musta done somethin' to 'cause all this racket."

"You did too do it!" Sherry screamed.

"Not another peep out of you, Terry," Rev. Youngun said. "And you also, young lady. He made his bed, now he'll have to lie in it."

Sherry shook her head. "Terry's never made his bed."

"Just finish your supper, Sherry."

Rev. Youngun cleared his throat. Then he thought about Larry. *And now I've got a girl wantin' to play kissing games with my son. What am I gonna do?*

They finished the meal in a silence that was broken only by the booming thunder outside. Sherry felt the locket against her neck and shivered. Her conscience said she'd done something wrong in taking it. *I'll put it back tomorrow. No one will know.*

What she didn't know was that Michael Sutherland was on his way back to Mansfield to get the locket back.

22

Night Tears

Sutherland ran through the woods, going south toward Mansfield. The smell from the prison fire hurt his nostrils, and the running made his heart beat faster.

Though he'd been confined without much exercise for five years, Sutherland pushed his body hard. He cut through the prison cornfields and the neighboring wheat fields that were worked with prison labor.

The sound of the bloodhounds seemed headed his direction. *Maybe some others ran off too,* Sutherland thought as he climbed over a fallen tree. *They can't be on me that quick.*

His heart pounded through his matted prison shirt. Sutherland paced himself, knowing that to escape, he had to keep going at an even pace.

He took twists and turns, hoping to shake the dogs, but they seemed to be coming his direction. Like a cornered animal, he let his instincts guide him. *They're after me,* he thought, licking the sweat from his lips. The salty taste made him gulp. *Them guards will whip me to death if they catch me out here alone. Got to get Jamie's locket in my hands again . . . then I'll go see her. Got to get there before she gets married.*

He could almost feel the guard's whip cutting into his shoulders. Seemed like everyone had beat him down. His daddy, Jamie's father, the guards.

Switching directions, Sutherland headed west toward a creek he remembered crossing over when they'd brought him to the prison in shackles five years before. *Old wooden bridge is up here somewhere. Creek cut through the woods. Got to lose the dogs.*

With the bloodhounds less than a quarter-mile behind him, Sutherland found the creek and ran west along the bank, making sure he left a trail. Then jumping high into the air, he landed in the water.

Without losing stride, he doubled back down the middle of the shallow creek, careful not to touch any of the exposed rocks.

Making good time through the knee-high water, he prayed that he wouldn't disturb any nests of snakes. *Don't need to get bit now, Lord. Keep the serpents away from me.*

He heard the dogs follow his false trail but didn't slow his pace. With the moonlight as his guide, Sutherland headed toward Mansfield.

"Got to get to Jamie," he whispered, over and over.

In the woods less than a mile back, two guards gripped the leather harnesses that held the bloodhounds together. "We're gainin' on him. I can feel it," the tough-looking sergeant said. He called back over his shoulder to the rookie guard. "Come on. We can't let him get away."

"I'm comin'," the rookie said, fearful of what lay in the woods at night. He also knew that a man sent to prison for life had nothing to lose in killing a guard.

The sergeant looked around, the lust for blood in his eyes. "When we catch him, there won't be nothin' left to bring back."

A half hour later, with the barking dogs struggling at their leashes, the rookie shook his head. "We've lost his trail."

"He's probably runnin' up the creek. Let's keep goin'," said the sergeant.

From out of the woods came a third guard with his front teeth missing, holding on to a set of dogs. "I think this con fooled you boys," the toothless man said. "If he was headin' upstream, dogs would have caught scent on things floatin' down."

"Maybe he's hidin' in the trees?" the rookie suggested.

"And how'd he get up there? Fly?" the sergeant mocked. "The dogs would have smelled where he climbed up."

The toothless man struggled with his dogs. "Think he's headin' west to the state line?"

The sergeant thought for a moment. "Kansas is closer than Arkansas. But he's from Mansfield. Bet that's where he's headed."

The toothless guard looked down the stream and nodded. "I think you're right. Convicts always run for home. They're like old dogs with no place else to go."

A mile away, Sutherland was running down another creek, which crisscrossed a road. An old delivery wagon with a swaying lantern was on the dirt road heading south. Heading toward Mansfield.

Quietly climbing up the creek bed, Sutherland sneaked up in the dark behind the wagon and climbed up onto the back. The driver was talking to the horses, which were visible in the circle of light that the lantern threw off.

Sutherland covered himself with a loose burlap bag and lay quietly watching the moon. *Got to stay awake,* he told himself. *Got to get off at daylight.*

To keep awake, he thought of the moment when Jamie gave him the locket and said they were going to get married.

That's the only happy memory I've got in my whole life, he thought. *Nothin' good ever happened to me before Jamie. But she understood me. She knew how to fix my broken brains.*

As he closed his eyes, Sutherland felt a bad memory coming on. A film of sour, sticky sweat came over him. His father was trying to get him to recite a vow to burn a list of his supposed enemies.

Sutherland stared blankly at the stars, counting his heartbeats. When the memory passed, he counted the hoofbeats of the mules as they clumped toward Mansfield. All he thought about was seeing Jamie again.

At that same moment, Jamie was thinking of Michael Sutherland as she walked along the path she'd worn on the hillside around their property. Her life had become one of routines. Hiding from daylight. Existing with her father. Writing to Michael. Waiting for darkness so she could go out again.

Her journeys to the edge of the wilderness always brought a sense of calm and wonder. Like Alice in Wonderland, she felt too small for the world around her.

The tall trees backdropped by the knife-edge ridges made her seem small and out of place, yet it was the place where no one bothered her.

She remembered how the bluff near the house was by day emerald with mosses and lichens from the shading of the waterfall-like flowing ferns. How cool the creek water was. The still pool of water in the cup of the cliff filled with a trickle that ran from a crack in the rock.

Sitting there with Michael, looking into the still water. The reflection of the girl she'd once been. A reflection that she'd never see again.

"I wonder if Michael has forgotten those moments." She sighed, then remembered how he always told her he had a memory like an elephant.

She stopped and felt the huge boulder at the base of the cliff. It was squared off like some stone carried over from the pyramids of Egypt. Spiderwebs and plant life clung to its sides.

The heat and humidity were almost overpowering, but for Jamie, the night was release. Moving along the old bluffs and among the old boulders, she breathed deeply, feeling like a survivor who had nowhere to go.

The blooming prickly pear flowers, which signaled the end of spring and the onslaught of a Missouri summer, sat securely in their precarious rootholds on the sides of the rocks. The heat and drought of the summer that was upon them had already parched the hills. Withering plants and flowers were testimony to the dry weather.

Jamie moved with uncaring grace, shaking her hair free from the scarf she kept draped around her face in the house. When she was alone, with only the trees and sky to look upon her, she felt free of her face. Free of the hideous scars that had left her sickened the one time she had looked in the mirror.

Though she hadn't been a great beauty before, she had been pleasant to look at. But not now.

At the same pool that she and Michael had tried to see their future in, Jamie turned away. She didn't want to see her reflection even by moonlight.

Turning in a circle, touching the walls of the timeless boulders, Jamie felt like she was standing in some prehistoric ruin. Like she was the queen of ruin.

I feel like Humpty Dumpty, and I've fallen off the wall, she thought, *looking at the boulders around her. No one will ever want to love me . . . not with the way my face looks.*

Jamie stopped to watch a bolt of lightning hit the distant ridge, then reached down and plucked a yellow-fringed flower from the bottom of the bluff. It was an Ozark orchid.

She held it up to the night sky. *This was Michael's favorite flower,* she thought, twisting it in her hand. For a moment she imagined that she'd found the last orchid on Earth. That the wallflower had found the last trace of beauty that existed.

She saw irony in her thoughts and smiled grimly. It was like she held a miracle of the rocks, and for that she cried her night tears that no one could see on her face.

23

Privy Monster

❖

Terry sat alone in the bedroom he shared with Larry listening to his stomach. "I might just shrivel up into a piece of string by morning if I don't eat somethin'."

But the thought of having to go downstairs and eat those carrots was enough to gag him. All he really wanted was gum, candy, honey, jam . . . anything with sugar in it.

"I wish I lived on a big rock candy mountain." He sighed, looking out at the hills beyond their property line. "I'd wake up every mornin' and just bite me a hunk of sugar from the ground."

His candy craving was so strong that he searched through all his hidden places, but found nothing. Then he found his empty candy stash bag.

"Might just as well sniff it," he shrugged.

Wiggling his nose, he took a deep breath and whiffed the final trace of gumdrops and Tootsie Rolls. "Wish I had me just a crumb of sugar," he said, shaking the bag, hoping against hope that a grain of sugar would fall out. Making a funnel with the lip of the bag, he held it over his head, hoping that a morsel of sugar remained. "Nothin' left!" he said disgustedly, throwing the bag over his shoulder.

"Just one grain of sugar, Lord, that's all I want."

Thunder boomed outside. Terry took it as a sign. "Lord, I'd give all Sherry's dollies to the poor for a spoonful of sugar right now," he said to the ceiling. "Yup, Lord, I'd even let dog-face Georgia kiss my cheek for a big old gumdrop."

Then he thought about what he was saying. *Don't think even sugar's worth lettin' slug lips touch me.* "Cancel that last request, Lord," he said.

Not knowing how to ward off another sugar fit, he took off his socks and threw them around the room. Then he drew an ugly picture of Sherry and pinned it on his wall.

"I'm bored and hungry for sweets," he moaned. He listened for conversation from the dining room but didn't hear anything. *Glad I'm not down there. Sounds like a graveyard havin' a bone party.*

Terry nervously skipped in a tight circle thinking up a rhyme:

"I'd trade Sherry for a piece of gum,
'Cause she's just a girl and really dumb.
And I'd trade Larry for a candy elf
Then I'd have the room all to myself."

I like that one. He giggled, skipping faster. He began another one:

"I'd eat bugs with maple syrup,
I'd eat flies with . . ."

He stopped and scratched his head. "Don't know nothin' that rhymes with syrup."

Raising his arms up, he began skipping again, slowly at first, then building up to his old speed.

"If you give me sugar here's what I'll do,
I'll kiss a girl and polish my shoes.
I won't be mean and I'll learn to dance,
I'll put a squirrel in my underpants."

At the last line, he burst out laughing. "I really like my poems," he said. "I wish everyone were like me." He grinned, trying to shake the sugar urge off.

Still smiling, he thought up another.

"Carrots are for rabbits,
Milk is for cows,
The only thing that Terry wants

Is a bowl of sugar now!"

He said the last line so loud that he stopped skipping and listened to see if they'd heard him downstairs. *Hope Pa didn't hear that.*

But his father didn't shout up for him to be quiet, so Terry started wiggling around with the sugar feeling coming over him. Unable to calm down, he wiggled over and sat on the windowsill.

Got to go to the privy, he thought, looking out the dark window. *Boy-oh-boy, it's dark out there.* He shuddered.

He squeezed his legs together, hoping that would do the trick, but it didn't. He still had to go. Now he had to do both.

Lightning cracked, illuminating the path to the wooden outhouse that sat behind the kitchen. *Bet there's a boogie man on the privy path. Bet he's just waitin' to eat a kid that's gotta go bad.*

But the boogie man on the privy path was not Terry's greatest fear. It was the privy monster who lurked below the seat in the muck.

"No sir, I'm not goin' out there. It's too dark to go sit down. This is the time the privy monster reaches up and pulls you into the muck. Yup, he pulls you down and turns you into a stink bug."

Terry got goose bumps over the thought. "Yes sir, the ol' privy monster knows just the instant when your pants drop below your knees. Then he reaches up and grabs you by the legs!"

Terry jumped around like he was fighting and kicking the privy monster away. "Keep your hands off me! I ain't gonna be no stink bug!" he shouted. Terry kicked so hard that he knocked over his night table.

"What's goin' on up there?" his father shouted from downstairs.

"Nothin', Pa," Terry said meekly.

He righted the table, then gave one last air punch to the privy monster. But he'd moved so much he had to sit down to keep from going.

Terry sat on the windowsill again, trying to will away the urge. *Rather sit up here like a water sack waitin' to burst. Better than bein' turned into a stink bug.*

24

Colored Water

❖

Dr. George sat on the edge of Cubby's bed. "That was nice of you to walk Frankie home."

Cubby shrugged. "It was on the way," he said.

"But you didn't have to. You did it because you wanted to. Isn't that right?" Dr. George asked.

"Maybe," Cubby said, thinking about the boys from Mountain Grove.

Dr. George sighed. "Cubby, I'm trying to compliment you. Some kids just make fun of Frankie, but you and the Younguns are really nice to him."

"We needed another soldier," Cubby said.

"But the point I'm trying to make is that you kids don't have to play with Frankie. I'm proud that you're kind to him."

"Frankie's Frankie. We needed another Johnny Reb to help defend the fort."

Dr. George looked into his son's eyes. "And that's another thing I've been meaning to talk to you about."

"What's that, Pops?"

"About you calling yourself General Cubby E. Lee and fighting for the Confederacy," he said, not knowing how to bring up the subject.

"What's wrong with that?" Cubby asked. "He was a good general, wasn't he?"

"That he was," Dr. George agreed, wanting to get to the point. "But I think you're fightin' for the wrong side and . . ."

Cubby sat up. "You want me to fight for the enemy?"

"No, no . . . I just want you to understand what the war was about."

"It's the grays fightin' the blues, that's what it's about."

"It involved color all right, but it was more about black and white."

Cubby looked perplexed. "That don't make sense. The lady down at the library showed me pictures that said gray troops and blue troops. Didn't say nothin' 'bout black and white troops."

Dr. George looked at his son, trying to decide what to do. He was concerned that his son, a black child, was playing Civil War soldier games and fighting for the Confederacy.

Should I stop Cubby from playing the game? he wondered. *What harm's it doing?*

He didn't want to have to disturb Cubby and force him to think about color. About racial problems.

But why can't they play something else? Something that doesn't have anything to do with race? He looked at the little boy.

"Somethin' wrong, Pops?" Cubby asked.

"Cubby," he began slowly. "I want to tell you a story about something that happened to me and my granddaddy a long time ago. It's about colored water."

"Colored water?" Cubby said, perplexed. "What's that?"

"Just listen for a moment. It's got something to do with this war game you've been playing." Cubby sat quietly, waiting for his father to continue.

"When I was about your age, just after the Civil War ended . . ."

Cubby interrupted him. "You were in the war?"

"No, just listen," Dr. George said. "Anyway, my granddaddy, who had been a slave, had . . ."

"He was a what?" Cubby asked.

"A slave. He was owned by a farmer."

"Owned? How can you own another person?" Cubby asked.

"That's what the war was fought about. Blues wanting to free the slaves that the grays owned."

Cubby didn't say anything.

"Anyway, my granddaddy took me to the cattle market in St. Louis to sell some cows. I was thirsty and wanted a drink of water.

"Well, my granddaddy hadn't come out of the office yet, so I walked over to two pumps with drinking cups hanging on them. I asked this white man which one I should drink out of, and he pointed to the one marked 'colored water.' Well, that made me curious."

Cubby nodded silently.

"So I walked over and began pumping that colored water pump like I was putting out a fire. I had never seen colored water before, and I was waiting for a rainbow of colors to come pouring out."

"Did you drink it?" Cubby asked softly.

"My granddaddy came out and stood next to that white man and began pumping from the other pump marked 'white.' The big white man pointed to the one I was pumping, meaning for him to drink from that, but my granddaddy said no."

"He said no?" Cubby said. "Weren't he scared?"

"He wasn't, but I was. Then all of a sudden, the ways of the world came exploding into my head, making me see things I'd never seen before. With his eyes burning into my soul, my granddaddy said loud and clear for everyone in that cattle yard to hear, 'The war was fought so we don't never have to be satisfied with colored water again. Son, you come over here and drink from this.'"

Dr. George paused, letting his words sink in. "My granddaddy told me later that it doesn't matter much what happens. It's what you do when it happens that matters."

Cubby sat quietly for a moment, then whispered, "If the Civil War was fought over colored water, how come those pumps are still around?"

"The Civil War was just one episode in a long war for our people's rights. Nothing comes easy when you're asking other people to change their ways. But it's better today than it was yesterday, and it'll be better tomorrow."

He stood up and patted Cubby's head. "Just don't ever settle for colored water, and always stand up for what you believe. The blues won that for us in the Civil War . . . for us . . . heck, for everybody here in this country."

"Tell me another story," Cubby asked.

"We'll talk about it more in the morning. Now you'd best get some sleep and think about that story."

"Night, Pops," Cubby said, pulling the sheet up.

"Good night, Cubby," Dr. George said, turning out the light.

"Pops?" Cubby called out.

Dr. George stopped in the hall. "Yes, son?"

"I forgot to get the matches back from Frankie."

Dr. George paused. "What matches?"

"Frankie found some matches in town and was talkin' 'bout lightin' them. I told him not to play with matches and to give them to his Grammie."

"That was the right thing to do. Now go to sleep."

Dr. George thought about Frankie and his grandmother, June Schmitt. *Things could be worse than worryin' about Cubby playing Confederate soldiers. I could be facing the end of my life like that woman is.* He shook his head. *What's going to happen to Frankie? Lord, I wish I had an answer to that.*

Then he remembered the letter that had come from the hospital in Springfield and knew he had to call over to Frankie's grandmother. It was a call he dreaded to make.

25

Frankie's Dream

❖

June Schmitt had tried to put the fears of those test results behind her for a while. In her small, neat house, she held Frankie's hands as they said the evening prayers. His next day's clothes were laid neatly on the chair beside her.

Since Frankie had a hard time remembering any of the prayers he heard in church, he'd made up a special prayer of his own.

He'd hum while June said it, then she'd hum while he repeated the verse. It had been that way every night for more than twenty years.

His grandmother began humming when it was Frankie's turn to say the prayer.

"God's in my head.
God's in my eyes.
God's in my mouth.
God's in my heart.
God's my friend."

"I could say that every night until I go to heaven." She smiled, kissing his forehead.

Frankie thought for a moment, rubbed his eyes, then asked a question he'd never asked. "Are you going to heaven soon, Grammie?"

"All good people go to heaven," she said carefully.

"One day soon?" he asked quietly.

"I hope not too soon." She smiled bravely.

"I don't want Grammie to ever leave Frankie," he said.

Please, God, don't let him find out until I'm ready, she thought.

"Wanna know a secret?" he whispered.

She nodded. "Yes."

"God really does love you." He smiled and threw his arms around her neck. "And you know what?" he asked, putting his nose against hers.

"What?"

"What—that's what!" He giggled, hugging her again.

She was glad he couldn't see the grimace of pain she made. It was all she could do to keep from crying out, but she bit her lip, holding back the pain.

Before she left him each evening, she asked him the same question. "Do you have anything you want to tell me?"

Frankie thought for a moment about the matches he'd hidden in his drawer. He was about to tell her when the wall phone in the kitchen rang out. "Phone, Grammie," Frankie said.

"You go to sleep," she said, standing up by the bed. The phone kept ringing.

"Answer it, answer it," he said nervously.

"I will. Good night."

"Night. Night. Frankie loves you."

"And I love you."

She went into the kitchen and took the mouthpiece off the hook. "Yes?" she said.

"June, this is Dr. George. I got the letter from Springfield. I think you should come see me as soon as you can."

She paused for a moment. "Is it bad, Doc?"

"It's not good," he said quietly.

In the bedroom, Frankie Frank was asking God to take care of his friend. "God, watch over Michael Sutherland. And tell him Frankie kept the secret."

For a moment Frankie thought of the bad secret that had given him nightmares, then closed his eyes and gritted his teeth, trying to think of something else. But it was hard, because of his disjointed thinking process.

In a moment he was off to sleep, dreaming his favorite dream where he could be anything he wanted. He was in his special place. In his dream, Frankie was running like the other boys, with long legs and a slender body. There was nothing different about him.

"Hey Frankie, come on, we've been waiting for you to come play ball with us," Larry Youngun shouted.

"Frankie's comin', Frankie's comin'!" he answered, his strong, young legs running with the wind.

"Tell us a secret," Terry cried out.

Frankie laughed, jumping high to touch the tip of the branch in front of him.

"Frankie's as fast as a cheetah and as brave as a tiger."

"Come on, Frankie, tell us a secret." Sherry laughed.

"God's Frankie's bestest friend!" Frankie shouted.

"Tell us a real secret," Cubby shouted.

Frankie shook his head and jumped up to touch another branch. "Frankie don't tell secrets!" he shouted, landing in their arms.

The children linked hands and ran up the hill. Racing like there was no tomorrow, trying to catch the sun. And Frankie was leading the way.

That's when Frankie was in his happy place. The place where he was a healthy, normal boy.

And it was only a million smiles away.

26

Second Thoughts

Having second thoughts about the supper conversations, Rev. Youngun decided to talk with Terry. He climbed the stairs quietly.

Terry's probably huddled under the sheets, worried about the thunder being God's anger, he thought.

But he was surprised to find Terry sitting on the windowsill, looking out at the lightning storm over the hills. Rev. Youngun cleared his throat.

Terry turned and smiled. "Oh hi, Pa." He turned back to look out at the storm. "God's puttin' on a big fuss over my carrots, ain't He?"

Rev. Youngun sat by his son, looking out into the storm. "God's not doing this over a carrot. This is just a storm."

Terry watched the lightning dance across the sky. "Guess it's pretty darn lonesome up there in heaven for God. Don't you think, Pa?"

"God's not lonely up there."

"Does that mean I won't have to sit outside of heaven's gate 'cause I didn't eat my carrots?" Terry asked hopefully.

Rev. Youngun patted his son's head and thought, *I'm sure you'll probably be charging admission at the gate after you get up there.*

"Does it, Pa?"

"I'm sure you'd find a way through the gate," he said quietly.

"I don't understand."

"We'll talk about it all in the morning, son. I'll send Larry and Sherry up so you kids can get to bed."

Terry remembered he had to go. "Pa, will you walk me out to the privy?"

"Walk you out? Why don't you just run out yourself?"

Terry looked down. "Just want you to come. That's all."

Rev. Youngun started to speak, then remembered his own fears as a young boy. "There's nothing to worry about out there," he said softly.

"I know there ain't nothin' really out there." Terry shrugged. "But I'm worried about the things that are out there that ain't supposed to be out there."

Rev. Youngun started laughing and took his son by the hand and walked him out the door and along the privy path. Terry did his business so quickly that he forgot to drop the carrots in his pocket down the hole.

I'll do that in the morning, he thought as they climbed the stairs back to his bedroom.

Terry got under the covers and looked up at his father. "You know what we need, Pa?"

Rev. Youngun stopped at the doorway. "What?"

"We need to go on a vacation. Go someplace we've never been."

"Like where?" Rev. Youngun asked, feeling a wave of guilt come over him. They didn't have enough money to go anywhere.

"Since we ain't never really been anyplace, why I'd settle for wherever you want to take us," Terry said.

"That would be nice," Rev. Youngun smiled. "Maybe one day we'll go someplace."

Terry got up and hugged his father's leg. "I wish it was one day and we were at that someplace."

"So do I, son. So do I."

"Sorry that I made you mad. Hope you still love me."

Rev. Youngun looked at his son. "I want to tell you a secret about a father's love, all right?" Terry nodded. "Love isn't something I give you every now and then," he said, pausing to put his arms around Terry. "A father's love is never ending. No matter what happens, it's a love that knows no end."

"I love you, Pa," Terry said, with all the sincerity in the world.

"And I love you, Terry," Rev. Youngun said, remembering the nights his father had told him the same thing.

27

Call in the Night

❖

Andrew Jackson Summers was going over the final copy of the next day's *Mansfield Monitor*. Todd Watson, the paper's sometimes writer and generally cranky know-it-all, watched the editor check for errors.

"Summers," Todd chuckled, "why do you spend so much time proofreading? You know half the people in this town can't read and the other half can't spell."

Summers didn't even look up. He had long grown used to Todd's jokes, wit, and generally sarcastic nature. "It's what I'm supposed to do."

Todd shook his head. "There's lots of things I'm supposed to do. Like run up stairs and be able to bite into an apple, but heck, my body just forgot about it and started getting old."

Summers managed a smile. "Why don't you write that down in a column? I've got a hole to fill in the paper, and there's a lot of middle-aged folks worryin' 'bout gettin' old."

"Maybe if you paid me more, I'd have more reason to write."

Summers looked up. "But you only write now and then as it is."

"And you only pay me now and then, and lately it's been a lot more then than now."

"Business is down. You know how it is."

Todd cleared his throat. "I *do* know how it is. There's not a businessman in this country who don't use the same excuse. Being cheap must be part of being in business."

Summers started to answer, but the wall phone rang loudly. He looked at it, then continued proofreading.

"Aren't you going to answer it?" Todd asked, irritated by the ringing.

"You answer it. I've heard enough bad news today."

It rang three more times before Todd picked up the receiver. "Monitor. Yeah, this is Todd Watson."

Summers tried to make sense from the one side of the conversation he could hear.

"Charlie? Yeah, of course I remember you. What news do you have?" Todd said.

He listened for a moment, then turned solemn. Summers looked up, trying to figure out what Todd was hearing.

"Escaped! No! You're kidding. When? . . . Tonight? . . . Where's he heading? . . . You don't know! . . . Here? . . . You think so? . . . You called Sheriff Peterson, didn't you? . . . Good. . . . All right. . . . I'll tell Summers. Bye."

Todd hung up the phone and took a match out of his pocket. Rolling it between his fingers, he waited for Summers to ask him what the conversation was about. Though Todd was trying to make light of things, what he'd heard bothered him more than he would let on.

Summers tried to keep editing the paper, waiting for Todd to tell him what the conversation was about. Finally, he had to ask. "Aren't you going to tell me what that was all about?"

Todd shrugged. "You told me to answer it. If you're so fired up about what was said, then you should have picked up the dang phone."

"But I didn't and you did. What were you talking about?"

Todd picked up his hat. "Sheriff knows. That's enough. Guess I've got to go now." He really did need time to think about what he'd heard.

"Todd!" Summers commanded. "You can't leave here until you tell me who that was. I've got a hole in my paper and could use some more copy."

Todd walked over and looked at the tiny space that was left on the bottom right of the front page. "Not big enough," he mumbled, turning toward the door.

Summers stood up. "Now hold on just one minute! You answered *my* phone, so I have a right to know what that was all about."

"I said," Todd smiled, speaking slowly, "you should have answered it."

Exasperated, Summers took out a five-dollar bill. "Here's what I owe you for last week's story. Now, tell me what's going on."

Todd took the bill and put it in his pocket, then opened the door.

"Wait!" Summers said. "I paid you, now tell me."

Todd shook his head. "You still owe me for two stories I did at Easter."

"But you said they were a gift and . . ."

Todd coughed loudly, signaling for Summers to be quiet. When he was able to speak, Todd said, "I said my writing was a gift . . . a gift from God. Not a gift to you."

"But . . . but . . ."

"No more buts. Ten more bucks, and I'll let you in on the biggest story of the year."

Summers's eyes went wide. "Bigger than the rabies outbreak?"

"Makes that look like momma's milk. Well?" Todd said, waiting.

"Well, what?"

"Where's my ten bucks?" Todd held out his hand.

Summers got a disgusted look on his face, then reached into his pocket again. "Okay. Here's your money. Now tell me."

Todd walked to the front page layout and pointed to the headline: "Watermelon Seed Spitting Contest Planned for Independence Day Celebration!"

He shook his head. "Do you think that should be the headline?"

"People are interested," Summers said, defensively.

"And I thought you were a journalist," Todd chuckled. "Your headline should read, 'Michael Sutherland Escapes! Barn Burner's Son May Be Heading This Way.'"

"No!" whispered Summers in awe.

"Yes," whispered Todd.

"What else did they say?" Summers asked. "I'll change the headline, and you write the story and . . ."

"And hold your horses there, Mr. Mighty Pen. You're forgetting one thing."

"What's that?" Summers asked.

"For this story, you have to pay me five bucks up front. No more IOU's."

Summers reached into his pocket. All he had left was a five-dollar bill. "If I give you this, I'll be broke."

"And if you don't give me that," Todd said, taking the bill from Summers, "you won't have a story."

He walked back to the general desk, which was used by the part-time writers. "Now clear the headline, and give me space for about five hundred words."

"Five hundred words!" Summers exclaimed. "You were only on the phone about a minute and . . ."

"And I've got a good memory and an even better imagination. I know all about the Sutherlands, father and son. This story is hot. I'll write something that will make people's hair stand on end . . ."

But suddenly, Todd went silent.

"What's wrong?" Summers asked. Todd got up. "Where you going now?" Summers asked.

"Need to think about what I'm going to write," Todd said. "If that's all right with you."

"But I've already paid for my story," Summers stammered, "and . . . and . . ."

"And you'll get your story. There's more to this Sutherland thing than just a headline," Todd said impatiently.

"Yeah? Like what?"

"Like . . . I gotta think about it," Todd said, letting the door slam behind him.

Summers stared at the door. *Bet he's thinking about Sutherland's father. Bet the whole town's going to be thinking about him by tomorrow.*

With a deep sigh, Summers went to the back room. Lighting a lantern, he looked at the bank of wooden, four-drawer filing cabinets.

Looking along the tab markers, he came to the "S" file and opened it. He ran his fingers along the almost illegible notations on the top of the files, then came to a whole section marked "Sutherland Family."

Summers gathered up the files and carried them back to his desk. He had a long night of reading ahead.

28

Crazy Man

❖

Abolt of lightning electrified the top of Devil's Ridge across the ravine from the Younguns' house. The eery shape that momentarily glowed in the dark made Rev. Youngun shiver.

The dancing, slithering snake of a lightning bolt disappeared as quickly as it appeared. Then the phone rang.

Todd Watson told Rev. Youngun about Sutherland's escape and about the list of names that Jack Sutherland had vowed to take revenge on.

"I know," Rev. Youngun admitted.

"You do?" Todd exclaimed over the phone.

"Michael told me about it when he was jailed for the Johnson fire."

"What'd he tell you?" Todd asked solemnly.

"Said that his father had a list of names which included the sheriff, the doctor, the undertaker, my name, and maybe some others. Michael said his father made him swear to carry out that act of vengeance for him."

"We've got a crazy man heading this way," Todd said.

"Not crazy, but he's probably got a lot of resentment. He said he was innocent, that he didn't set that fire," Rev. Youngun said.

"You know the old man turned his son bad, don't you?"

Rev. Youngun took a breath. "I just can't figure why no one knew what was going on at the time. Someone must have known he was hurting that boy."

Todd cleared his throat. "These hills keep good secrets. There's a lot of things that happen that shouldn't happen."

"I'm going to pray for guidance."

"You do that. I'm going to see the sheriff," Todd said, hanging up.

Todd went over to the sheriff's office and told him what he'd heard and what he'd told Rev. Youngun. Then he paused.

"You got somethin' I ain't heard already, Todd?"

Todd paused, then said, "Just that Sutherland might not be all there, you know what I mean?"

"He's an escaped barn burner who tried to kill a girl. That's about all I need to know, ain't it?"

"Maybe it isn't all his fault, Sheriff."

"Are you sayin' that someone else burned up that Johnson girl?"

Todd hit the wall with his fist. "Darn it, Sheriff, you listen to me! What that Sutherland boy went through from his daddy is *worse* than you can imagine. He still carries those scars."

"Todd, how come you know so much and no one else heard 'bout it?"

"I heard most of it firsthand a long time ago. From Sutherland."

"And did Sutherland tell you why he escaped and why maybe he's comin' back to Mansfield?"

Todd took a deep breath and exhaled slowly. "Sheriff, maybe Michael Sutherland's coming back to punish the town for not helping the little boy who was left to suffer at the hands of that crazy father."

The sheriff sipped his coffee. "Guess I've heard rumors of parents gettin' too hard on their kids and . . ."

"No one has the right to do to a child what that man did."

"What'd he do?" the sheriff asked quietly.

Todd cleared his throat, then told the sheriff what had haunted him for five long years. What Michael Sutherland had told him when he was arrested. About the evil things that his father had done to him.

Sheriff Peterson sat in an uncomfortable silence, hearing about an Ozark secret which was no secret any longer.

When they finally got around to calling Leonard Johnson, the sheriff was subdued. "Want me to do it?" Todd asked.

The sheriff paused, then said, "No. It's my job. I'll call him."

"Wonder how Jamie will take the news?"

"Don't know," Sheriff Peterson said. "I don't know anyone who's spoken to her in years."

"She hides her face away," Todd said.

"Guess I don't blame her for doin' that," the sheriff said. "Thanks for comin' by."

At the newspaper office, Summers sat reading the files. It was worse than the rumors he'd heard. There was one note saying a neighbor was afraid that Jack Sutherland was going to beat his son to death.

The man who was sheriff at the time checked it out but passed it off as just a discipline problem that Jack Sutherland was having with the boy.

And there was the story about Jamie Johnson being burned in her barn. "And he's coming back," Summers said out loud, looking at the picture of Michael Sutherland being led off to prison. "God help us."

Thunder boomed above as if the heavens were amening his plea. Thirty miles away, Michael Sutherland pulled the burlap sack around him, trying to ward off the chill from his wet clothes. He was miles away from the prison.

I'm goin' back to Mansfield, he thought, trying to stay awake. *I'm goin' back to set some things straight.*

29

Welcome Back

❖

Johnson picked up the phone, and the sheriff identified himself. "Only news you'd be callin' 'bout at night is bad news," Johnson said gruffly.

Peterson gripped the phone. "Leonard, I know it's late, but I wanted you to hear the news from me and not from any rumors."

Jamie sat on the edge of her bed, straining to understand her father's side of the conversation. The single candle by her bed flickered from the slight breeze that came in through the window.

Leonard Johnson exploded, "You got to catch him. He can't go free!"

"I'm goin' to get a posse together if we get a sighting, but we've got no proof he's comin' back here."

"He's comin' back, Sheriff," Johnson said coldly, "and this time he's mine." A mental image of a shot of whiskey going down his throat came over him. *Can't even have one. Can't start drinkin' again.*

Jamie came to the bedroom door. "Who's coming back?" she asked, but her father didn't answer.

Sheriff Peterson shouted over the phone, "Don't be tryin' to take the law into your own hands!"

Johnson was in a world of his own. He was battling an overpowering urge to drink and hadn't heard the sheriff.

"*Leonard,* I said don't be tryin' to take the law into your own hands."

"Sheriff," Johnson said, shaking off the drinking thoughts, "my hands are the only way he'll suffer for what he did to Jamie."

"That's what the law's for."

Johnson shook his head. "Then you just catch him first. If I catch him, I'll do things my way this time. What I should have done five years ago."

He slammed the receiver against the wall, then hung it on the hook. "What's happened?" Jamie asked.

"Nothin'!" Johnson snapped, pulling on his boots.

"Who's coming back? Is it Michael? Have they set him free?" she asked, grabbing her father's arm.

He stared coldly into her eyes. "He escaped. The man that ruined your face escaped from prison."

"Has anyone seen him?" she whispered, feeling her heartbeat increase faster and faster.

"No. But I'm hopin' I'll be the first," he said, taking his shotgun off the rack.

"Where you going?" she called out as he let the door slam behind him.

"Keep the door locked," he shouted back.

Jamie wrung her hands together. *Why's Michael comin' back here?*

Then she knew. *If he's comin' back, it's to see me. He's never forgotten. I know there's a reason he never wrote me.*

She smiled for a moment, remembering how he used to joke that he had a memory like an elephant. "But elephants always return to where they were born to die. That's what you told me, Michael. Is that why you're coming back?" Jamie wondered out loud.

In the moonlit darkness, Johnson walked. The liquor urge came back over him, but he tried to shake it off.

A stab of hurt hit him in the gut. It was the same pain he felt every time he thought about the night his daughter had been burned, wondering why he'd ever chosen to move to Mansfield.

He walked back to the burned shell of the barn and took out a cigarette. He struck the wooden match against a half-burned beam. The flame leaped up.

Johnson eyed the flame, then lit his cigarette. He watched the flame on the match burn down until only a curved, charred stick remained, then he blew it out.

It's fire time again. Feels like the summer when the barn burned down. I can feel it in my bones.

Though Johnson was only fifty, he looked seventy. The loss of his wife and then his daughter's accident had prematurely aged him. It had turned his hair snow white.

He looked at the remains of the barn as if it were a skeleton. Neighbors had urged him to tear it down, but he let it stand so that he'd never forget the hatred he felt for the man he blamed for his daughter's scarred face.

He stepped through the burned wall posts that were still standing. In his mind, he remembered everything that had happened. He ran his hand down the side of a board. *I couldn't get to her. She was screamin', "Help me, Poppa . . . save me!" but there was nothin' I could do. I couldn't think straight.*

Wincing at the memory, he put his arm over his face. But there was no stopping it. He was back there again.

The flames were too tall. Kept burnin' the skin off my arms and face each time I reached in.

He could smell the burning animal flesh again as he thought about the barn burning. Jamie, his pride and joy who had made the passing of his wife bearable, was trapped in the burning barn.

He covered his face. *I had come out to see if that Sutherland boy was still hangin' around. But I was too drunk to understand what she was sayin', and then I slapped her and knocked her unconscious. I fell back and knocked over the lantern and . . .*

It was a blur in his mind. Stumbling backwards. The lantern falling over. The flames scaring him. Running from the barn, leaving Jamie behind. Then finding Frankie hiding by the barn. In the blurred memory of alcohol, Johnson remembered staggering forward, screaming at the top of his lungs.

"Help, help!" Frankie shouted, running to the barn door.

"Shut up!" Johnson slurred, his mind too confused to know what to do. He took a step forward, then the barn's roof collapsed.

"Call fire people!" Frankie screamed.

Johnson tried to open the barn door. But the burning rafters had blocked it, and Jamie and the animals were trapped inside.

Frankie crawled through the window and braved the fire. He found Jamie under a burning beam. He kicked it off and dragged her out.

Johnson grabbed his daughter from Frankie, left her against the fence, then grabbed Frankie by the collar, and stared into his eyes. His sour whiskey breath made Frankie feel sick.

"Listen good, retard," he said, his eyes flaring. Frankie's eyes were wide. "I hear you don't tell secrets."

"Frankie don't tell secrets," he mumbled.

"Good. Don't you never, ever tell anyone—not a living soul—what you saw up here. You understand?"

Frankie nodded. "Frankie don't tell secrets," he whispered.

"You keep that secret and you'll live." Johnson let go and staggered backward. "It was that Michael Sutherland who did this, you remember that! Michael Sutherland caused the fire." Johnson struck Frankie across the face. "Do you understand?"

"Frankie don't tell secrets," he whispered, looking down.

"You keep this a secret or I'll kill you!" Johnson shouted into the man-boy's face. "Now get out of here and forget what you saw!" he screamed, booting Frankie down the hill toward town. Then Sutherland had come back. "Jamie . . . Jamie . . . where is she?" he cried out, as if in a daze.

All Johnson could do was nod toward her burned body, which lay crumpled by the fence. Sutherland broke down in tears.

I didn't want to admit what happened. Admit that my drinkin' burned up my daughter. That I left her in the burnin' barn because I was too scared . . . that the retard saved her.

So I blamed Sutherland. Blamed the barn burner's son. Lied in court to keep from admittin' what I done.

Going down to the shed, Johnson grabbed a lantern and walked purposely through the woods toward the Sutherland homestead. *That's where he'll be headin',* he thought as he walked.

He remembered the night after the trial when he'd come along this same path and burned Sutherland's house down. *But it wasn't even enough,* he thought. *This time I got to stop him for good.*

But when he arrived at the Sutherland homestead Sutherland wasn't there. In the light of the lightning bolts and shrouded moon, Johnson stood within the burned frame of the house, then walked over to the fort the Younguns had built.

"Kids shouldn't be playin' round here," he said, kicking away the brush gate. Nosing around, he found the list of names that Sherry had dropped.

I swear by the flame of my soul that these people will burn:

Doctor
Sheriff
Undertaker
Frankie
Rev. Youngun

He looked at Jack Sutherland's signature and then at the unsteady signature of Michael. It gave Johnson an idea. He reread the names. *Sheriff, doctor, undertaker, Frankie, Rev. Youngun . . . Gonna make sure that everyone's gunnin' for him this time,* he thought, as he headed toward town.

When he came to Sheriff Peterson's, he hid the lantern in the woods. He quietly edged up to Peterson's barn and sneaked inside.

Careful not to disturb the animals, he found a can of paint in the back of the barn and went over to the woodshed.

With bold strokes, he painted the list of names on the woodshed wall and left the letter on the ground. Then he went back behind the barn and piled brush and sticks against it, took matches from his pocket, and set the pile ablaze.

The flame raced across the dried brush, growing bigger and bigger as twigs ignited sticks which set fire to branches . . . soon the barn was in flames. The crackling cinders flew into the air, competing with the fireflies and lightning bolts.

"Welcome back, Michael Sutherland," he whispered, staring into the blaze. "Welcome back to Mansfield."

Then Johnson disappeared into the darkness. He wanted to get home to protect his daughter from the escaped convict.

On the outskirts of Mansfield, Michael Sutherland slipped off the wagon and headed to his Secret Tree to sleep until daylight. He wrapped himself in the memories of better times, and settled down to sleep.

He had no idea that Sheriff Peterson's barn was being burned in his name. That the son of a barn burner was accused again, without even striking a match.

30

Morning

Terry slipped out of his bed, hoping not to awaken his brother so he could be first into the privy. On the way down he thought about sneaking a lick from the sugar bowl but decided against it.

Opening the back door, he smiled at the rising sun. Sunup was a time that Terry liked. The world was coming awake with excitement. It was also the time that Terry believed the privy monster was asleep.

Skipping along the outhouse path, Terry warily eyed the small, wooden structure. He tiptoed forward, trying not to make a sound.

Maybe the privy monster is still waiting to pull me in, he thought, trying to be brave. *Maybe he's been waitin' up all night just to bite me.*

He looked around for a stick to protect himself with. *Bet he's gonna grab me with my pants down and pull me into the stinkin' muck.*

He stopped at the door, peering carefully around the edge. He poked inside with the stick. *Must be thousands of bees, wasps, hornets, bats, and rats in there just waitin' to eat me.*

He saw a cockroach scurry out and batted at it with the stick. *Must be a trick of the privy monster. Tryin' to make me think everything's okay.*

Opening the door a half-inch at a time, Terry looked up and down. *Bet there's bats, rats, and skunks waitin' to jump out and bite me when I drop my britches.*

Then a dark shape bounced against the door. Terry swung the stick around and screamed to high heaven. "Help!!!!!!"

He rolled backward down the slight incline and stopped. Staring back at him from the doorway of the outhouse was a porcupine.

"You again," Terry said.

It was the same porcupine that had been sneaking in at night and gnawing on the privy seat. Terry picked up a rock and tossed it near the pesky creature to shoo it away. The porcupine ran for the woods.

Terry went back to the privy and called through the door, "Mr. Privy Monster, you best leave me alone. I'm not worth turnin' into no stink bug. Ain't supposed to be no redheaded stink bugs on this earth."

He knocked on the door for good luck, then said, "So don't be pullin' at me when I drop my britches. I got some good food for you, so you best leave me alone or you won't get the best treats in the whole world."

Terry went into the privy and opened the door wide to let out the trapped night air. He took last night's supper carrots from his pocket and dropped them down the dark hole.

"Hope you like 'em, Mr. Privy Monster," he said to the dark hole below. The only answer was a splat.

"Best place in the world for carrots," Terry mumbled. He spit down the hole, joking to keep from being scared. "Hope you like carrots, Mr. Privy Monster."

Terry sat on the seat, feeling the warmth of the morning sun come through the opened door. The awful night stench had left with the breeze that came at ground level over the ravine behind their property.

There was nothing much to look at except for a bucket of lime, the corncob box, a fly swatter hanging from a nail, and a stack of old magazines that his father kept for reading and the kids used for other things. So Terry contented himself with thinking about candy and making up poems.

Dangit the dog peeked in through the door.

"Hey Dangit, listen to this:

Roses are red,
And slugs are slow.
To the privy monster I say,
Look out below!"

"How'd you like it?" he giggled to the dog. Dangit sat on the privy stoop and howled.

"Hush, dog, you'll wake everyone up!" Terry said.

Then he remembered who was down below and quickly got off and pulled his britches up. *Don't want to wake* him *up,* Terry thought as he hauled out the door.

On the other side of Mansfield, Missouri Poole awakened from a beautiful dream. She'd dreamed that she and Larry were married and had a dozen little Larrys running around.

"I bet that's just what he wants." She smiled.

At that moment, Larry was awakening from a nightmare in which he'd been forced to marry Missouri and move away from home. He saw himself plowing fields, cooking, cleaning, and doing everything except having fun. He sighed, wondering how he was going to keep avoiding Missouri.

"Might have to have my lips cut off."

31

Catch the Worm

Leonard Johnson was up an hour earlier than usual. He tried not to awaken Jamie.

Got to get back up to the Sutherland place, he thought, fixing a cup of coffee. *I know in my bones that he's gonna be back up around there. Early bird might just catch the worm this morning.*

"What are you doin' up this early?" Jamie asked, her face half covered by the sheet.

"Got some business to do in town," he lied, picking up his shotgun again.

"This early? Feed store doesn't even open until eight." She rubbed the sleep from her eyes and looked at him. "You're goin' after Michael, aren't you?"

"I'm sure they're callin' up a posse to hunt the barn burner down. I want to be there when they catch him."

She tried to dissuade him from going, but he wouldn't listen.

"He's burned again," he said.

"He has?" Jamie asked. "How do you know?"

"That's what the sheriff was callin' about last night."

"What was burned?"

Johnson paused and looked at his daughter. "Burned the sheriff's barn. Killed all his animals."

"Oh, Lord," she moaned.

"And he painted a list of names on the sheriff's woodshed of people he's gonna burn too. Left a written list too."

"But why?" she whispered. "Why is he doing this?"

Sutherland shook his head as he walked toward her. "He's crazy. He tried to kill you, and he's come back to try and kill others. If we don't stop him now, he might succeed."

Jamie watched her father trudge up toward the back field. *That isn't the way to town,* she thought.

Slipping into a loose dress, she started after him, then stopped at the door. *Can't go out into the light. Can't let anyone see the way I look.*

Returning to her rocker, she sat and wondered why she kept feeling a tingle on her spine. Why she kept having goose bumps run up and down her arms.

It's because Michael's back. I can feel him in the air. He's come back to see me.

She started to look in the mirror, but stopped. There was no erasing what had happened. No makeup or beauty tricks could change the way she looked.

She broke down in tears at the thought of seeing him again. Her inner desire to see him, to hold him, collided with the hurt and emotions from the fire.

It was like it was all happening again. Her father upset, Michael coming back. She looked out at the shell of the barn on the hill, worried now that her father had gone off to town to drink again.

The phone rang, and she walked to the corner wall and unhooked the receiver. Sheriff Peterson was calling to tell her father about the barn fire. He said that her father was the first person he was calling about it.

"But you already told him that last night," she said.

"Nope. Told him that Sutherland escaped. But the barn fire happened after the call."

Jamie hung up the receiver and wrapped her arms tightly around her waist. She rocked on her heels, trying to figure out what was going on.

She worried about what was coming. It all seemed to be happening again. Her father and Michael Sutherland seemed to be on a collision course of death and destruction.

32

Morning in the Secret Tree

❖

Michael Sutherland awoke, curled stiffly against the inner bark of the tree hollow. He opened one eye and saw the words "Don't Tell Secrets" that he'd carved in it years before. *Guess my escapin' is no secret now,* he thought, lacing up his shoes.

He thought of all the secrets, good and bad, that he'd pledged to keep over the years. Secrets that he only repeated in the Secret Tree.

He patted the inner bark. "You know more 'bout me than anyone, except . . ." He choked back a sob. "Except for Jamie. She knew it all. I told her everything."

Lost in his thoughts, he hugged himself, wishing it were Jamie's arms around him instead. *She knew how to heal my wounds. She knew the words to make me feel good.*

For a moment he was back at the bottom of the rock bluff near her farm. Both of them hunting for Ozark orchids, then finding the pristine pool of water that was kept in balance with the pure water that leached out from the crack in the rock.

We looked into each other's reflections and pledged our love forever. Saw in each other what we wanted. Saw the inner beauty that had been beat down in us both.

Sutherland shook his head. *Inner beauty? Jamie's face got burned. Wonder if she still knows that her inner beauty is what I really saw? Her face wouldn't matter to me.*

Then a pain stabbed his heart. *And I guess it don't matter to someone else neither. She's gettin' married. Gonna honeymoon with another man.*

Give him the love that was to be mine. Was to be ours together. Till death do us part.

Sutherland looked at the words he'd carved years before into the Secret Tree and spoke slowly. "I will not let her marry someone else until she knows the truth. Once she hears it, then she can do what she wants."

He knew that he'd die of a broken heart if she married someone else. *Please, Lord, give me the strength to see this through. Give me the strength to show her the truth.*

It had been a long time since he'd gotten on his knees in the Secret Tree to pray for help. But this time it wasn't to keep his father away from him.

"I will see her before this day is done. Before another dawn rises," he said, standing up in the hollow tree.

He inched his way through the tight opening and looked warily around. *Got the feelin' that someone's around,* he thought, looking for faces in the dense woods.

He passed the feeling off as just being nervous. He inspected the remains of his property and found the piled brush and logs near the burned-out shell of his home. Not recognizing it for the fort the children had built, he passed it off as just the doings of someone trying to clear part of the area.

Sutherland wanted to find Jamie, but he was hungry. It had been a day since he'd last eaten. He knew he couldn't go freely into town for food—the law was probably looking for him.

Then he thought about Frankie. "Frankie will get me somethin' to eat."

He took the invisible trails that he still remembered, avoiding all paths of civilization. Along the way he thought about the horrid list of names that his father had forced him to memorize and sign off on.

I ain't like Daddy, he thought, over and over. *I'll convince Jamie of that.*

He didn't know that Leonard Johnson was following him as he made his way through the woods to Frankie's house.

Frankie was up early to feed his bunnies and change their bedding. It was something that he did everyday, rain or shine.

He was as proud as a little boy could be with how many bunnies he had. Starting with two given to him as a gift, he now had thirty-four rabbits of all sizes and colors.

Though there were times that his grammie had run short of food, there was never a thought of eating the bunnies. Frankie called them his little children and had named each one.

That was the thing that amazed the people who'd stop by and talk with him. Here was a man who couldn't read or write, yet he'd memorized the names of thirty-four rabbits.

"Josh, don't jump on Zeke. John, leave her alone!" he admonished in his singsong voice.

"And you, Michael Sutherland Rabbit. Come over and talk. I kept your secret."

"Hey, chipmunk!" a deep voice called out behind him. "You talkin' to yourself now?"

Frankie turned. It was Kindrick, the assistant butcher from the meat market. "Leave Frankie alone."

"Don't you want to make some money, chipmunk?" Kindrick laughed. "We're short of rabbit meat, and yours sure do look tasty."

"Frankie's never gonna sell my little bunnies. Never!" Frankie screamed.

"Them bunnies are for eatin'." Kindrick chuckled, enjoying the torment.

"No!"

Kindrick held up a rabbit's foot he kept for luck. "After we cut 'em up, we'll sell the feet for good luck."

"You leave!" Frankie screamed.

"Can't take them to the state home," Kindrick leered.

"To where?" Frankie asked, confused.

Grammie stepped out from the back door. "Mr. Kindrick, what are you trying to do? Scare my boy half to death?"

"Sorry, ma'am," Kindrick muttered. "Just wanted to see if Frankie was ready to sell those bunnies. Got a need for 'em down at the butcher shop."

"Frankie won't be selling his bunnies, so you have no need to keep asking."

Kindrick muttered under his breath, "I'll just wait till after you're gone, old lady." He tipped his hat and kept walking toward town, not letting on that he'd heard a rumor about June Schmitt's failing health from the telephone operator.

"Frankie, it's time to get dressed. Your ride will be here soon," Grammie said.

"Is Frankie's flag ready?"

"It's waiting for you." She smiled.

"Just a minute. Frankie's got to close the bunny doors."

Grammie watched him skip around the bunny cages, bumping his head on the doors as he latched them. *I heard what Kindrick said. What does he know? Who could have told him that I'm sick? I haven't told anyone.*

She went into the parlor and sat down, deep in thought. *Please, God, don't let Frankie find out yet. I want to be the one to tell him . . . after I've got things ready.*

Sutherland had hidden behind the shed, watching Frankie, waiting for his grandmother to go inside. In the woods behind Sutherland, Johnson waited patiently for his chance.

"Pssst, Frankie," came a voice from the bushes next to the house.

"Yes, yes?" Frankie smiled looking around. He recognized the voice. Michael Sutherland stuck his head out. "Did you keep my secret?"

"Michael, Michael!" he squealed, hopping around. "Grammie said you were never comin' back," he said with glee.

"Shhh, Frankie. Don't let anyone know you seen me."

"Is it a secret?"

"It's a secret." Sutherland nodded. "You can't tell anyone."

Frankie puffed up his chest. "Frankie didn't tell anyone 'bout your Secret Tree."

"I trusted you. You were my friend, Frankie, and you still are." Sutherland winked. "How's your Grammie? She's an angel from heaven, that woman is."

"A what?" Frankie asked.

"An angel from heaven. I wish my Auntie Gee was like your Grammie."

Frankie puffed up with pride. "Frankie will go tell Grammie she's an angel right now."

Sutherland shook his head. "Can't Frankie. It's a secret between us."

Frankie thought for a moment about the other secret he knew. The one he hadn't told anyone, not even his grandmother.

"What you thinkin' 'bout?" Sutherland asked.

"'Nother secret."

"Tell me." Sutherland winked.

"Can't. Don't tell secrets." He smiled.

Sutherland laughed quietly. "That's my Frankie. Now go back inside and get me some food."

"But should Frankie tell Grammie?"

"Don't tell her a thing. Drop the food out the open kitchen window. I'll be there to catch it. Remember, it's a secret." He gave Frankie a hug. "God still your bestest friend?"

Frankie nodded. "And Frankie named a rabbit for you," he said proudly.

"That's good, Frankie. That's what I always wanted." He smiled, looking at the rabbits. "Now you go on in and drop me out that food."

"Shhh," Frankie said, looking around, "that's a secret."

"That's right." Sutherland nodded, crouching down.

"Can you play with Frankie?"

Sutherland patted Frankie's head. "Wish I could, but I don't have time. Maybe tomorrow."

"Will you pull Frankie in the wagon again?" he asked, remembering how Sutherland used to take him for long rides through town.

"I'll see."

"Frankie's a soldier near your house."

"A what?" Sutherland asked.

"We built a fort near your house."

Sutherland shrugged. "Didn't know what all that mess was up there. Now go get me that food."

"Frankie's got matches," he said proudly, showing Sutherland what he'd kept hidden in his pocket.

Sutherland shook his head. "I told you, don't play with matches They'll get you in trouble," he said, his mood souring. "And they can hurt people."

"Fire's bad," Frankie warned.

"I know," Sutherland nodded. "Give the matches to your grandmother, but first go on and get me somethin' to eat."

Frankie smiled and did as he was told. Sutherland took the rolls and apples that Frankie gave him back into the woods and ate them greedily.

Johnson watched him eat, then crept down past Sutherland toward

Frankie's house. He knelt down by the shed and took out his own matches. *Soon the whole town will be wantin' to lynch Sutherland.* He chuckled to himself.

Inside the house, Grammie looked at Frankie. "What's this?" she asked, picking up a match on the floor that he'd dropped from his pocket.

Frankie was silent. He felt so guilty that he couldn't say anything.

"Frankie, what are you doin' with matches?" she asked, reaching into his pockets. "And there's more in here!" she exclaimed.

Frankie stood silently.

"I told you fire is dangerous. That you should never, ever play with matches."

"Frankie don't play with matches."

"And I hope you never do," she said, wagging her finger.

Then the smell of fire hit her nose. "Oh no!" she said, looking out the window. The shed was on fire!

"What have you done, Frankie? What have you done?" she cried, rushing to the door.

Bad Boy

❖

Sheriff Peterson had been awake all night. First the call about Sutherland's escape, then he fought a losing battle against the raging fire that took his barn and animals.

The evidence seemed to point to Sutherland. But then he'd gotten the call about June Schmitt's burning shed and Frankie being caught with matches, and now his theory was in a jumble.

He arrived at Frankie's house and went around to the backyard. "June, you okay?" he asked, seeing the gaunt look on her face.

She nodded, then looked down. "Frankie came in from the yard, and then I found the matches in his pocket."

"You think he was playin' with matches and set the fire by accident?" Sheriff Peterson asked, taking off his hat.

"I just don't know," she said, feeling faint.

He didn't want to ask but had to. "Was Frankie in his bed all night?"

The old woman turned and looked at him closely through her left eye. "I tucked him in early. Why?"

"'Cause my barn burned down last night and . . ."

"Sheriff!" she exclaimed. "My Frankie was in his bed! He didn't go out anywhere."

"Had to ask. You know that." He took out his handkerchief and wiped his brow. "With Sutherland escaping from prison, and my barn burnin', why . . ."

"What did you say?" she gasped.

He looked at her. "Don't you know? Michael Sutherland escaped from prison last night. Warden thinks he might be headin' this way."

"Oh, Lord," she whispered, "I hope he doesn't come back 'round here."

The sheriff motioned for Frankie to come over. "Frankie, did you set your shed on fire?"

Frankie shook his head. "Frankie don't play with matches."

Sheriff Peterson put his hand on Frankie's shoulder. "Did you do it? Were you a bad boy, Frankie?"

"No."

The sheriff looked at him. Frankie was shaking with nervousness. His eyes were blinking rapidly. "Do you know who might have done it?" he asked softly.

Frankie thought for a moment, then put his finger to his nose and pinched his nostrils.

"What's he doin'?" the sheriff whispered to June.

"Thinkin'," she said. She didn't want to tell the sheriff that Frankie had been Sutherland's friend.

They watched Frankie concentrate. He began taking deeper and deeper breaths, then his eyes went wide. His grandmother recognized the sign of a thought coming to her grandson.

"Frankie, tell the sheriff what you think," she said sternly.

"Can't. It's a secret," Frankie said, looking down.

"What secret?" the sheriff asked. "Do you know who done it, boy?"

Frankie stood mute.

Sheriff Peterson looked at June. "Make him tell me what he knows."

"Can't." She sighed. "Frankie will never reveal a secret he's promised to keep."

Frustrated, the sheriff pressed on. "Have you seen Michael Sutherland? Have you, Frankie?"

Except for Frankie's blinking eyes, he didn't move.

"He knows somethin'. Make him tell me," the sheriff commanded.

Frankie's grandmother shook her head. "Frankie doesn't ever tell his secrets."

The sheriff looked at her. "June Schmitt, we got a crazy lunatic runnin' 'round, and this boy either knows somethin' or has been playin' with matches and settin' fires."

"Frankie wouldn't do that," she said defensively.

"You're not sure of that, are you?"

She looked down. "If he was playing with matches, he wasn't meanin' no harm. He's just curious. Like all children are."

"June," he said, taking her hand. "Frankie's not a child. He's a twenty-five-year-old man in the eyes of the law."

"He's just a child," she said, then remembered that Frankie was listening.

"Frankie don't play with matches," he pouted.

"Frankie," she said, pushing him along, "why don't you go check on your bunnies."

"Yes, Grammie," he whispered, walking slowly away.

Sheriff Peterson shook his head. "Folks are worried 'nough as it is with Sutherland escapin'. If people start thinkin' that Frankie's out settin' fires, why . . ." he paused, "why, they'll force you to put him into an asylum."

"It'd kill him," she whispered.

"And fire kills innocent people."

"But if he did it he was just curious and . . ."

The sheriff interrupted her. "And people don't want a curious retarded man who plays with matches runnin' around. They'll turn on him overnight and send him packin'. No one wants a fire bug around whose mind ain't right."

Frankie stood by his bunny cage, trying to understand what they were saying. *Frankie can't tell secret. Frankie didn't play with matches.*

He tickled the bunny's ear against the cage. *Frankie's not a bad boy. Frankie's not a bad boy*, he thought, his eyes moving faster and faster.

The bunny that he'd named after Michael Sutherland hopped up. Frankie started to call out the name but stopped. He knew instinctively that it was not a good time to say Sutherland's name.

The sheriff said, "June, you got to keep an eye on Frankie. Don't let him out of your sight after dark and . . . don't let him have no more matches."

"But I didn't and . . ."

The sheriff interrupted her. "And folks are gonna suspect that you catchin' Frankie with matches right after your shed burns looks mighty bad. If other fires start and they don't catch Sutherland, they'll come lookin' for someone to blame."

"But people in town like him. They call him the Mayor of Mansfield and . . ."

"June, I don't think you should be lettin' Frankie go runnin' into town this mornin'. Might should keep him home today."

"But he's got to go raise the flag. He thinks that's his job," she exclaimed.

The bunny nipped Frankie's hand. "Michael Sutherland Rabbit, no, no!" Frankie exclaimed.

"What did he say?" the sheriff asked.

Frankie's grandmother shook her head. "Named a rabbit after Michael Sutherland."

"What's he know about Sutherland?"

"He just knew him . . . that's all."

The sheriff looked at Frankie through the screen door. "I think he knows more than he's lettin' on. I think he's hidin' somethin' with this secret business." From the corner of his eye, he watched Frankie. *He's not tellin' me the truth,* he thought. *Frankie knows somethin' 'bout all this.*

Frankie stood, half listening to what the sheriff and his grandmother were saying. He knew they were talking about him, but he wasn't sure what it all meant. But he knew the sheriff was asking a lot of questions about his friend.

"Frankie don't tell secrets," he mumbled to Michael Sutherland Rabbit.

34

Back to the Fort

Sutherland took the paths through the brush and bushes, unaware of the fire at Frankie's. He crept alongside the abandoned road toward his old homestead, keeping out of sight.

Seeing Frankie and the houses of Mansfield had brought back a lot of old emotions. *Got to see Jamie before the sun rises tomorrow,* he thought over and over as he walked. With each step he unconsciously counted his heartbeats, trying to calm himself down.

The tree branches drooped in places, blocking the road. Bushes and plants in other places had grown wild across it.

When he got back to the shell of his house, he felt bile rising in his throat. His mouth was sour. Sticky sweat clung to his shirt. Seeing the remains brought back the feeling of being hated and unwanted. Of being treated like an outcast by the town. Of the memory that no one ever tried to help the young boy who reached out to anyone but found no one there.

They put me in prison for somethin' I didn't do. Now they've turned my house into a shooting target, he fumed, kicking away some of the debris around the burned out shell. *They couldn't leave it alone. They had to abuse me even after they convicted me of somethin' I didn't do. Believed Leonard Johnson over me. Then they burned down my house.*

I had already left the barn. When I came back, it was on fire. Johnson came after me with his bullwhip.

The judge took his word over mine. 'Cause I'm a barn burner's son. But I didn't do nothin' wrong.

He looked at the fort that Frankie had told him about but decided he'd investigate it later. It was time to step into the remains of the house that held so many bad memories.

Sutherland walked between the small chimney and the door frame, as if measuring off memories in his mind. Though it had been small, it was the only home that Sutherland had ever known, and he had come back as soon as he could to escape Auntie Gee's coldness.

He looked around, trying to find the memory of a happy thought. Stepping carefully, then erratically, Sutherland went from corner to corner, trying to remember something good that had happened in his home.

He went back to one of the few moments he cherished. Jamie. He thought about Jamie giving him the locket.

Then he remembered why he'd wanted to come back. Why he'd escaped from prison.

He wanted to touch and hold the locket again. Look at Jamie's picture. Remember that one moment in his life when no evil touched him. When she made him feel like a good person.

Got to see Jamie before the sun rises, he thought. *Convince her that I didn't hurt her. That she shouldn't marry anyone else because I still love her.*

He remembered the locket and the tintype picture of Jamie and him together. Remembered the moment he and Jamie had posed in town for the picture. How they'd had to stand for what seemed like hours while the photographer got their positions right.

"I need to touch it again," he said, stepping carefully over a burned rafter. "It'll give me the strength to talk to Jamie."

At the stone base of the fireplace, he pushed the dirt away from the right-hand floor stone. Digging carefully, he looked for the metal box.

He dug deeper and deeper. "It was right here," he said, pushing the dirt away.

He panicked and dug deeper and deeper. He pulled out all the base rocks of the fireplace but still didn't find it.

"It was right here," he moaned, then collapsed on the stones he'd dug up. He dropped his face onto his hands. "I'm goin' crazy. It was right here. Right here's where I put it."

He felt exhausted. Things weren't going the way he'd planned. "Got to rest," he mumbled, heading toward the Secret Tree. He had to sit down for a while in the place where he felt safe. After that, he'd try to figure out what happened to the locket.

"Got to find it," he whispered, slipping into the Secret Tree.

Sherry Youngun had the locket and was determined to keep it. She half listened to her father, thinking instead of the feel of the gold on her neck.

"You children need to finish your chores before you go out to play," Rev. Youngun said as he put his papers together.

"Yes, Pa," the three Younguns chorused. He looked at his daughter. "Sherry, you're going to be hot in that shirt. Why don't you put on something cooler?"

"I feel okay, Pa," she answered.

"Well, at least unbutton the top button before you sweat to death."

"Perspire, Pa," Terry said. "Horses sweat and people perspire."

Rev. Youngun sighed. "Yes, I know." He looked at Sherry. "At least roll up the sleeves."

Sherry still had the locket on. She'd slept with it. It was the most beautiful thing she'd ever seen, and she was determined to keep it. That's why she kept her collar buttoned. "I will, Pa," she said, rolling up her left sleeve.

While their father was still at the house, the Younguns did their chores very carefully, but the moment he got into his buggy and headed to Mansfield, they rushed through the chores like they were practicing a fire drill.

"Come on, let's go!" Terry shouted, kicking off his shoes.

"But we're not finished yet," Larry said.

Terry shrugged. "Let's finish tomorrow. Pa'll never know."

"He will if I tell him," Sherry said.

Terry gave her the eye. "And if you do, you can also tell him I walloped you," he warned, brandishing his fist. But Larry prevailed, and they finished the morning chores. Then, like a starter going off, they headed out. Running barefoot down the path to the fort and slipping under the honeysuckle vines, they avoided every sharp rock and thorn. They knew every inch of the trail to their secret place in the woods near the Willow Creek Bridge.

Their feet were already toughened from days of no shoes, so they had no trouble running over the path roots and creek stones without flinching. There, away from the eyes of adults and unwanted kids, they could keep adding on to Fort Mansfield.

"Gonna fight the Yankees today!" Larry screamed out, jumping over a finger of the creek.

At the fort, Terry picked up a barrel-stave sword and waved it in the air. "I say we're pirates, and we make Sherry walk the plank!" He laughed, swishing it toward Sherry.

"Stop it!" she screamed.

Sutherland heard her shriek from inside the Secret Tree. It startled him awake.

Blinking his eyes open, Sutherland peeked out through the hollow tree opening. He could see the Younguns playing at the fort they'd built on his property.

Larry stopped, looking around. "Someone's been foolin' 'round with our fort."

"Looks the same to me," Terry said.

"Got the feelin', that's all," Larry said. He inspected the brush gate that Johnson had kicked. "This has been stomped."

Sherry shrugged. "Maybe it was a bear or somethin'."

"Maybe," said Larry, "maybe."

Sutherland watched them chase each other, jumping over the graves of his parents. It didn't bother him that they jumped on his father's grave, but he felt anger building when he saw Sherry standing on his mother's grave.

Terry chased Sherry around the edge of the gully near the fort until she stopped and pointed. "Save them!" she shrieked, pointing to the two Missouri box turtles on their backs in the water. "Get 'em, Larry."

Larry eased himself down the small, dirt-clod bank that crumbled underfoot.

"Are they dead?" Sherry asked, making a sad face.

Larry picked up the closest one. It was a three-toed box turtle that wiggled to life in his hands. "Got this one in time," he said, handing it up to his sister.

The other turtle came to, turning itself over. Larry reached down and grabbed the colorful, yellow-striped turtle. "You got two more for your collection." He smiled.

"Let's take 'em home now," she said.

Sutherland watched the children march off, turtles in hand. He waited, then walked over to inspect the fort. It really didn't bother him that the kids had made a fort on his property. Poking through their stick weapons, hospital lean-to, and brush tunnels, he came across the small tunnel they'd dug. Inside he saw the box. The box where he had put Jamie's locket.

Crawling in, he grabbed the box and took it out. Inside he found the pictures of his family, which brought back a flood of memories.

These pictures hide the truth, he thought, gritting his teeth and remembering how his father had forced him to smile for the family photography. *Nothin' ever, ever to smile about in this home,* he thought.

"It's got to be in here," he mumbled, taking everything out.

But the locket wasn't there. He put everything back in the box and crawled back out of the fort.

He looked in the direction that the Younguns had headed. "Those kids know where Jamie's locket is. Can't go see her without it." Sutherland looked toward the horizon, then toward the direction of Jamie's home.

"I don't care what she looks like. My ma used to say that beauty's only skin deep." He paused, thinking about how beautiful he'd found Jamie—not for her looks, but because she listened to him, understood the hurts that lurked under his skin, and made him feel like a person.

She made me feel like there was nothin' wrong with me. That what my daddy did was not my doin'. Jamie understood. That's why I loved her then and I'll always love her. Got to make her understand. Got to.

35

Seed of a Bad Seed

❖

Sheriff Peterson sat at his desk answering calls about Sutherland's escape and the two fires. Rumors were spreading faster than the wind that fluttered the curtains behind him.

Most people were more concerned with Frankie than with Sutherland. They wanted to know if "the retard" was still running around loose.

Here we've got an escaped barn burner running around with a list of people to burn, and they're more concerned with Frankie. The sheriff drew a deep breath and let it out slowly. *But if it's Sutherland, why ain't he burnin' down the houses if he wants to get revenge and hurt people like his daddy did? Why just sheds and barns? And why would he write that list of names? Don't seem logical.*

He chuckled at the irony of his own thoughts. *Logic? What logic is there to what he done to Jamie? Or what his daddy done? Maybe the abuse his daddy did to him warped his mind or somethin'.*

Another call came in about Frankie. It was the second person who "thought" he'd seen someone lurking behind his barn.

Things are gettin' out of hand, he thought. *Someone's gonna shoot at shadows and end up killin' some innocent kid.*

Sheriff Peterson banged his boot heel down on the desk. *His grandma caught him playin' with matches right after the shed caught fire. My barn burned last night. No one's seen Sutherland. Maybe Frankie found the list of names playin' at the fort, and he painted the names from the list on my barn.*

As implausible as it sounded, he had to consider all possibilities. *Maybe some of the kids he plays with painted the names as a joke and ran when Frankie started playing with matches. And he's keepin' their names secret.*

Looking at the wall phone, he thought about calling June Schmitt to tell her to bring Frankie in so he could talk to him some more. Then he decided against it. *Can't get much straight talk from him anyway. Don't know much more I can do 'cept keep an eye on him.*

Wish I could just catch Sutherland. If the fires stopped, well, then I'd know who'd done it. Then he paused. *Wish I knew if Frankie's seen him. Namin' that rabbit after a crazy man won't sit well with the town. If people start thinkin' that a barn burner and Frankie are teamed up somehow, why, no tellin' what they'll do.*

He pondered the thought, then went back to his files and reread the meager information his predecessor had kept on Jack and Michael Sutherland. He got more from the cryptic notes that were scribbled on the sides of the poorly typed documents than he did from the court records.

Sheriff Peterson's knowledge of the Sutherlands came from the stories he'd heard and the articles he'd read that Summers had delivered from the newspaper's files. It was hard to separate the facts from the rumors that had been told and retold by the rural Ozark grapevine of news, gossip, and distortion.

He hadn't been sheriff when Jack Sutherland was hanged, or when Michael Sutherland was sent to prison five years ago. But you couldn't live in Mansfield without hearing the stories about the infamous barn burner. And then there was the information Todd Watson had given him about Michael's pain as a child.

At that moment Todd came through the door. "What's this I hear 'bout Frankie Frank burnin' his shed down?"

Sheriff Peterson hit his fist into the palm of his hand. "I'm not sure if Frankie did anythin'. His grandmother caught him with matches and . . ."

"And it looks bad. I just left Bedal's General Store, and folks are talking all over the place about Frankie being sent to a state home for people like him. To keep the town from being burned down."

Sheriff Peterson sighed. "Frankie's goin' nowhere soon. I don't know what he did or didn't do."

"Don't bet your badge on that. I also heard folks sayin' that they heard rumors of Frankie sneaking out of his grandmother's last night and burning down your barn."

"June Schmitt said he was in bed all night."

"And everyone knows she's old and getting older. Old folks can't hear half the things you tell them let alone whether someone slips out the window at night."

"Todd Watson, you're letting this go to your head."

"No, *I* don't think Frankie done it. But fire puts fear into folks living in wooden houses."

"They should be more concerned about Sutherland runnin' loose."

"Heard Frankie named a rabbit after that barn burner."

Sheriff Peterson nodded. "That he did."

"Some folks think that Sutherland and Frankie are doing this together, and some think that Frankie's smarter than we give him credit for. That he just wants to hurt those that helped him," Todd continued.

"Frankie's not smart enough to do what everyone's sayin'," Sheriff Peterson said.

"Don't take much smarts to strike a match," Todd said. He pretended to strike a match against the wall.

"And it takes even less to believe what you're sayin'," the sheriff said. "Bad 'nough folks thinks the Missouri Ozarks are filled with dummies without you talkin' nonsense."

"Mind you, Sheriff, I'm from Arkansas."

"Sorry 'bout that." The sheriff smiled. "I was half-worried myself 'bout Frankie playin' with matches until you came 'round here sayin' your ignorant talk."

Todd shook his head. "Remember, Sheriff, everyone tolerates Frankie because he's kind of like the town pet. He's like a big, goofy kid who doesn't know any better." He paused.

"Go on," the sheriff said.

"All I'm saying is that you have the badge to nip this in the bud. You and I both know that Frankie's no barn burner. But you can't make scared folks think logically . . . not with an escaped lunatic maybe running around who he's friends with."

"You heard anythin' more bout Sutherland?" Sheriff Peterson asked.

Todd shook his head. "I have the feeling he came back for his own reasons."

The sheriff looked at Todd. "Hope that man ain't the bad seed of a bad seed."

"Heard an old boy down at Tippy's Saloon say Sutherland was born bad and should have been strung up like his pa."

"You believe that?" the sheriff asked.

Todd coughed to clear his throat. "There's no such thing as a boy born bad."

"Some folks might say you're naive."

"Sheriff," Todd said, "I'd rather be naive than so calloused that I can't tell right from wrong." The sheriff raised his eyebrows but didn't say anything. "He wasn't born bad. His father turned him that way. Made him crazy in the head."

Sheriff Peterson scratched his chin. "But he's the one that burned Jamie up. Not his daddy. His daddy was long dead."

The door slammed open, and Leonard Johnson barged into the office. "Sheriff, you got to call up a posse. Get some armed men together so we can hunt down Sutherland 'fore he burns the whole town down."

"You been drinkin', Leonard?" the sheriff asked, sniffing whiskey in the air.

Johnson shook his head. "I gave up the bottle a long time ago." But the sheriff wasn't sure.

Johnson started to tell him about seeing Sutherland then stopped. *Can't say I followed him to that boy's house.*

"Sheriff," Johnson said, "there's three more names on that crazy man's list. He already got to you and Frankie. But there's still the doctor, the undertaker, and Rev. Youngun. You need to put some guards night and day 'round their properties."

"Leonard, why don't you calm down. I got everyone around keepin' an eye out for Sutherland."

"You gonna leave a minister unprotected?"

"Rev. Youngun's been warned."

"Warned? We got to go out and find him."

"It's not just that simple. Sutherland's escaped, but with Frankie bein' caught with matches, everythin's all confused."

Johnson thought hard. *Frankie's the only livin' soul who knows the truth of what happened to Jamie that night. He's the only one who knows what my drinkin' did. Can't trust him to keep a secret forever.* "What happens to Frankie if he's been settin' fires?" he asked.

The sheriff looked at his fingernails, then shook his head. "They'd send him away to a home his grandma told me about. A home for mentally ill people up in Jeff City."

"Be a long time 'fore they let him out of somethin' like that, don't you think?" Johnson asked.

The sheriff stood up and looked out the window. "They'd never let Frankie Frank back out. He'd be there till he died."

After a moment Johnson walked out the door and down the street and entered Tippy's Saloon, believing his tracks were covered.

36

The Mayor of Mansfield

❖

Bye-bye, bye-bye, bye-bye," Frankie shouted in his odd voice, blowing kisses to his grandmother. "Feed bunnies, feed Frankie's bunnies."

"Stand by the side of the road, and wait for your ride," she called out. *I shouldn't be lettin' him go. But it means so much to him*, she thought, looking out at her grandson.

"Frankie will, Grammie." Frankie nodded. "Please feed my bunnies."

"And you come right back and don't pick up any matches."

"Yes, Grammie," Frankie nodded, kicking at a fly. "Frankie don't play with matches."

"Don't even pick any up."

She saw him step into the road. "Stay on the side, and wait for your ride to pull up next to you."

"Yes, Grammie."

"And say the pledge loud and clear so everyone can hear you when you raise the flag." She sighed. *I know the sheriff said to keep him here today, to watch him, but I don't feel up to walkin' with him. Just don't feel good today.*

Frankie stood by the road with his hand on his heart, shouting loudly in his odd way of speaking, "I pledge allegiance to my Flag and to the Republic for which it stands." He paused and took a deep breath, then continued, "One nation indivisible, with Liberty and Justice for all."

His grandmother clapped. "That's good! Now go raise the flag and say the pledge just like that, so everyone can hear you." It was the same thing she said to him each morning.

"And Frankie don't play with matches. Frankie don't," he said sincerely. He waved again, his hand flapping like a leaf in the wind. "Frankie loves you, Grammie."

"I love you too, Frankie." She smiled and waved him on.

She watched Frankie stand by the side of the road, his hands clutched, patiently waiting for his ride. The sharp pains in her stomach had not left her since daybreak, and they were getting worse.

Frankie stood outside his house every morning waiting for a ride to town. He never knew who was going to pick him up, just that someone would. No one made a special plan to be there at a certain time, but the road into Mansfield was well traveled. He'd never had to wait more than thirty minutes—even in bad weather.

People just stopped and gave him a ride, because they knew he had a job to do. They knew it was important that Frankie get to town as early as he could, so he could raise the courthouse flag and say the Pledge of Allegiance to the birds in the square. It was one of his duties as the honorary Mayor of Mansfield.

Frankie was very proud that he could say the Pledge of Allegiance, but he had no idea what it meant. All he knew was that adults took off their hats and put their hands over their hearts every time he raised the flag and said the pledge. It made him feel like they were showing him respect as the mayor.

Rev. Youngun brought his buggy to a halt. "Mr. Mayor, you want a ride to town?"

"You're late," Frankie said, climbing up. It was the same thing he said to anyone who picked him up.

"I'll try to be on time tomorrow, Mr. Mayor." Rev. Youngun smiled, playing along. "How come you're not up playing at the fort?"

"Frankie has to raise the flag," he said. "Frankie's job."

"Well, I'm sure the children are up there waiting for you," Rev. Youngun smiled.

"You bring me any sugar?" Frankie asked.

Rev. Youngun fiddled around in his pockets. "Think I have one of Terry's sour balls in my pocket somewhere." He found one in his pant pocket. "Ah hah, here it is," he said, handing it to Frankie.

Frankie put it in his mouth and began sucking. "Thank you. Thank you. Thank you."

"You're welcome."

Frankie shook his head. "Grammie says you can never say thank you enough."

"How's your Grammie doing?"

Frankie bobbed his big head up and down. "Grammie fine. She made Frankie breakfast and ironed my pants," he said proudly, pointing to the fresh-pressed crease. "Frankie's old enough to wear long pants you know." He bobbed his head up and down.

"How old are you now?"

Frankie closed his eyes and counted on his fingers. "Frankie's one, two, three . . . Frankie's four years old, four years old, fours years old." He smiled, clapping for himself. "Grammie says that I'll be four years old forever. That I'm special."

"That you are," Rev. Youngun agreed.

"Grammie's special too," Frankie added.

"That's right. She's a good, good woman," Rev. Youngun said, clicking the reins.

"She's an angel from heaven," Frankie said, running his tongue over the candy.

"That she is, but who told you that?" Rev. Youngun asked curiously.

"Can't tell," Frankie said, "it's a secret." He looked up at the sky, held out his hand, then shook his head. "God won't be dropping tears today."

Rev. Youngun smiled. "No, I guess He won't."

Frankie held on to the wagon bench as Rev. Youngun giddiyapped the horse. "You got any sugar?" Frankie asked again.

"I already gave you that candy in your mouth."

Frankie stopped and felt the sour ball with his tongue. "Thanks," he nodded. Then he became serious. "You paid your taxes yet?" he asked, holding out his hand.

"Why, I'm sorry, Mr. Mayor, I forgot." Rev. Youngun reached into his pocket and pulled out a nickel. "Hope this is enough. Don't want to be in trouble with the mayor."

Giving Frankie tax money was another dimension to the game that the whole town played with him. Everyone knew he gave the money to his grandmother for food and clothes, which was part of the town's way of taking care of them without making June feel like it was charity.

Frankie took the coin, examined it, and then bit it. He'd once seen an old prospector do the same thing when he was testing to see if a coin was gold or not. Frankie had imitated him ever since with every coin he was given for taxes.

"It's just a nickel. It's not gold." Rev. Youngun chuckled.

Frankie bit one more time to make sure. "It's a real nickel," he said, putting the coin into his pocket. He turned and asked, "Want to know a secret?"

"You got a good one?" Rev. Youngun smiled. Though Frankie had asked him the question a thousand times over the years, he always acted like it was the first time. It was another part of Frankie's game with the town.

"God loves you," Frankie said matter-of-factly.

"I'm glad to hear that," Rev. Youngun said. "In my field, it's comforting to know that."

"Yup. Don't tell no one. God told Frankie that He loves you." Then Frankie suddenly became quiet.

"What's wrong?" Rev. Youngun asked. Conversations with Frankie were always erratic, since you could never tell what he was thinking.

Frankie began blinking faster and faster. He touched the tip of his nose and pinched his nostrils.

"Don't do that," Rev. Youngun said, concern in his voice.

But Frankie kept holding his breath, his head turning a darker purple by the second. Then he exhaled like an explosion. "Frankie didn't do it!" he said, crossing his arms.

"Do what?"

"Burn the shed. Burn the barn. Frankie don't play with matches."

Rev. Youngun was confused. "What are you talking about?"

Before Frankie could answer, a sputtering automobile came toward them. Rev. Youngun tipped his hat to Sarah Bentley, who was riding with her husband.

William Bentley owned the largest logging operation in the state and was the wealthiest man in the county. Sarah had come from New York City and thought she was the social queen of Mansfield.

"Have you heard the news, Reverend?" Sarah asked.

"What news is that?" Rev. Youngun asked, pulling the buggy to a halt.

"Tell him, William."

William Bentley looked uncomfortable. He cleared his throat. "Someone burned down the sheriff's barn last night."

Rev. Youngun's eyes registered his shock. "Who did it? Sutherland?"

"They don't know," Bentley said.

"And someone burned the shed at . . . at . . . at his house," Sarah said, nodding toward Frankie. Her disdain for Frankie was well-known. She felt that he belonged in a state home.

Rev. Youngun looked at Frankie. "What happened?"

"Frankie don't play with matches. Frankie didn't do it." He moaned, squinching his eyes tight.

Sarah shook her head. "He shouldn't be out by himself."

"Frankie didn't do it," Frankie said, looking at Rev. Youngun with imploring eyes.

"What does the sheriff think?" Rev. Youngun asked.

Bentley cleared his throat again. "He said that he doesn't know who burned his barn, but with Sutherland runnin' loose, and until he's caught, everyone should be careful."

"And tell him the rest." Sarah nudged her husband.

Bentley took a breath, not looking at Frankie's face. "And he said that Frankie was found with matches in his pocket just after the shed caught fire."

Sarah looked at Frankie, shaking her head. "You ought to take him right back home, Reverend. I think he's a dangerous fire bug."

"Frankie didn't do it," Frankie moaned.

Sarah looked at Frankie, then turned away. "We've got to go, don't we, William?" she said, nudging him again.

Bentley nodded. "Talk to you later," he said, starting the car forward.

37

Missouri Turtles

❖

Maurice drove his wagon slowly down the road toward Mansfield. Eulla Mae had sent him into town to buy supplies.

"Gonna be leavin' soon for my vacation," he said to his mules, who flicked their ears in response. "Gonna leave all this behind and go to my wonderful cousin Speedy's cabin. This place ain't nothin' compared to where I'm goin'."

A mockingbird called out and Maurice laughed. "Why, I might just like it so much that I'm gonna move away from here. Yes sir, move down to where the livin' is real, real good."

He pulled his mule team to a halt to let the Youngun children pass in front of him. Sausage sat next to him on the bench and barked out a hello.

"Hush, dog," Maurice said good-naturedly.

"Hi, Mr. Springer," the Younguns said in unison.

Maurice nodded. "What you carryin' there?" he asked.

"Got two more turtles for my collection," Sherry said proudly.

She stopped in a small puddle from the creek runoff in the middle of the road and proudly held up her turtles.

Sutherland watched them from his hiding place in the woods. Sausage barked at the turtles, trying to get down. "You're too fat to jump," Maurice said.

The thick, round dog wagged its tail, still trying to get to the turtles.

"Sausage likes the turtles," Sherry said.

"Sausage looks like he likes to eat." Larry laughed.

"Does Sausage eat turtles?" Sherry asked, pulling them back from the dog.

"Sausage likes to eat anything." Maurice smiled.

Sausage wiggled around, barking loudly. Maurice rubbed the dog's head. "Calm down 'fore you let loose on the seat. I told you, it happens again and I'll never take you ridin'."

"What happens again?" Terry asked.

"You know," Maurice said in embarrassment.

"If I knew I wouldn't be askin' you," Terry answered.

Maurice looked at the auburn-haired scampster. *I know he knows what I'm talkin' 'bout . . . I just know it.* Sausage wiggled around, trying to get down. "Dog has a plumbin' problem . . . just sort of leaks at the wrong time."

The children giggled. Terry reached up to pat the fat dog. "Sausage just gets excited. That's all."

"You like my turtles?" Sherry asked.

"They look hungry to me," Maurice said, half in jest.

Sherry turned the turtles around to look at their faces. "My turtles love strawberries. Wish we had some."

"Strawberries," Larry said. "That's what my ma used to love."

Maurice saw the look of hurt and memory that came over Larry's eyes as he spoke. He didn't want thoughts of their late mother to cloud their day, so he tried to be lighthearted.

"What do turtles eat? Why, girl, turtles like worms most of all."

Sherry made a face. "Worms?"

"That's right. They like to start at the head and eat them down to the tip of the tail."

"How do you tell the head from the tail on a worm?" Sherry asked.

Maurice chuckled. "You don't know? Why, the pointy end is always the head. Helps in diggin' through the ground too."

Maurice looked at the hapless turtles, feet trying to climb out of Sherry's hands. "You best wash your hands after holdin' them," he said.

"These are clean turtles," Terry said. "They already had a bath."

"Yeah, we found 'em in the creek," Sherry said.

"They don't look like water turtles," Maurice said.

Larry just grinned and shrugged. "They're not."

"You still better wash 'em," Maurice said. "My daddy told me that turtles carry some disease that can give you the runs."

Terry looked at the turtles. "The runs? Turtles can only crawl. So how could they give you a runnin' disease?"

Maurice made a face, trying to ignore Terry. He looked at the children's bare feet. "How come you kids are runnin' 'round without shoes, lookin' like hoboes?"

"'Cause it's summertime," Larry said.

Maurice shook his head. "Don't you know you can get lockjaw if you step on a rusty nail?"

"What's lockjaw?" Terry asked.

"That's where you can't talk and you got to eat through a tube down your throat for the rest of your days."

Larry looked at his shoeless feet. "I'll watch out for nails, don't you worry."

"And puddles," Maurice said, seeing the puddle they all were standing in. "You best be not standin' barefoot in puddle water."

"What's wrong with puddle water?" Terry asked, stepping out of it.

"Don't you know 'bout puddle water?" The children shook their heads in unison. "Why, puddles are full of invisible deadly bugs. Little wormlike things, that crawl under your big toenails and get into your body."

"What do they do?" Larry asked.

"They get in your liver, crawl into your lungs, and sometimes slide out your nose."

"Like when you got a cold?" Terry asked, knowing that Maurice was pulling their legs.

Sherry stamped the puddle water off her feet. "Get 'em off me," she pleaded.

"What's done is done," Maurice said solemnly, looking down at her feet. "But I think you were lucky this time."

"Don't you got somethin' nice to tell us?" Sherry asked.

"How 'bout see you later. I got to go to town." He giddiyapped his team of mules and guided the wagon toward Mansfield. Sausage barked happily. "You kids be good," Maurice said, over his shoulder.

"Buy me some candy. I need somethin' sweet," Terry called out.

"Go eat a piece of fruit." Maurice laughed.

"Come on. Buy me some candy. Please."

Maurice stopped the wagon. "Got any money?"

"I'll owe you," Terry said.

Maurice shook his head. "And no thank you. Last time you gave me an IOU was for that candy at the picture show. You ain't paid me back yet."

"That's 'cause you ate half," Terry said.

"But you ain't even paid me for your half yet," Maurice retorted.

"But I'm hungry for some candy food," Terry said.

Sausage started barking. Maurice patted the dog's behind gently. "Calm down, Sausage, he ain't got none."

"But I want some candy food," Terry said.

The dog started barking again. "Stop sayin' the word *food*. Every time this dog hears that word, his stomach just goes crazy."

"Smart dog." Larry laughed.

"So smart it looks like it ate a dictionary," Maurice said.

"Will you think about gettin' me some candy?" Terry asked.

"No need to waste my thoughts," Maurice said. "What you need to do is get yourself a summer job. Earn yourself some money."

"Summer's for fun," Terry said.

"You just don't like workin'," Maurice said.

"You ain't kiddin'," Larry said. "Terry would rather climb a tree upside down than do any extra work."

Maurice shook his head. "Why, when I was half your age, I was up at five every mornin', feedin' the chickens, cleanin' the barn, and then helpin' my father deliver milk to town." He sighed, remembering those times fondly. "I did all that every morning, and I thought nothing of it."

"I don't blame you," Terry said, "'cause I don't think much of doin' all that either."

Sherry giggled.

Maurice took a deep breath, then fluttered his lips. "Guess I'll be movin' on."

Terry wiggled around. "Hold on. There was somethin' else that I was goin' to be tellin' you . . . but you got me so upset talkin' 'bout work that I just can't seem to remember it."

"Maybe it was good-bye." Maurice laughed, urging the mules on.

Terry watched until Maurice was around the bend. He turned to Larry and asked, scratching his head, "Think he'll buy me some candy?"

"Don't hold your breath. Come on," Larry said, "let's get these turtles home."

Maurice rode off, thinking about his vacation. At that moment, however, Eulla Mae was reading a telegraph message that had just been delivered. It was from Speedy.

Telegraph Message—Telegraph Message
Dear Eulla Mae and Maurice STOP Change of plans STOP Cabin sold STOP I still owe you ten dollars STOP Sorry if this is problem STOP Speedy

'What am I ever goin' to tell Maurice?" She sighed heavily, feeling like crying for her husband who at that moment was on his way to town but in his mind was already fishing down at Speedy's cabin.

Rumors

Sheriff Peterson watched Rev. Youngun drop Frankie off at the courthouse and flagged the wagon down on the corner.

"You heard the news yet about Sutherland?"

Rev. Youngun nodded. "Todd called me last night. Anybody seen him yet?" he asked.

The sheriff shook his head. "Like tryin' to find a ghost from what I hear."

Rev. Youngun nodded. "He knows the ways of the woods. He'll be hard to catch."

"Heard he's like a bobcat, sneakin' 'round, strikin' where you least expect him."

"He's no bobcat, but he's someone to be reckoned with." Rev. Youngun paused, then asked what was on his mind. "Do you think Frankie burned his shed?"

Sheriff Peterson licked his lips, choosing his words carefully. "Don't look good, him bein' caught playin' with matches." Then he shook his head. "I told June to keep him home. Keep an eye on him."

"I picked him up on my way in. I didn't know anything about it until I ran into the Bentleys and . . ."

"This is fuel for Sarah Bentley's fire. She don't like Frankie havin' the run of the town. Been tryin' to have him put in the state home for years."

"What are you going to do?" Rev. Youngun asked.

"About sendin' Frankie away?"

"No, about people thinking he might have set the fire."

"Can't help what people talk about. All I can do is get everyone to keep an eye out for Sutherland. Catch him, and maybe these fires will stop."

"But no one's seen him and . . ."

"We got my barn and that list of his daddy's and . . . ," he paused, "what else do we need?"

"Proof that it was him that did it and that he's even come back."

The sheriff held up his hand. "Where else is he gonna go?"

Rev. Youngun didn't say anything.

"Don't be spreadin' any rumors," the sheriff warned.

"You know I won't."

"Sorry, I shouldn't have said that," the sheriff said. "Just that rumors are like a cancer. They'll turn this town overnight into a mean, armed camp, and the next thing you know some kid or field hand's gonna get shot by a nervous widow."

"I'll try to calm my congregation down."

"You can see it in the eyes of the boys down at the feed store. Talkin' 'bout shootin' first and askin' questions later." The sheriff shook his head. "I heard some of 'em talkin' like they was goin' into battle. Singin' 'Mine eyes have seen the glory of the coming of the Lord.'"

"Who's stirring things up to a fever point?"

"You know how whiskey and big talk go hand in hand with trouble."

"Well," Rev. Youngun said, "tell them that I'm readin' from the same Bible they are. They don't have both ears of God on this one."

"You tell 'em that. You're the minister."

"I'll counsel everyone I can to be calm."

"Thanks," Sheriff Peterson said, tipping his hat. "Best be gettin' on up to see Gee Sutherland."

"Oh no," Rev. Youngun said. "I hadn't thought about her."

"She's got a right to know," Sheriff Peterson said. "I don't want her findin' out through the grapevine about Sutherland's escape."

"How did Leonard take the news?"

"How do you think? Last time I was up there, all he wanted to do was walk me to the barn where his daughter got burned. Go over how it happened. Like he was testifying at the trial again."

Rev. Youngun cleared his throat. "I feel so sorry for that girl."

Sheriff Peterson nodded. "I just caught a glimpse of her face through the window. Looked like someone that would scare you on a dark night."

"I used to go up there, but she wouldn't come out," Rev. Youngun said. "Made me talk through the door."

"Sad thing, him and his daughter movin' here to start a new life and then she gets burned up. Well," the sheriff said, "got to be goin'."

Rev. Youngun watched the sheriff walk away, then he looked over to the county jail, which was where he had last seen Michael Sutherland. He remembered going to counsel him after they'd put him in jail for burning Jamie Johnson.

Rev. Youngun moved the buggy forward. *God help you, Michael Sutherland. God help your poor tormented soul.*

Truth and Consequences

Sheriff Peterson went back to his office and found the phone ringing. It was the telegraph office down at the train station saying they had an important message to deliver.

He waited impatiently for it to come, heating up fresh coffee and fiddling with paperwork he didn't really look at.

Stephen Scales, the telegraph operator, came through the door and handed him a folded, yellow piece of paper. The sheriff read it quickly, then looked at Scales. "Anyone else know 'bout this?"

Scales shook his head and licked his lower lip. "Strange, ain't it?"

"That it is," the sheriff said.

"I ain't heard nothin' 'bout her gettin' hitched," Scales said. "Matter of fact, I ain't heard 'bout anyone even seein' her in years."

"Comes out of the blue to me too."

Scales went to the door. "Got to get back."

Sheriff Peterson reread the letter from the warden at the Missouri State Prison. They'd found a letter on the floor near Sutherland's cell and telegraphed what the letter said.

It was Sutherland's letter to Jamie Johnson.

Sheriff Peterson stood by the window, trying to make sense of the news. *Who's she marryin'?* he wondered. *Maybe this was what it was all about. Sutherland escaped from prison to stop Jamie from marryin' another man. He's come back to burn the town down in revenge.*

There was one way to get some answers. He cranked the receiver and had the operator ring up the Johnsons. After what seemed like several minutes, Jamie answered.

"Hello," came her whispered voice over the static-filled line.

"Jamie, this is Sheriff Peterson."

"My father's not here."

"I'm callin' to talk to you."

"It's about Michael, isn't it?"

The sheriff cleared his throat. "Uh, Jamie, reason I'm callin' is to tell you 'bout a telegraph message I got 'bout you and the good news, I guess."

Jamie spoke each word as if she were etching it in stone. "What good news?"

Feeling like he was on thin ice, the sheriff proceeded cautiously. "The news 'bout you gettin' married. Guess I should have first said congratulations."

Her words chilled the line with her icy tone. "Sheriff, if this is your idea of a joke, I'm not pleased. Is that what you called for?"

He stammered his way through an explanation about the telegraph message.

"Read it to me," she said, without emotion.

As he read the words over the line, he had no idea of the tears that flowed crookedly down the scar lines under her eyes. He had no idea of the shivers and silent sobs that were racking her body. When he finished, there was silence on the line.

"Jamie? Are you still on the line?"

"I'm not getting married, Sheriff. Thank you for calling."

He looked at the wall phone after the line went dead, trying to make sense of it all.

Jamie thought about the telegraph and about all the letters she'd sent to Michael over the years. She was trying to make sense of it all, also.

I didn't write him saying I was getting married. I never once told him to not write me again.

She stood at the window, rocking on her heels, staring at the burned shell of the barn where her life had changed.

My father's not been telling me the truth, she thought. *He lied about the sheriff calling last night about the barn fire. It didn't happen until after he called.*

Maybe he's been lying over the years about Michael not writing to me. But why? Why?

Wrapping a scarf over her head, she opened the door and stepped into the daylight. It was the first time she'd done it in years.

But she had to go to the remains of the barn. Had to think about the unthinkable. Make herself go over everything she'd been told to figure out what the truth was.

Each step was painful. The flames of that night lurked behind her thoughts.

In the barn she found a burned piece of her letter that she had asked her father to mail the day before. It was ground into the ashes of others. And she knew. She knew that her father had been lying to her.

But she didn't know what to do. The betrayal she felt cut her like a knife, ripping apart her fragile hold on the reclusive life she'd built for herself since the night of the fire.

All she could do was cover her face and weep.

40

Looking for Maurice

❖

Eulla Mae was holding Speedy's telegraph on the back porch when the phone rang. It was Stephen Scales from the telegraph office.

"Eulla Mae, we got another telegraph down here for you and Maurice."

"Would you read it to me, Stephen?"

"Hmmm. Okay. Says here, 'Dear Eulla Mae and Maurice: New owners of cabin might rent it to you at $15 week STOP Interested? STOP Speedy Springer.'" Scales paused. "That's all it says."

"Just send an answer saying no."

"That's it?"

"I'd like to add a few more words 'bout what a no-good, thievin' skunk he is, but that wouldn't be the Christian thing to do."

Scales chuckled. "So I'll just say, 'No, you thievin' skunk.'"

"Just no will do."

She finished her cup of coffee and left the letter on the kitchen table. Hoping to find Maurice, she headed over to the Younguns', knowing he liked to stop there and talk to the kids on his way to town. From the garden she took another fresh bunch of carrots along with her.

She crossed the fields, stepping carefully to avoid the mole hills that plagued the north fields. "He's gonna be heartbroken. I've never seen his heart more set on something."

The Younguns were nearly home when Crab Apple the mule came walking up the path. "What's he doin' loose?" Larry asked.

"Grab him 'fore he runs away," Terry said loudly.

The mule hee-hawed and backed up in circles around them. "Come on, Crabbie," Larry coaxed quietly. "Let's go back to the barn."

But Crab Apple would not cooperate. He kicked and bucked and moved faster than the Younguns could grab for him, knocking them down and turning them in circles.

Finally, Larry threw up his hands in disgust. "Let's just leave him." He looked at the mule and shook his finger in the air. "Go on. Go live with someone else who'll make you pull a plow."

Larry started to walk away. Terry said to him, "You can't leave Crabbie."

"It's the only way that fool mule will come back. Come on, he'll follow us."

So they walked, pushing and shoving each other, kidding and tripping, until they got near the barn. Crab Apple followed behind them, but he stopped each time they turned to look at him.

They found Dangit growling at a mound of dirt next to the barn. Bashful the fainting goat was lying on the ground.

"What made Bashful faint?" Sherry asked.

"Probably saw his shadow," Terry sneered.

Dangit was furiously digging at the ground, kicking dirt behind him. "What's down there, boy?" Larry asked.

Dangit ignored him. He smelled a badger and stuck his nose down into the tunnel.

"You bury a bone down there or somethin'?" Terry asked.

"Hope he ain't found a skunk," Larry said.

Bashful lifted his head up, blinking his eyes. "You okay?" Sherry asked quietly.

Larry pulled Dangit by the tail and shouted, "Get out of there!" so loudly that Bashful fainted again.

Dangit turned his head, snarling. "Stop that!" Larry said, raising his hand in the air.

T.R. the turkey came out, pecking at the barn wall for bugs. "All the animals are loose!" Terry exclaimed.

"Crab Apple must have kicked the door open." Larry looked down at Dangit. "Whatever Dangit's after must have gotten the animals upset."

Dangit lowered his head, then dove back toward the tunnel. "Hope it ain't a monster down there," Terry said.

"Maybe it's a dragon," Sherry said, thinking about the fairy-tale book her brother had read her.

"And maybe he's diggin' to China," Terry said, pushing her. Larry tugged Dangit back out of the tunnel and tied him to the fence. Terry peeked at the hole. "What's down there?"

Sherry stood behind him. "Bet it's a snake . . . a monster snake."

"You knucklehead," Terry said. "No such things as monster snakes."

Larry got down on his hands and knees, peering respectfully at the hole. He sniffed the scent that he'd smelled once before. "I think we got ourselves a badger."

"Get a gun and shoot it," Terry exclaimed.

"He ain't hurtin' anyone," Larry said.

"But what about Dangit?" Sherry asked. "He'll get the badger."

Larry shook his head. "That badger will learn Dangit a lesson. He'll be lucky if he only gets his nose nipped a few times till he learns to keep out of the hole."

"What's a badger look like?" Sherry asked.

Larry shrugged. "Sort of like a cross between a skunk, a bear, and a polecat."

"That's just great," Terry said. "We got ourselves a two-hundred pound stinkin' skunk cat livin' under the barn!"

"What you kids looking at?" Eulla Mae called out.

Terry looked at what was in her arms. *Oh no,* he thought, *more carrots.*

"We got ourselves a giant skunk cat livin' under the barn!" Sherry cried out.

"A what?" Eulla Mae laughed.

"A badger," Larry said.

Sherry gasped suddenly. She thought she saw someone staring at her from behind a tree. Her nervous fingers climbed up the buttons on her shirt until they came to the locket, which was hanging out. Looking around, she put it back under her shirt and looked back toward the tree, but the face was gone. A chill ran up her spine.

"What should we do, Mrs. Springer?" Larry asked.

"Just leave him be," Eulla Mae said. "Have you kids seen Maurice?"

They all nodded. "He was just here," said Sherry.

"Said he was headin' to town," Larry said.

"Is he in trouble or somethin'?" Terry asked.

"No, I just got somethin' to tell him. Is your pa here?"

Larry shook his head. "He went into town. Left us to fix the noon meal for ourselves."

"Are you hungry?" Eulla Mae asked. They all nodded. "Well, come on inside and I'll fix you some food."

"What you gonna cook?" Terry asked, feeling sick at the sight of the carrots.

"One of Eulla Mae's specialties."

"What's in it?" Terry gulped, feeling as if he were going to get sick.

"Carrot stew." She smiled. "I hope you're hungry."

As they walked to the house, all Terry could think about was how he would get out of eating the carrot stew.

"What are you so quiet 'bout?" Larry asked him.

"Got somethin' on my mind."

"What?"

"Carrot stew, that's what."

"Maybe we'll eat carrots every day," Sherry teased.

"And maybe I'll be runnin' away from home," Terry said. Then he brightened. "Hey, Sherry. I got a poem for you."

"If it's not nice don't tell me."

"It's nice. Listen:

Cockroaches are brown
And worms are too.
You've got a whole bunch
Living in you."

Sherry ran screaming to the house. Terry grinned. *I'll have to remember that one. Good way to get rid of her.*

From behind the barn, Michael Sutherland watched them go into the house. *She's got the locket. That little girl's got my Jamie's locket.*

41

Frankie's Secret

❖

Missouri Poole walked down Main Street looking for her Larry. She'd used the phone at the general store to call his house, but there wasn't an answer.

Merchants had hung out their goods, hoping for customers, but the town seemed subdued, full of whispers. Missouri didn't take the time to listen or find out what was going on. The only thing she was interested in was finding Larry.

A sprightly old Mexican man, who seemed to come and go in his own world, was playing dominos by himself in front of the feed store. Missouri was staring at him so intently that she almost walked under a ladder, but stopped in time. She wished she had salt to toss over her shoulder but settled for a quick prayer and crossed fingers. *Should have brought my rabbit's foot,* she thought.

She stopped at the pushcart operator who was carefully quartering his watermelons. The sections were arranged against a big block of ice he'd cracked into a wet, melting bed.

Missouri peeked under the faded tan canvas top and held up a penny. "Got a little one for me?"

The little man with the heavy-jowled face laughed and pulled out a plug from the watermelon he was working on. "This one's on me," he smiled, handing her the round, rosy piece.

Missouri knew he had three little children and gave him the penny.

"You don't have to do that," he said.

"I know," she smiled, biting into the watermelon. "That's why I want to do it."

A half-block on, she saw Todd Watson sitting on the bench by the town square and headed over to him, passing by two women loaded down with assorted dry goods.

"I'm lookin' for Larry Youngun. You seen my boyfriend around?"

Todd made a show of expressions with his ruddy face, then looked at his pocket watch. "It's about dinner time. He's probably eating his noon meal at home."

"If you see him, tell him Missouri's lookin' for him."

Todd shook his head. "Aren't you a bit young to be running after boys?"

Missouri shrugged. "I'm ten. Almost eleven."

Todd coughed, showing his displeasure. "Wonder what Reverend Youngun's congregation at the Methodist church would think about what you're doin'?"

"Let them wonder." Missouri smiled.

"Or what your momma would think," Todd said slyly.

Missouri ignored him. "I figure Larry and me'll be gettin' married next year. Gonna live at my house, he and I."

"You asked Larry yet?" Todd laughed.

"I know he's ready, but he don't know it."

"You're as crazy as a monkey stuck in itching powder."

Missouri turned to go. "See you, Mr. Watson."

"You heard about the fires?" he called after her.

"Anybody hurt?" she asked.

"Naw," Todd said, "but people say it could have been . . ."

Missouri cut him off. "Could have been the fire in my heart for Larry. Got to go," she said.

Missouri looked down the street and waved. "Hey, Frankie, wait up." She ran to where Frankie was waiting. "Hey, Mr. Mayor. You already said the pledge?"

Frankie nodded. "And Frankie raised the flag." His expression changed. "Frankie don't play with matches."

"Heck, I know that." She smiled, ruffling his hair.

"Grammie's mad at Frankie."

"For what?"

"Matches. Found matches in my pocket."

"Did you do something bad?" she asked.

Frankie shook his head. "Frankie didn't do nothing."

"Good," she said. "Just don't keep any more, and you won't get in trouble. Okay?"

Frankie nodded and brightened. "You want to know a secret?" Missouri shook her head yes. "God loves you," he said, trying to wink, but closing both eyes at the same time.

"And do you want to know a secret?" Missouri whispered.

Frankie looked around to make sure no one was listening, then nodded. "I won't tell."

"Good. 'Cause this is a doozy." Missouri made a big show of looking around, checking for eavesdroppers, then said, "I'm gonna kiss Larry Youngun on the Fourth of July 'cause I got itchy lips for that boy."

Frankie's jaw dropped. "Kiss? You mean kiss-kiss?"

Missouri grinned. "I mean kiss-kiss on the lips-lips."

"Does Larry know?" Frankie asked, feeling giddy all over.

"He knows I'm gonna try, but he doesn't know when or how. That's why it's a secret," she said, puckering her lips.

Frankie was embarrassed and turned his head.

"And if I don't kiss Larry . . . why, maybe I'll just kiss you." She smiled.

"No kiss-kiss for Frankie. Got to go help Mom," he stuttered, racing down the street as fast as his stubby legs could carry him to Mom's Cafe.

Sheriff Peterson rode slowly out to see Gee Sutherland to warn her of her nephew's escape, then decided to make a stop on the way. He rode his horse up the back road to the old Sutherland homestead.

Wonder who did burn the place down? he pondered, looking at the remains. *It had to be Leonard. On one of the drunken sprees he used to be famous for.*

He dismounted and tied his horse to a tree. *What's that?* he wondered, noticing the Younguns' fort.

He made his way over the dirt wall. "Kids," he smiled. "Made themselves quite a fort."

He poked around, admiring their handiwork, then he saw where the grass had been beaten down in a path toward a stand of trees. Following it from the side, the sheriff came close to the Secret Tree but didn't know it.

"Sutherland or someone's been around here," he said to himself. "Or maybe it's just the kids . . . That's it." He nodded, somewhat relieved. "Just a path the kids made."

He took the ridge road to Gee Sutherland's house. He found her sitting on her front stoop, smoking her pipe.

"Mornin', Gee," he said, tipping his hat.

She blew a ring of smoke toward him. "He's back 'round, ain't he?"

"Who told you?" he asked, alarmed. He knew she didn't have a telephone.

"No one," she said, puffing slowly. "I just know it."

Sheriff Peterson considered what she said for a moment, then let it pass. Dealing with Gee was always strange.

"Cat got your tongue, Sheriff?" she cackled.

"Just wanted to ask you to be on the lookout. Some say his mind's not right."

"Nothin' 'bout him's right," she said. "His father, my brother Jack Sutherland, cursed all that came around him."

Sheriff Peterson didn't pursue the past. "If you see him, get word to me."

"I don't expect to be seein' Michael. We never got along so good."

"But you're his only living relative and . . ."

"He won't be comin' round here. I never did him no good. No good at all," she muttered, staring away.

"All I know is we got an escaped convict that might have come back. We've had two fires and . . ."

"Might?" she snickered, interrupting him. "*He is!* You can count on that."

"Why you so sure?" the sheriff asked.

"'Cause his daddy broke his brains and made him sign the list."

"You know about the list?" the sheriff asked.

Gee nodded. "Jack lived for revenge. Took it out on everyone around him for what he thought others done. Took it out worse on Michael . . . yes he did," she said, drawing from the pipe.

The sheriff told her about his barn being burned and the list that had been painted on the shed. "And we found this list of names, signed by your brother."

Gee looked at the old paper. "Names on that list are the ones who got to worry," she said quietly. "And your name's on there, Sheriff. But he already got you."

"But I wasn't even 'round back then. That was another sheriff."

"Didn't matter none to my brother. One sheriff was like another. Revenge is all that mattered to Jack."

"But we're talking about his son. About Michael."

Gee shook her head. "We're talkin' 'bout my brother Jack. He wanted Michael to help him get revenge. I heard what he made the boy vow."

The sheriff looked at Gee. "Michael burned up Jamie in that fire, we know that."

"And you best believe it's him settin' these other fires."

"You sure you don't know where he might be holin' up?"

She pointed her pipe toward the clouds. "Michael Sutherland was just like the clouds. Some days he was sunny, and some days he was stormy and rainin'. Michael could change like the clouds," she said, staring off toward the horizon.

"But what's the weather like for him today?" the sheriff asked impatiently.

Gee half-closed her eyes. "He had a place, some secret place, that he'd always run to when he was hurtin'. Find that place, and you'll find Michael Sutherland."

"You know where it is?"

Gee shook her head. "Somewhere in the woods near his home. His pa looked to find it for years but never could. Never could," she repeated, looking down.

Sheriff Peterson rode off, confused. The pieces of the case were creating a bigger puzzle that he seemed no closer to solving.

Frankie's got a secret and likes to play with matches. Sutherland's like the clouds and has a secret hiding place. Todd said the Ozarks kept secret the abuse Michael suffered. And Jamie didn't know anything about her own weddin'. He coughed, then spit toward the bushes. "The real secret is, I don't know what to make of all this," he said aloud.

Frankie stopped at the back door of Mom's Cafe. He was supposed to help bus the tables and clean the dishes in the kitchen, but a dark cloud seemed to cover his mind.

It was as if he were being punished, but he didn't know for what. His eyes began blinking faster and faster. His arm began to twitch.

"Breathe slowly," he told himself, taking deep breaths.

He touched the tip of his nose, then pinched his nostrils, trying to figure out what was bothering him. Then he saw it again.

"Bad secret," he mumbled, grabbing onto the door frame.

The secret that made him feel bad was back on him again. He remembered following Michael Sutherland that night five years ago because he wanted to watch him kiss Jamie.

It just was something he wanted to do. He didn't know why he wanted to see them kiss, but it made him shiver to think about it.

Frankie had hidden behind a wagon outside the Johnson barn and watched from the corner window. He thought they would put their lips together, but instead they hugged and talked a lot more than they kissed.

Michael Sutherland seemed happy, and he didn't want to go. Jamie told him to wait until tomorrow and sent him away.

Frankie wanted to follow, but then he saw Leonard Johnson staggering toward the barn. The same way he'd seen men leave the saloon in town.

Frankie didn't know that Leonard Johnson was drunk or what being drunk meant. He just knew Johnson wasn't walking right and that his grammie said that something called whiskey was evil.

Frankie wanted to run and find Michael, but he was worried for Jamie, because she seemed frightened of her father. Johnson staggered forward, screaming at the top of his lungs.

Frankie cringed at the window, feeling something bad was about to happen.

He remembered Johnson slapping Jamie. Hitting her face. Knocking over the lantern. *Fire went fast,* he remembered.

Sweat broke across his forehead. "Bad secret," he moaned, wrapping his arms around his chest.

He closed his eyes, trying to block out the thoughts of that night, but he couldn't shut it off. *Frankie tried to help Jamie. Frankie wanted to call firemen.* Tears welled up in his eyes. *But Johnson said no. Johnson hit Frankie.*

Whimpering like a lost child, Frankie was in the barn again in his mind. Crawling through the window. Grabbing Jamie and pulling her outside.

Johnson said it was a secret. To never tell. That he'd hurt Frankie if Frankie told the secret. That Frankie was to blame Michael Sutherland.

"Frankie don't tell secrets," he whispered to himself, looking down. He kicked his shoes in the red dust, trying to make himself feel better.

Mom Carter came to the back door of the cafe and found Frankie in tears, trembling. "What's wrong, Frankie?" she asked, putting her arm around him.

Frankie tried to talk, but he couldn't find the words.

Mom patted his head, whispering softly, "Just come on in and sit down. I'll get you some milk and cookies. Then you'll feel better. Mom's gonna take care of you. Don't you worry."

Mom had wanted to tell Frankie about the sheriff's barn and ask him what really happened to his shed. But his tears washed the thoughts away. Frankie looked into her face and then buried his head into her chest. *Wonder what's goin' on in his mind?* she thought, softly stroking the back of his head.

42

Sweet Dilemma

❖

Sutherland watched the Youngun house patiently from the bushes. *That little girl's got my locket. I need to catch her alone and talk to her. Got to get it back, so I can take it to Jamie.*

Inside, Terry and Larry did the dishes, while Eulla Mae sat in the parlor, teaching Sherry how to sew.

"How come you always get to wash?" Larry grumbled.

Terry moved the dishes around in the soapy water. "'Cause I'm not tall enough to put the dishes away."

Larry handed Terry a dirty plate. "Yuck," Terry said, looking at the remains of the squishy boiled okra. "I can't believe Eulla Mae would try to poison us with this stuff."

"You sure cleared your plate," Larry said, putting away the cups.

"Yeah, into my pocket," Terry smiled. He pulled out a soggy napkin full of okra.

"If you don't eat somethin', you're gonna shrivel up to a skinny redheaded string bean."

Terry shrugged. "I ate the ham. But okra makes my mouth feel like I've been eatin' paste."

Outside, Sutherland heard footsteps on the road and moved deeper into the brush. He saw a pretty girl coming down the path toward the Younguns' house.

Missouri Poole took the back stairs two at a time and knocked on the back door. "Yoo-hoo, Larry," she called.

"Kissy lips is here," Terry jeered, puckering his lips.

"Hush," Larry said, quickly running his fingers through his hair.

Terry cocked his head, as if he were judging a beauty contest. "You look pretty 'nough to get married."

"Yoo-hoo, sweet thing," Missouri called again.

"Missouri! I'm right here," Larry said, embarrassed.

She looked through the screen. "Is that you?"

Terry mimicked under his breath. "Is that you?"

"I didn't recognize you holdin' the dishcloth. Guess you're gettin' in practice for when we get hitched."

Terry poked Larry in the stomach and whispered, "First comes love, then comes marriage, then comes an ugly baby in the baby carriage."

Larry shoved him and turned to Missouri. "What do *you* want?"

"Let's go for a walk. It's such a nice day."

"It's such a nice day," Terry mimicked.

"Hush," Larry said, under his breath.

Missouri winked with an all-knowing smile. "Terry Youngun. I was talkin' to my sister Georgia 'bout you. Maybe we could have us a double weddin' and . . ."

Terry spun around. "And maybe I might just take your sister to the dog pound."

"That's not nice," Larry whispered.

"And Georgia's 'bout as nice as a dead toad," Terry retorted.

Missouri looked Terry up and down. "You and Georgia would make a fine lookin' couple walkin' down the aisle." Larry caught her wink and smirked.

Terry was agitated. "Only aisle we'd walk down is me walkin' her to the butcher shop. I ain't never gettin' married."

"Come on, Larry," Missouri said, "I got somethin' I need to talk to you about."

"You promise you won't try to kiss me?"

"Sugar," she said, "I'll promise you anythin'." She crossed her fingers behind her back.

Terry grinned devilishly. "Maybe you two ought to run off and get married. Be a lot less dishes to do without this here horse eatin' every-thin'," he said, nodding toward his brother.

Missouri laughed. "Come on, Larry. Let's go walk. I got some candy."

"Not until he finishes the dishes," Terry said, upset that Larry was being offered candy and not him.

"Come on," Larry pleaded, "you owe me for doin' your barn chores two weeks ago Saturday."

Terry shook his head. "All right. But you got to give me a bite of that candy."

Missouri broke him off an almost invisible piece of the gumdrop. Terry looked at it with disgust. "This wouldn't even make an ant smile."

"That's all you get," she said. "Or I can send Georgia over, and she'll give you somethin' really sweet." She puckered her lips.

"No thanks," Terry said, sticking the small dot of sweet on his tongue. He watched them run off down the road, then finished washing the dishes.

Wiping off his hands, he slowly began putting the cups and plates away, one at a time. The big plate had to go on the shelf in the pantry, so he pulled a chair into the small storage room and put the plate on the third shelf up. He came face-to-face with the sugar bowl.

Oh, Lord, why you temptin' me like this?

He started to climb back down, then stopped. *One little peek won't hurt,* he thought, taking the lid off.

He looked inside at the sparkling white granules and closed his eyes. *That must be what heaven looks like, where everythin's sweet and good.*

He pushed the sugar around with the tip of his finger. *Wish I lived in this sugar bowl. Wish my bed was made of sugar.*

He stuck another finger into the bowl. *Just one little lick won't hurt.* Carefully wetting his whole finger, he stuck it deep into the sugar bowl. He held it up in the air and looked at it, then he put it into his mouth and sucked on it like a new baby.

"I needed that," he said to himself, as he put the lid back on.

Just one more little lick won't hurt a thing, he thought, sticking his finger back in. The second lick led to the third, and before he knew it, he had the sugar bowl tipped above his head.

Sugar was everywhere. All over his clothes, his face, and on the floor. Terry was eating up the sugar like he was famished.

"Terry, is everything all right?" Eulla Mae called out from the living room.

Terry coughed sugar all over the pantry. "Itsallright, Mrs. Springer," he managed to mumble. The shelves were covered with sugar.

"What did you say?" she asked.

Terry gulped the mouthful of sugar down. "Everythin's all right. I'm just cleanin' up a bowl."

"That's good, Terry. Keep doin' your chores like this, and maybe your pa will reward you with a sweet treat tomorrow."

"That would be nice," Terry said, licking the inside of the bowl.

"'Cause I know how much you love sugar treats."

"That I do," he said.

"If you got some white sugar, maybe I'll even make you a cake today," she continued.

"We got a whole bowl of sugar," Sherry squealed from the parlor.

Terry stopped licking and looked into the empty sugar bowl. "Yes, that's what I'll do," Eulla Mae said. "After we finish our sewing lesson, I'll make you both a cake."

Oh no, Terry thought to himself, looking at the empty sugar bowl. *What am I gonna do now?*

It was a lot to think about, so he licked the sugar bowl one more time. He didn't notice the ants coming up the edge of the pantry shelves.

A sudden awkwardness came over Larry as he and Missouri Poole walked along the thickly wooded path. *What if she tries to kiss me?* he worried. He looked at her. *What if she breaks her promise? What am I gonna do if she grabs me and tries to eat my lips off?*

Missouri kept up a running conversation about anything and everything. "I know you don't want to think about gettin' married, but I've been doin' some figurin'."

"Missouri, can't you talk 'bout somethin' else?"

"Honey," she smiled, "I just like to be prepared. Now I figure that with your five cents allowance and my two cents, why that's seven cents a week, and we could be savin' for things."

Larry picked up a rock and threw it at a tree. "What are you talkin' about? Savin' for what?"

"For our babies. They're gonna need clothes and shoes and . . ."

"And you can stop it right there," Larry said.

"What's wrong, Larry?" she asked softly, moving toward him.

Oh man, Larry thought, *I can't hit her. I know she's gonna try it.* He felt her hand creep into his. *She's tryin' to hold my hand,* he thought, wanting to shrivel up and die.

"Larry, all I was trying to do is figure out how much five cents and two cents a week would be after a month."

Larry figured for a moment. "That'd be 'bout twenty-eight cents."

"That's right! Boy, are you smart." She squeezed his hand. Larry blushed. Missouri held onto his hand and kept talking. "Then if we saved for a year, that would be 'bout . . ."

Larry's knees were getting weak. Holding her hand was making him very nervous. So he concentrated on his math. "Three dollars and forty cents."

Missouri squeezed his hand again. "You are just a gene-e-us." She winked. "So if the marriage license costs only fifty cents, that would leave us . . . hummmm . . . let's see."

"Two dollars and ninety cents," Larry said.

Missouri stopped and looked at him with adoring eyes. "You know somethin'? With a sharp mind like yours, we're gonna do real good. You might even be a businessman when you grow up. You can teach math to our babies."

Larry coughed, trying to get the courage up to change the conversation. "Missouri, you gotta *quit talkin'* 'bout gettin' married. We're too young. Heck, I just turned ten."

"Sugar," she said softly, putting her head on his shoulder, "here in the mountains, we do everything early. That's why it's okay to get married while you're still goin' to school."

Larry stepped back. "I don't want to get married now. You're nice, but I want to do some more schoolin', not have children." Missouri's eyes started to well up. "Missouri, I got enough trouble with my squirrel-headed brother and sister. I can't imagine havin' some kids of my own to take care of. Gosh, I can't hardly even read or write yet, and you want me to marry you?"

Tears came down her cheeks. "But I told my momma that you were gonna move in with us."

"Then you just untell her. I like livin' with my pa. I got my own bed and clothes and slingshot and . . . and all the things that make me happy and . . ."

Missouri stepped closer. Larry stepped back. Missouri reached out. Larry blocked her.

"But Larry. You don't have a momma. My momma can be your momma."

Larry held up his hand. "I had a momma, and now my pa does his best to be both poppa and momma." He looked into her eyes. "I appreciate your likin' me and all, but we're just too young to be talkin' stuff like this."

"You want some sugar now?" she asked, getting the candy from her pocket.

I think she's puckering her lips. That's the kind of sugar she wants to give me, Larry thought, moving back. "I, ah, I don't feel so good," he said, moving away. He turned and ran back home.

"Where you goin'?" she asked. "Don't you want the candy?"

Test Results

Frankie put on the apron that "Mom" Higgens handed him. "Frankie's a good worker," he said proudly.

"You're a worker bee, you are that." She smiled, happy that the milk and cookies and a little hugging had made him feel better.

She watched Frankie carry a small tray of food to the front of the diner. She turned to her husband, Hambone, and smiled. "Frankie's a jewel. Wish everyone worked as hard as he does."

Hambone shrugged. "He just don't know no better."

Mom shook her head. "Frankie is one in a million."

"Better that way," Hambone said, scrambling a pan of eggs.

"What do you mean?"

"He's special, because he's like a big kid who never grew up. But don't think that his grandma don't work twice as hard raisin' a kid who's never gonna mentally grow up."

Mom thought about that. "Never thought about it that way."

"His grandma's a good woman. Not many folks would have taken Frankie in the way she did."

"No," Mom said, "I don't think they would."

"Can't understand all this talk about him playing with matches. I've never even once seen him mess with the lighted cookstove."

Frankie pushed the kitchen door open holding up a shiny penny. "Frankie got a tip!" he beamed.

"Good, Frankie, good." Mom smiled, looking out into the front of the diner to see who'd given it to him. Todd Watson winked back and Mom nodded.

At the doctor's office, Frankie's grandmother took the news as well as she could. "Are you sure?" she asked.

Dr. George paused, then nodded. "You don't have much time. I'm sorry."

June Schmitt wanted to cry, but the weight of her responsibility for Frankie's future pulled her together.

"You better start making plans for Frankie," Dr. George advised quietly. "There's a good state home up in Jeff City."

"No! I won't put Frankie in that place. He'd die there."

"Then who'll take care of him? You can't leave him by himself."

"I know," she stammered, feeling the tears coming. "But . . . but . . . I don't know what to do."

Dr. George put his arms around the old woman's shoulders as she broke down. Any idea he had of talking about the shed fire and Frankie being found with matches was gone. "It'll work out. If you and I put our heads together, we can figure this thing out."

He thought about Mom Higgens at the cafe. "What about Mom? Frankie likes to help out there, and she adores him."

Grammie shook her head. "I couldn't ask her and Hambone to take on the responsibility. Someone's got to help dress him in the morning, make sure he's fed. You gotta put his clothes out each night, and he likes 'em folded just a certain way and . . ."

He put his finger in the air to stop her. "But one thing's for sure. If you don't tell someone what Frankie likes, then no one will ever know and he'll end up in a state home for sure."

"But he's only a boy inside," she whispered.

Dr. George held up his hand. "There's nothing easy about taking care of a boy in a man's body. But you have to think about what you will do. If you'd like, I'll talk to Mom. I know she's got a big heart and Frankie likes her. Something's bound to work out." Dr. George stood up and walked her to the door. "Now you go home and start thinking about what you're leaving behind. Start thinking about what you'd want someone to do for Frankie. What you want them to tell him."

She nodded and closed her eyes. A tear squeezed between her lids. She started to tell him about the burned shed, but didn't for fear that it would stop Dr. George from helping her find a place for Frankie. The tear slid down her cheek. "I promise I'll try to figure something out for Frankie," she said.

After Frankie's grammie left, Dr. George couldn't concentrate. All he could think about was Frankie and what was going to happen to him. Finally, he grabbed his hat and headed out the door. Walking briskly down Main Street, he opened the door of Mom's Cafe and sat down.

"You hungry for food or gab?" Mom called out from the kitchen.

"Coffee will do," he said cheerfully.

"Last of the big-time spenders." Mom laughed. She walked out from the kitchen and poured him a cup. "Got any gossip?" she asked.

Frankie peeked his head out from the kitchen. "Hi, Dr. George. You paid Frankie's taxes yet?"

Dr. George smiled and handed Frankie a fifty-cent piece. "That's a lot of taxes!" Frankie exclaimed.

Mom smiled. "Frankie, you finish cleaning those dishes so you can earn your meals."

Frankie grinned and went back to the kitchen. Mom started to walk to the other end of the counter, but Dr. George grabbed her hand. "I have something to talk to you about," he said.

"And what's that?" she asked.

"You've got to promise not to tell anyone."

Mom laughed. "You mean it's a secret! Doc, you're soundin' just like Frankie!"

"Frankie's the one that can't hear what I'm about to tell you."

That got Mom's attention, so she came around the counter and sat on the next stool. Dr. George took the next twenty minutes trying to convince Mom to take Frankie in when his grammie died, but Mom was against it.

"Look, I like Frankie and all, but I've got a husband and a business to run and . . ."

"And Frankie's a good helper, and he likes you and he needs you."

"Doc," Mom sighed, "I'm sorry that his grammie's not goin' to be on this earth much longer, but I'm not Frankie's keeper. I've never had kids of my own, and I'm too old to start now. You got to find someone else."

"Like who?" Dr. George asked.

Mom thought for a moment. "How about Rev. Youngun? Men of the cloth are supposed to help the sick and lame."

Dr. George shook his head. "Rev. Youngun's got a hard enough time as it is, tryin' to raise those three kids on a preacherman's wages."

Mom closed her eyes and hummed to herself. "How about Father Tim up at the Catholic church?"

"He can't be takin' in someone and adoptin' him. Priests can't do that."

"Then how about the nicest man, the smartest man in town? The man who cares about people and goes out of his way to help them?"

"And who is that?"

"You."

"Me!" Dr. George exclaimed. "Why, I can't be takin' Frankie in!"

"Shoe doesn't fit, Doc, see what I mean? You can't just be askin' folks to take in Frankie like it was just for a weekend or somethin'. You're askin' them to take Frankie in for the rest of his life."

"Then who should I ask?"

"You better pray on it to the Man upstairs, Doc. He'll know what to do."

Busy Bee

❖

Terry sat in the garden behind the house, trying to figure out where he was going to get enough sugar to refill the bowl in the pantry. *Pa's gonna yell to high heaven when he finds out I ate all the sugar.*

He licked his lips. *But it sure was good.* He smiled. *Almost worth gettin' punished over.*

Sutherland watched patiently from the woods, wondering what Terry was up to. *Where's his sister?*

A bee buzzed around Terry's head, then went on to land on a flower. *Bees got the life,* Terry thought.

He watched the fat and happy bees float from flower to flower. *They don't got a care in the world. Just fly around all day makin' honey and . . .* Terry got an idea and ran into the barn. He came back out with a box.

"Come here, bee. Just fly into this box," he said, inching toward what he thought was a honey bee.

The wasp sat there, moving its blue-black stinger, twitching it around in a circle. "Nice bee," Terry said softly.

Wasps are not like honeybees. And they're not like bumblebees or even yellow jackets, which can easily be avoided. But Terry was only thinking about turning honey into sugar and didn't realize that he was trying to trap a slim, liquid fire-tipped devil.

The wasp whirred its black wings. Somehow Terry managed to trap the wasp in the box. "Gotcha!"

He stuck his ear to the side, listening to the upset wasp buzz and bounce around inside.

"Just fill this box with honey, and I'll let you go. Then I'll make the honey into sugar, and Pa won't be the wiser."

With his problem solved, Terry kicked back his legs and stretched out on the grass. "Yes-sir-ree, I'm gonna get a couple of quick licks of honey in and then I'll turn it into sugar." Though he had no idea how to turn honey into sugar, it was at least a step closer in the right sweet direction.

With no worries in the world, Terry picked a fragrant flower. "Where do you keep your smelling stuff?" he wondered out loud, picking the flower apart.

Not finding it, he pulled at another flower, then another until he had a lap full of petals. "Guess it's indivisible or somethin'," he said.

After twenty minutes of killing time, Terry lifted the lid of his box and peeked inside. "You got the honey ready?" he whispered to the wasp.

The box was dark and he couldn't see that the wasp had its stinger aimed at his face. "Can't wait to taste my honey," he said.

The stinger on the tip of the wasp moved in and out. Terry lifted the lid a little more and stuck his nose in.

The wasp jumped onto his nose and stabbed its stinger in and out. It was like a red-hot pin being stuck under Terry's skin. It felt like the end of his nose was going to explode.

Terry ran screaming through the yard. "Ahhhhh!!" he cried, trying to knock the wasp off.

Eulla Mae came running out. "What's wrong?"

Terry was jumping around, rubbing his nose. "Owohgollygee-owohwow."

Eulla Mae grabbed him. Terry pointed to his nose. "You been stung by a wasp," she exclaimed. She picked him up and took him into the kitchen. "How on Earth did a wasp sting you on the nose?" she asked, mixing a small amount of flour and water together to put on the sting.

"I was sitting out in the wildflowers and saw this honeybee and . . ."

She interrupted and put a glob of white flour paste on the tip of Terry's nose. "Bees love flowers. But you were stung by a wasp. You gotta be careful playing around the garden."

"It hurts, Eulla Mae," he winced, but it was starting to feel better.

"Sure it does." She dabbed some more of the mixture on his nose. "Just be glad they didn't swarm down on you like a bunch of Comanches around a wagon train. Wasps can kill you."

She stood back. "Let me see how you look."

Sherry came in and laughed. "You look like a clown."

"Hush, Sherry," Eulla Mae said, walking into the pantry to get a rag. Then she saw the ants. They were everywhere.

"Sherry, get me a bucket of lye soap. You got ants in the sugar bowl!"

Terry watched her clean up the mess in the pantry. *I just know I've had it now. She's gonna see the empty sugar bowl and tell Pa and . . .*

Eulla Mae came out of the pantry, wiping her hands on her apron. She was holding the empty sugar bowl.

"Terry, I want you to run over to my house and get a bowl of sugar. The ants ate all yours up."

Saved by the ants! Thank you, thank you! he thought, winking up toward the ceiling.

"Did you hear me?" Eulla Mae asked. "Maybe Maurice is back. If he's there, you have him call me."

"Yes, ma'am." Terry took the bowl. *Lord must be shinin' on me now.*

"Oh heck, I'll just call him while you're on your way over there. If he ain't there, just go on into the kitchen and fill up a cup."

"Right away." Terry smiled.

Eulla Mae looked back into the pantry. "Funny. I've never seen ants eat a whole bowl of anything."

"Guess they were powerful hungry," Terry said.

Sherry walked up to her brother. "What's this white stuff on your shirt?"

Terry looked down and his eyes bugged out. *Sugar!*

"Ah, that's . . . that's . . ." he mumbled, dusting off his shirt, "just some white dust and lint I got washin' and puttin' away the dishes."

"Fibber!" Sherry exclaimed.

"Just musta come from one of the cups or bowls," Terry said, struggling to tell a half-to-whole truth with his fingers crossed behind his back.

Eulla Mae thought about the ants, the empty bowl, and Terry's well-known sweet tooth. *Wonder if Terry's tellin' a big one?* She glanced at the empty bowl. *No one could eat a whole bowl of sugar without gettin' sick. Not even Terry.* She let the thought pass. "You run over and get that sugar."

"Right away, Mrs. Springer," Terry said, skipping happily toward the door with the empty bowl of evidence in his hand.

"And take Sherry with you."

Terry stopped dead in his tracks. "Come on. I can get over and back 'fore she even gets her shoes on."

Sherry's lip began to quiver. "I want to come."

"Let her go," Eulla Mae said. "Sherry, get your shoes on."

"But Mrs. Springer," Terry protested. "I'd rather take a mangy porcupine along than her."

"That's not nice," Eulla Mae said, shaking her head.

"Let her go alone then," Terry said.

"No. You both be on your way." She scooted them both out the door. "Faster you get back, the faster I'll start the cake."

Terry looked at his sister as they stood on the back steps. "If somethin' happens to you, it ain't my fault."

Neither knew that Michael Sutherland was hiding in the bushes, waiting for Sherry.

45

Give Me the Locket

Eulla Mae called over to her house and Maurice answered. "I just sent Terry and Sherry over to get a cup of sugar. I'm gonna bake a cake."

"That's good," Maurice said indifferently.

"What's wrong?" she asked, then she knew. "You saw the telegraph message, didn't you?"

Maurice looked at it again. "Can't understand why he'd change his mind. Why he'd do this to me?"

"I know, I know," she said, trying to console him. "But we can go on another vacation sometime and . . ."

Maurice wiped back a tear. "Workin' man don't ever get a vacation."

"Honey, why don't you bring that sugar over here, and I'll make you some coffee and we can talk, all right?"

Maurice thought for a moment, then nodded reluctantly. "I'll come on over. Don't feel like bein' by myself." He got the sugar bowl from the pantry and headed toward the Younguns' with Sausage waddling behind him.

"Hope you can make it all the way over there," Maurice said to the dog. "'Cause I ain't gonna be carryin' your fat self."

Terry and Sherry walked up toward the field that separated the property. Sutherland followed behind them as they climbed over the fence. He kept in the shadows of the trees that ringed the plowed ground.

Terry looked at his sister. "Why don't you run away from home? I hate you taggin' everywhere I go."

Sherry stuck her tongue out. "Sticks and stones will break my bones but . . ."

Terry tried to trip her. "And they really hurt a lot."

". . . and names will never hurt me," she said, finishing the rhyme.

"Made up a poem 'bout you," he said.

"Don't want to hear it," she said, covering her ears.

"You'll like this one," he snickered.

"When Sherry was born,
The doctor cried,
Because you were so ugly,
You hurt his eyes."

"I hate you!" she exclaimed.

"You know you're adopted," he said.

"Am not."

"Sure you are. Pa said he found you in a trash can behind the saloon. Said someone was throwin' you away, and he thought you were an ugly baby monkey."

Sherry's eyes welled up. "Stop it."

Terry was on a roll. "Said he brought you home and tried to feed you a banana, but you threw up everywhere, so he took you to the pigpen and had the big fat sow raise you."

"You're a meany," she sobbed, her lip puckering.

"So?" Terry shrugged. "If I was found in a trash can and raised in a pigpen, I'd run away and join the circus. Be part of the freak show!"

Sherry put her hands over her eyes and started running blindly. She was crying so hard that she didn't watch where she was going.

"Come back!" Terry shouted, worried that he would get into trouble.

But Sherry just kept on running and stumbled into a ditch over the rise. "Ohhhh," she moaned, "skinned my knee."

She couldn't stop crying so she lay down and curled up. The warm sun seemed to soothe her.

"Sherry, where are you?" Terry shouted. He ran past the ditch, not seeing her lying there.

Serve you right, she thought, fingering the locket through her shirt.

"Sherry, please come back," Terry called, now really worried. "You weren't found in a trash can."

Hee, hee, hee, she giggled, pulling the locket out from the shirt and opening it. "Wonder who this is?" she whispered, fascinated by the picture.

Sutherland began to move closer. He was only a few yards away from Sherry and the locket.

On the other side of the rise, Maurice waited for Sausage to catch up. "I swear, I'm gonna leave you here for the vultures to pick over." The dog yipped. "Yes sir, they'd feast for a week on you, Mr. Sausage."

When the dog got to him, he started forward again. "You best be keepin' up with me, 'cause I ain't stoppin' no more for you." He heard Terry callin' out for Sherry up ahead and shook his head. "Them kids are already up to mischief."

From the bushes, Sherry heard a voice. "Pssst. Hey, little girl." Sherry froze. It wasn't Terry's voice. She didn't say a word. "Hey, little girl, give me the locket," Sutherland said a little louder.

Sherry turned. It was the man in the picture in the locket! "Go away," she said, sitting up.

"Give me that locket," Sutherland said, inching closer. "It's mine. My girl gave it to me. I want to give it back to her."

Sherry stood up. "Go away!" she screamed.

Maurice heard her scream. "What's wrong, Sherry?" he shouted. But he didn't get an answer. "Come on Sausage, let's get on up there!"

Terry heard her but didn't see Sutherland. "I'm sorry, Sherry, don't tell Pa on me," he said, turning back in the direction of the voice.

"Look, Sherry . . . that's your name, isn't it?" Sutherland said, trying to stay calm. Sherry just nodded. "That locket belongs to me. It's got my picture in it. Look inside."

Sherry opened it again and nodded.

Sutherland inched closer. "Please, just give it back."

Sherry started to take it off then froze. "You're the man who set the fires."

"No, I didn't do anything."

"Yes, you did." She nodded, wishing she could run.

Terry was approaching. "Please Sherry, I'll be nice. Please come out from wherever you're hidin'," he said.

Sutherland's eyes scared her. Sherry's lip began to quiver. "Don't hurt me . . . please don't hurt me," she moaned.

Sutherland stopped. Suddenly it was as if he was watching himself, only here was another child who was scared of an adult. Just like he had been afraid of his father.

"Sherry, Terry, where are you?" Maurice shouted.

Sutherland looked toward the sound of the voice, then looked back at Sherry. "I won't hurt you. My daddy hurt me bad, but I wouldn't ever hurt a child."

Sherry began crying. Sutherland looked around, desperation on his face. "Please give me the locket, Sherry. My girl's gettin' married. I need my locket back."

"It's mine," she said, slowly standing up. She was so scared that it was the only thing she could think of to say.

"No, it's mine! My girl gave it to me," he whispered. "It's the only nice part of my life," he said, moving forward with his hands outstretched to grab the necklace.

"Leave me alone," she whispered.

He jumped at her, almost grasping the locket. Sherry managed to jump back, falling back down into the ditch. She crawled through the dirt and brush.

"It's mine!" he shouted, coming after her.

Terry shouted out, "Who's that with you?"

"Run, Terry!" she screamed. She came to a short drop-off and turned just in time to see Sutherland reaching for her.

Maurice came over the rise and saw what was happening. "You leave her alone!" he shouted. Sausage raced ahead, barking and growling like Maurice had never heard him.

"Give it to me!" Sutherland shouted, lunging at Sherry. But the dirt cliff of the drop-off gave way and Sherry fell backward.

Terry was standing below. "What are you doin'?" He laughed—then he looked up and saw Sutherland's face.

Sausage jumped on Sutherland and began ripping at his clothes. Sutherland pushed the dog away. "It's *my* locket!" he shouted, then crouched down, and rolled out of sight.

Sherry ran past Terry, screaming her head off. "Wait for me!" Terry shouted, running behind her.

Maurice ran to where he'd last seen Sherry's attacker, but he wasn't there. He heard Sherry screaming down the hill. "Hold on, baby, Maurice is comin'!"

He caught up with Sherry and tried to calm her down, but Terry didn't stop running until he was back home, telling Eulla Mae everything that happened. Terry said it was worse than facing the privy monster, and by the time Maurice arrived, Terry had built the events up to where he had single-handedly defeated the man.

Maurice related what he'd seen. "All I could get out of her," he said, "was that it was the man in the locket. She said he was the man setting the fires."

Sherry was sucking her thumb in his arms. "Best put her to bed," Eulla Mae said. "I'll call the sheriff."

Eulla Mae looked at the picture in the locket. "I know that face. Yes indeed I do. This is Michael Sutherland . . . and that girl, Jamie Johnson, 'fore she got all burned up."

From his hiding place in the woods, Michael Sutherland wanted to wait for another chance to talk to Sherry, but she didn't come out. "I'll be back," he whispered. "It's my locket. I got to give it back to Jamie before the sun rises tomorrow."

He disappeared into the dense Ozark woods.

46

Light the Darkness

❖

As nightfall came over the Ozarks, the thunder and lighting began again. It was a night made for self-doubt and dark thoughts. Sheriff Peterson recognized Sutherland's picture in the locket and added that piece to the puzzle.

Maybe Sutherland's crazy after all, he thought. *His tryin' to hurt Sherry Youngun means that I've got to call a posse. Got to keep the town safe.*

Now it's not just a hunch. Sutherland must be the one burning the barns. He's got a list of names and is actin' more and more like his father. The sheriff shook his head. *Somethin' bad's gonna happen.*

It didn't take long to round up a posse. They searched the woods around the Younguns' place, trying to find Sutherland's trail, but it was as if he'd disappeared without a trace.

Standing on the peak of the ridge near the Younguns' home, Sheriff Peterson looked toward Mansfield. A jagged bolt of lightning chased another across the horizon. *It's goin' to be another hot night. Trouble's in the air.*

He thought about taking the locket from Sherry and going over to see Leonard and Jamie Johnson, but decided against it. He didn't want to dredge up any more hurt for either of them than necessary.

But he did reach each of the people on the list to warn them again to take extra precautions—Dr. George, the undertaker, Frankie's grandmother, and Rev. Youngun.

They all took it seriously, but none knew what to do except keep an eye out for Sutherland. It was all anyone could do once darkness came on.

Auntie Gee Sutherland rocked on her porch and pondered the situation.

Michael's on a collision course with himself, she nodded. *He's got the devil of his daddy on his back. Makin' him ride the devil's horse over the cliff.*

"Hello, Auntie," came a voice from the darkness.

She froze in her chair. "Is that you, Michael?"

Sutherland laughed in the darkness, then stepped forward into the light.

"Go away," she said.

Sutherland laughed. "I'm not goin' to hurt you. And I'd never let anyone do to you what you let my father do to me."

"Leave me alone."

"Like you did me? I will, but I just wanted something to eat."

"I don't want nothin' to do with you," she said coldly.

Sutherland stepped up onto her porch. "I'm goin' in to your icebox and get somethin' to eat. I'll take no more than my fill, then I'll leave you alone."

Gee sat mutely on the porch, listening to the rustling sounds from the kitchen. Sutherland came out a few minutes later, wiping his lips. "Thanks," he said.

"You're just like your daddy," she said with intensity.

"I'm nothin' like him."

"You're doin' the list," she said, shaking her head. "You're gettin' his revenge on the people on Jack's list."

"You're crazy."

"Then why'd you burn the sheriff's barn? Why'd you burn Frankie's shed?"

Sutherland stopped and stared. "I didn't burn anything."

"Sheriff was by here. Told me 'bout the fires. Told me 'bout you paintin' Jack's list of names on his shed and . . ."

Sutherland grabbed her arm. "I didn't do any of that. Someone's tryin' to do me in again." He dropped her arm and walked to the porch rail. "Again. It's happenin' again. They're accusin' me of things I didn't do."

Then Sutherland turned and disappeared into the darkness. Gee closed her eyes. *God help those on the list,* she thought, gulping for air.

In Mansfield, Dr. George was worrying about Frankie's grandmother. At the same time, Grammie was worrying about Frankie. About what would become of him when she died.

Frankie lay in bed, pinching his nostrils, trying to think about anything besides the secrets he wished he'd never been told. He wanted to tell Grammie that Michael Sutherland didn't burn Jamie's barn. But it was a secret.

He wished he could just lie down and dream his dream. Dream he was a million smiles away. That he was a normal boy, running and playing. Just like the other children.

But the dream wouldn't come. He turned over and over in his bed, then got up and sat by the open windowsill, looking out.

Up in the woods, Sutherland sat curled up in the Secret Tree, thinking about Jamie and his father's list. Trying to figure out what was happening.

"You made them think I'm bad, Daddy," he said to himself, then shook his head. "Can't start talkin' to myself. That's the first sign of goin' crazy."

He put his hands to his head and rocked back and forth, counting his heartbeats. Hoping that he could figure out what to do.

Slipping out of the tree, he watched the lightning hit Devil's Ridge and counted the thunder booms until he got to ten. *Frankie knows somethin'. Said he knew a secret that he couldn't tell me. I got to find out what he knows.*

He headed toward Frankie's. *I'll just tap his window. Frankie will tell me.*

He thought about his father as he walked. About the list of names and how his father had drilled into him the importance of revenge.

The image of his father appeared in front of him.

"You got names still on the list."

"Leave me be, Daddy."

"Not until you finish the list." Jack Sutherland laughed, shaking his head. *"Couldn't even grab the locket from that little girl. Always knew you were a sissy."*

"*Don't say that.*"

"*Do what I tell you to!*" his father ordered. "*Get the doctor and the retard tonight. Then go get the undertaker and the Younguns. You can't forget Rev. Youngun. You put him on the list yourself.*"

"You made me do that, Daddy," Sutherland whispered to the image in front of him, then he shook his head. "You're not real! I'm just not feelin' well."

"*I didn't make you do anything. You did it all yourself,*" his father laughed, fading away. "*Light the darkness, son. Light the darkness.*"

"I don't want to light the darkness!" Sutherland screamed out to the woods.

He walked away through the dark woods, mumbling to himself.

"He's crazy," Leonard Johnson whispered quietly. He had returned to the Sutherland homestead after a few drinks at Tippy's Saloon, knowing that Michael would come back.

He followed until he saw where Sutherland was going, then crossed over the ridge to Dr. George's house. "If Sutherland needs to light the darkness, I'll just help him along," he whispered.

A few minutes later Johnson stood looking at Dr. George's house from the bushes. Right next door to it was the undertaker's house. "Two names that are on the list. Light the darkness," he said, taking out his matches.

47

Bedtime Story

Sherry was scared to sleep in her room, so she sneaked into the boys' bedroom. "Keep seein' his face," she whispered.

"That's okay," Larry said. "You can sleep in here."

"You didn't ask me," Terry said to him.

"It's my room too," Larry said.

"Well," Terry said, "just make sure she stays on your half of the room.

Larry ignored him. Sherry came up and lay down on his bed. "He's a bad man," she whispered.

"He went to jail for settin' a fire," Larry said.

"And Pa says he burned the sheriff's barn," Terry said.

"Don't want to talk 'bout it," Sherry whispered.

Terry lay still, then fluttered a long stream of air through his lips. "Wish I had some candy. Can't sleep on an empty stomach."

"Eat candy 'fore you sleep, and your teeth will fall out," Larry chastised.

"With everythin' that happened, Eulla Mae forgot to bake us a cake," Terry complained.

"You'll live," Larry said sarcastically.

"Do you want to live forever?" Sherry asked.

Larry thought for a moment, then shook his head. "No, I think I'd get too tired."

Terry listened for a moment, then said, "I'd settle for one tooth fallin' out so I'd have some tooth fairy money."

"For what?" Sherry asked, picking her blankey up and sucking her thumb.

Terry threw his dirty socks onto Larry's bed. They landed on her face. "For candy, silly."

Sherry began to sniffle. Larry put his arm around her. "Don't cry, sis," he said quietly. Then he turned to Terry. "And don't throw your socks over here," he warned, tossing the socks back.

"Sorry," Terry said insincerely. He looked at his sister. "Why don't you get outta here? This is a boys' room . . . girls ain't allowed."

The house shook from a deafening clap of thunder. Sherry began to cry again. Larry picked her up. "It's okay . . . there's nothin' to be scared of."

"But I don't want that bad man comin' into my room . . . I'm scared."

"Just lie on my bed till you fall asleep. Pa won't mind," Larry said, fixing his pillow for her to rest her head on.

Thunder pounded in the distance. "Think my turtles are okay?" she whispered.

"They're fine," Larry assured her. "Now go to sleep."

Terry thought for a moment. "Want me to read you a bedtime story, Sherry?" he asked with a glint in his eye. Larry tried to figure out what his brother was up to.

Sherry nodded cautiously, then sucked her thumb.

Terry listened to the thumb-slurping sound for a moment. "You sound like you're suckin' on a juice orange. Keep it down so I can hear myself read. Okay?"

Sherry nodded and sucked as quietly as she could. Terry picked up a book from the nightstand, held it upside down, and pretended to read. "This is the story about Sherry's best friend, C.R. Good old C.R. Sherry's best friend and twin look-alike, ol' C.R."

"Who's C.R.?" Sherry asked.

Terry paused. "C.R.?" He smiled, looking over the top of the book. "You mean you forgot who C.R. is?"

Sherry nodded. "Don't remember."

"You don't remember the name of your look-alike best friend?"

"Don't know any C.R.," Sherry mumbled.

"Sure you do." Terry grinned. "Matter fact, you love kissin' C.R."

Sherry pulled her thumb out. "Don't know any C.R."

"That stands for cockroach," Terry smiled. Sherry started to whine.

"Lay off," Larry warned his brother.

But Terry jumped into his pretend bedtime story. Neither Larry nor Sherry saw the cockroach in his hand.

"Yes, this is a story about little C.R., the cockroach. He is big, black, and very, very horrible looking. Why, every night when Sherry goes to sleep, C.R. crawls over her pillow and into her open mouth . . ."

"Stop it!" Sherry screamed, but Terry continued, "He likes to sleep on Sherry's tongue and . . ."

"Stop it! I'll tell Pa!"

"Okay, okay," Terry said.

"You never do anything nice for me," she frowned.

Terry slowly fingered the cockroach. "Got somethin' for you."

"What?"

"Just open your mouth and close your eyes, and I've got a big surprise."

Before Sherry could turn her face, Terry threw the dead cockroach at her. She screamed loudly, trying to brush the bug away.

"I hate you!"

"Shouldn't hate," Terry teased.

"Why'd you do that?" Larry asked.

"'Gettin' even for tryin' to make me eat carrots at the table." He pointed his finger at Sherry. "I always get even . . . you better 'member that."

Larry sniffed the air and went to the window. He saw a blaze in the distance. "Fire!" he said, pointing toward town.

48

Frankie Don't Play
with Matches

❖

Frankie sat on his windowsill, watching the lightning. He felt sorry for his bunnies, who were frightened and moving nervously around in their cage.

Frankie sniffed the air. It smelled like fire. He touched his nose and pinched his nostrils, but he couldn't figure it out.

He decided that it must be just the smell from the burned shed. Since he couldn't sleep, he slipped out the window to pet his bunnies to calm them down. He took the forbidden matches and a candle along because it was so dark outside.

Carefully lighting the candle, he placed it on the edge of the cage. He heard a voice.

"Psst, Frankie," came a voice from the bushes.

"Who is it?" Frankie whispered, hearing the clang of the volunteer fire wagon in the distance.

"It's me. Michael."

"You go away. Sheriff was here. You got Frankie in trouble."

Sutherland looked at the burned shed. "I didn't do that."

"Who did?" Frankie asked, looking around.

"Don't know," Sutherland said.

He heard a bell clanging. Frankie looked toward the sound. "Fire wagon."

"Wonder what happened?" Sutherland said.

The fire wagon was getting closer. The smell of Dr. George's burning buggy shed filled the air.

Sutherland knew something was happening, and it was very, very wrong. Everything seemed to be crashing down on his head.

"Fire," was all Frankie said.

"Did you tell the sheriff that you saw me?"

"No," Frankie said, shaking his head. "Frankie don't tell secrets."

"You're a good boy, Frankie."

Frankie sniffed the air. "Fire. Frankie don't play with matches."

"That's right," Sutherland said. "Now you got to tell me that bad secret you're holdin' back on."

Frankie looked around. "Can't."

"Frankie!" Sutherland said, raising his voice slightly. "I gotta know."

"Grammie will hear you."

Sutherland looked toward the house then at the houses nearby. People were opening doors and windows.

"Just tell me the secret. You know somethin' 'bout me and Jamie, don't you?" Sutherland asked, worried that the neighbors would see him in the backyard.

Frankie thought about the shed. "Did you burn Grammie's shed?"

Sutherland shook his head. "I told you no."

Frankie was confused. He didn't know what to think or believe. "Sheriff said you did," Frankie said, shaking his head.

"Just tell me what you know. Please," Sutherland said.

Frankie stepped back. "Fire's bad. You did bad."

"I did not!"

The clanging of the fire wagon was just down the street. The blaze of Dr. George's shed cast a glow against the sky. The undertaker's buggy barn was also ablaze.

Frankie sniffed. "You set more fires!" he screamed.

"No, Frankie. You know me. I'm your friend," Sutherland said, moving forward.

Frankie backed up, bumping against the cage. He knocked the lighted candle off onto the loose straw. Everything burst into flames.

Sutherland backed off, shaking his head. Frankie started screaming, slapping at the flames, but his clothes caught fire. Sutherland ran forward and knocked Frankie to the ground and rolled him over until the flames went out.

He burned his hands but he didn't stop. Grabbing a burlap sack, he tried to put out the spreading flames. The rabbits were bouncing around in their cage, shrieking to get out.

"Frankie, what are you doing?" his grandmother shouted from inside the house.

"Frankie's bunnies, Frankie's bunnies!" he screamed, over and over.

Sutherland looked at Frankie. "Don't get near the fire," he said, then added, "and don't tell anyone 'bout seein' me." He looked around, then ran off toward the woods.

Frankie watched in shock as his grandmother tried desperately to put out the flames. Even when the sheriff came and shook him, he didn't say a word.

"We got to do somethin' 'bout him, June," the sheriff said as the neighbors poured buckets on the remains of the burned cages.

"What can I do?"

Sheriff Peterson shook his head. "Can't have him loose no more. He burned your shed, and it looks like he burned Dr. George's shed and the undertaker's buggy barn. And then he came back and burned up his own rabbits."

"I'm so sorry," she moaned, "so sorry. I should have watched him better and . . ."

"He's been talkin' to Sutherland, hasn't he?"

"I don't know," she moaned. "Frankie," she called out, "have you seen Michael Sutherland?" Frankie stood mute. "Answer me, honey."

"June," the sheriff said, "I think that he's been with Sutherland and that Sutherland's twisted his mind."

"No," she said weakly.

"Yup. Took advantage of the boy and has been gettin' him to set fires. He's been gettin' Frankie to do his biddin'. Think about it," he paused, "your shed, my barn, Dr. George's shed, and the undertaker's buggy barn. They're all on the list."

"What am I going to do?" she whispered, trying to hold back the pain which seemed to be taking over every inch of her body.

"Can't let him stay here. You know that don't you, June?"

"I'll watch him."

Sheriff Peterson took Frankie by the hand. "Come on, Frankie. I got to lock you up until we can figure out what to do."

"Can't he stay with me?" she begged. "I'll watch him."

The sheriff shook his head. "Next thing he might do is burn down your house . . . or one of the neighbor's houses and kill somebody."

Tears welled up in Frankie's eyes. *Frankie's not a bad boy. Frankie didn't play with matches.*

He touched his nose and pinched his nostrils, but he couldn't figure out a way to tell the sheriff what had happened without telling a secret.

"Please don't take Frankie," she gasped, grabbing her chest.

"Grammie," Frankie cried out, trying to hold her up.

But she collapsed on the ground. Sheriff Peterson knelt beside her. "Go get Dr. George, quick!" he shouted to his deputy.

"Grammie, Grammie," Frankie moaned.

She looked into his eyes and squeezed his hand. "Oh Frankie," she whispered. "What's gonna happen . . ." She stopped in mid-sentence. The pain was too much.

"Grammie, Grammie," he moaned.

"Don't keep bad secrets," she whispered, squeezing his hand with what strength she had left. "You understand?" she wheezed.

Frankie nodded. "I love you, Grammie," he whispered, feeling like his world was spinning apart.

"Say your prayer with me, Frankie," she whispered.

Frankie began to cry but managed to say it with her.

"God's in my head.
God's in my eyes.
God's in my mouth.
God's in my heart.
God is my friend."

"Don't ever forget the prayer," she said, squeezing his hand again feebly.

Dr. George ran into the house carrying his black bag. His clothes were covered with soot from fighting the fire in his shed.

"Move back," he said to Frankie and the sheriff. He took her hand. "June, speak to me."

"Hurts bad, Doc. Hurts real bad," she whispered.

Dr. George saw death in her eyes. Lifting her up, he took her back into the house.

"Grammie," Frankie cried, tears streaming down his face. "Help Frankie's Grammie."

"I'm trying," Dr. George said.

"Easy, son," the sheriff whispered, putting his hand on Frankie's shoulder.

"Put your ear down here," she whispered to Dr. George, who did as instructed. "Find someone to watch Frankie. Find someone to give him a lot of love and . . . and . . ."

"I will," Dr. George whispered, squeezing her hand.

She gulped, trying to speak. "And . . . don't let him be sent to the state home . . . he needs a real home . . . with love and . . ."

Dr. George felt her wrist and looked into her eyes. Then he turned to the sheriff. "She's gone."

Sheriff Peterson took off his hat. Frankie got down and grabbed her hands. "Grammie, Grammie, it's Frankie. Frankie loves you. Don't leave Frankie . . ." He began humming the prayer, then said, "God's in my head. God's in my eyes."

Sheriff Peterson took him by the arm. "Come on, son," he said, "let the doc take care of your grandma."

Frankie continued saying the prayer. "God's in my mouth. God's in my heart. God is my friend." When he finished he broke down sobbing.

"Where you taking Frankie?" Dr. George asked the sheriff, closing the old woman's eyes.

"Got to take him to jail. She caught him burnin' down the rabbits' cage just after your place and the undertaker's caught fire."

Dr. George looked at Frankie. "Did you do it, Frankie?" Frankie didn't say anything. "Did you light the fires?"

Frankie struggled with what to say. *Frankie don't tell secrets,* he thought, over and over, tears streaming down his face.

The sheriff shook his head. "Guess he just cracked up or somethin'. Jail's the safest place to keep him."

He walked Frankie to his buggy and helped him up onto the bench seat. "Frankie, wait here. I got to go ask the doc somethin'."

On the ridge above the houses, Johnson stood, matches in hand, looking at Frankie. He lit one.

Frankie saw the flicker of flame. He touched his nose and pinched his nostrils, blinking rapidly. Then it came to him. He knew what to do.

Johnson held the match higher. *Light the darkness,* he thought, then blew it out and headed toward the Younguns' house.

Frankie looked around and, not seeing the sheriff, he slipped off the wagon and headed up the ridge. *Got to stop Michael,* he thought. *Frankie don't play with matches.*

49

Last Name on the List

❖

Sutherland was watching from the bushes as Johnson lit the match. "It's him. He's tryin' to blame me again."

He followed Johnson through the woods, not knowing where he was going but knowing he had to stop him from hurting any more people.

Behind them both, Frankie came running as fast as his short, stubby legs would carry him. *Grammie said to tell bad secrets,* he thought, trying to figure out what to do. *Got to find Michael.*

He didn't know why, but he thought he knew where Sutherland would go next. Frankie remembered a shortcut that Cubby had showed him and ran through the woods.

Owls hooted overhead. A bat swooped over him. Frankie wanted to hide and scream. He wanted to run into his grammie's arms.

Though he didn't really understand life and death, he did know that things stopped moving. Grammie had once had a dog who died. Frankie remembered that when the dog stopped moving, they buried it. *Grammie stopped moving,* he thought as he ran. *They'll put Frankie's grammie in the ground.*

Tears streamed down his face, but he kept going as if he were running a race. His grammie was going to be put in the ground. His bunnies were going to be put in the ground. His mother was already in the ground.

"Frankie wants Grammie back," he cried out, but only the owl answered back.

Got to stop Michael. Frankie's got to stop Michael, he thought as he came over the rise to the Younguns' house. But Frankie didn't know that Sutherland had stopped running to pick an Ozark orchid for Jamie. When he bent over in the darkness he had twisted his ankle, and now he had fallen far behind Johnson.

Sheriff Peterson found Frankie gone from the wagon. "Has anybody seen Frankie?" he called out, but none of the neighbors had seen him go.

"Where do you think he went?" Dr. George asked.

The sheriff looked at the list. "There's only one name left," he said, pointing to Rev. Youngun's name.

"Oh, Lord," Dr. George said, "you better call him."

"No," the sheriff said, "I'm goin' to the Younguns'. *You* call him." The sheriff borrowed his deputy's horse and rode off into the night.

Maurice sniffed the air that drifted through their bedroom window. "Eulla Mae, you smell somethin'?"

She sat straight up. "Smells like fire," she said, a worried look on her face.

"Better check the barn," he said.

"You think that Sutherland's come 'round here?"

"Hope not," he said, picking up the shotgun, "but best be prepared." Eulla Mae got up and put her robe on. She found Maurice in the kitchen, trying to call the Younguns. "Dang line is blocked!" he snapped. Sausage lay asleep under the kitchen table.

"You don't think he'd hurt those kids, do you?" she asked.

"Sheriff said their name was on some list he found. Rev. Youngun didn't make much of it, but . . ." he paused. "You keep tryin' to reach 'em. I'm headin' over there."

"Be careful," she said. But Maurice was already out of earshot. She nudged Sausage awake. "Go on, follow Maurice."

The dog looked up and yawned. "If you don't get goin' I'm gonna put you on bread and water for a week." Sausage got to his feet and trotted out the door.

Sausage caught up with Maurice beyond the woodpile. "What you comin' 'long for?" he laughed. "You must have smelled the smoke and think we're headin' to a barbecue or somethin'."

Frankie got to the Youngun house first and stumbled as he came up the steps. He banged on the door. Dangit jumped up, trying to lick his face. "Down, Dangit," Frankie said.

He banged again. "Rev. Youngun, Frankie needs you."

Rev. Youngun looked at the clock beside the bed. "What the . . ." He came out of his room into the hall. Larry and Terry were already standing there. Sherry peeked out from their room, the locket hanging on top of her nightshirt.

"Sounds like Frankie, Pa," Larry said.

"It's late. What would he be doing here?" Rev. Youngun said, walking slowly down the stairs.

Larry, Terry, and Sherry followed behind. Rev. Youngun opened the door. "Frankie, what are you doing out this late?"

"Michael Sutherland's comin'," Frankie said, breathing hard.

"He's coming where?"

"Frankie knows he's comin' here."

The phone rang in the kitchen. Terry answered it. "It's for you, Pa."

Rev. Youngun left Frankie at the door with Larry and went to the kitchen. Dr. George told him everything that had happened. That Grammie was dead. That his shed and the undertaker's barn were burned down. That Frankie was on the loose and suspected of lighting the fires, maybe even working with Sutherland.

"Keep an eye on him until the sheriff gets there," Dr. George said.

"I will!" Rev. Youngun exclaimed, hanging up the phone. He started back toward the front porch. "Where's Frankie?" he asked, finding him gone.

"He just took off," Larry said. "Like he'd seen a ghost."

"Took off where?"

"Toward the barn," Larry pointed.

Frankie found Johnson lighting a brush pile behind the barn. "Bad man," Frankie exclaimed. "Fire's bad."

"Shut up or I'll burn you," Johnson snapped, pushing Frankie away. The pile of brush went up in a blaze.

The animals inside the barn were acting up, smelling the fire. "Pa, look!" Terry shouted. "The barn's on fire!"

Sherry screamed, "Save Bashful! Save Crab Apple!"

"Come on," Rev. Youngun shouted.

Behind the barn, Frankie jumped up on Johnson's back. "You bad man!"

Johnson tried to throw him off, but Frankie held on for dear life. Staggering under the weight, Johnson fell against the ground. His hand went into the badger hole, and he began screaming. The badger inside was ripping at his hand.

"Get off!" Johnson screamed, tearing his hand from the badger's jaws. His fingers were torn and bloody. "I'm leavin'," Johnson snarled, "and don't tell no one 'bout this, or I'll burn your grandma's house down."

"Grammie's dead," Frankie said, stumbling forward, swinging his fists blindly.

Then Sutherland limped up and grabbed Johnson by his arm. "You're the barn burner! You're the one who should have been in prison!"

"Keep away from me," Johnson said, shaking free.

"You talked Jamie into marryin' someone else, didn't you?"

Johnson couldn't pass up the chance to hurt him again. "She don't love you anymore. She got married tonight. You're too late. They're already honeymoonin'."

"I hate you," Sutherland shouted. "You're goin' to jail this time."

"They'll never believe you," Johnson said, smacking Sutherland in the jaw. Sutherland staggered backward, knocking his head against the barn wall.

Frankie didn't know what to say and watched Johnson run off over the hill into the woods. Sutherland got to his feet.

"Michael," Rev. Youngun said, standing by the side of the burning barn, "it's over. It's time to put the past behind you and stop the fires."

"You've got the wrong man, Reverend," Sutherland said. "It was Johnson. Leonard Johnson. Frankie will tell you."

"Leave Frankie out of this," Rev. Youngun said, "you've gotten him into enough problems as it is."

"I got to catch him," Sutherland said, running after Johnson.

"Come back!" Rev. Youngun called out. He had no choice but to follow with Frankie close behind.

The wall of the barn was ablaze. Larry threw open the doors, and Crab Apple and Lightnin' the horse stampeded out, followed by T.R. the turkey and Bessie the pig.

"Where's Bashful?" Sherry cried.

The smoke was suffocating. "He's in there!" Terry screamed.

Larry looked through the smoke and flames. He saw Bashful. The goat had fainted in the middle of the barn.

Sherry started to race in, but Larry grabbed her hand and stopped her. "Please save Bashful," she cried.

Larry picked up a burlap feed bag that hung from the wall and dipped it into the water trough and put it over his head. Then, with more courage than sense, he ran into the barn.

Maurice came over the rise and saw the barn ablaze. "Come on, Sausage," he shouted, running down the slope.

He heard Sherry screaming that Larry was inside the barn and ran as fast as he could. "Move back," he said, trying to get his breath.

"You gotta help him," Terry said, fear on his face.

"I'll try," he said, looking at the wall of smoke and flames in front of him.

Inside the barn, the flames licked at Larry's face and hands. The smoke made him dizzy. *Got to get to Bashful,* he thought, his heart pounding.

"Larry, you in here?" Maurice called out.

"Mr. Springer? I'm here!"

Maurice looked around through the smoke. "Can't see you. Just follow my voice." He looked up and saw that the roof was burning. *Not much time,* he thought. "Come on now, boy, get on over here."

"Got to get Bashful," Larry shouted.

"Forget him!"

"He's right around here," Larry said, then he saw him. "Come on," he said, picking the goat up.

He stumbled into Maurice. "Got him," Larry smiled, his face all smudged with smoke and ashes.

"Now, let's get outta here 'fore the fire gets us," Maurice yelled. "Follow me."

He took two steps then pushed Larry back. "Watch it!" he cried, as a beam from the roof crashed down in front of them.

Larry couldn't see Maurice. The smoke was too thick. "Where are you, Mr. Springer?"

"I'm right here," Maurice coughed, getting to his feet. He made it over to where Larry was holding the goat. "Stay right with me."

They made their way around the flaming roof beams and went low through a thick wall of smoke and flame. As they stepped out of the barn, the flaming roof collapsed behind them.

"Here's your goat." Larry handed Bashful to Sherry.

Maurice put his arms around the kids while Sausage jumped up and down. "Where's your pa?" he asked. They pointed toward the hill.

"Larry, you keep your brother and sister here. I'll be right back," Maurice said, picking up his shotgun.

Near the top of the hill, Rev. Youngun tried to grab Sutherland, but he was not fast enough. Sutherland dropped to his knee, tripping Rev. Youngun. Frankie shivered, his eyes blinking in anger.

Sutherland looked at Rev. Youngun, with tears in his eyes. "All I wanted was my locket . . . Jamie's locket. I never set no fires, and I didn't hurt your little girl. I just wanted to hold the locket again."

"That's all right, Michael," Rev. Youngun said, remembering the last time they'd spoken in the cell five years before. "Just calm down. It's all over. You don't have to do any more bad things."

"I didn't do any bad things. I just want my locket," he said, tears streaming down his cheeks. He felt like everyone—the whole world—was against him now as Rev. Youngun walked him back toward the crumbling barn.

Maurice came and stood beside Rev. Youngun. "You need some help?"

Rev. Youngun shook his head. "Just wait. Sutherland's not goin' to hurt anybody."

"Can I just have my locket back? Will someone just give me my locket back so I can give it to my girl before she gets married?" Sutherland pleaded.

"Married?" Maurice whispered. "What's he talkin' 'bout?"

"Just give me the locket, please?" Sutherland begged.

Sherry came toward Sutherland. "Here it is," she whispered, holding the locket in front of her.

Sutherland stepped forward. "Sherry, get back," Rev. Youngun commanded. Maurice lifted his shotgun.

Sutherland shook his head. "I won't hurt her. I'd never hurt a child."

Frankie watched the standoff for a moment, then took the locket from Sherry and handed it to Michael.

Sutherland looked at Sherry. "Thank you, Sherry. You won't ever know what this locket means to me."

"I think I do," she whispered.

Sutherland looked into her eyes. "Yes," he smiled, sniffing back tears, "I think you do."

"Go now, Michael Sutherland. Go away," Frankie said.

"Can't," Michael Sutherland said. "Got to prove I didn't burn my girl. Or set any of the other fires." He looked at Frankie. "You know somethin', don't ya?"

Frankie stood mute.

"You were there that night, weren't you?" Sutherland asked.

"Frankie don't tell secrets," he mumbled.

"Some secrets aren't worth keepin'," Sutherland said. "You remember that," he whispered, looking into Frankie's eyes.

Suddenly, the barn wall behind them collapsed. When Rev. Youngun turned, Sutherland was gone.

"Frankie don't play with matches."

"No, you don't," Rev. Youngun said, putting his arm around the boy-man.

"Grammie's going in the ground," he said, collapsing into Rev. Youngun's arms.

The sheriff raced up to the flaming barn, fearing the worst. "I'm sorry, Reverend. I should have kept a watch on Frankie and . . ."

"Frankie didn't do it," Rev. Youngun said.

For a moment, everyone was silent as Frankie cried for the stable part of his world that was collapsing around him. When he calmed down, Rev. Youngun told the sheriff about the fight with Sutherland.

The sheriff looked at Frankie. "Son, you got to tell me what you know."

"Frankie don't tell secrets," he whispered.

"Frankie, there's folks' lives at stake. This ain't no time for games. If you know where Sutherland went, tell me now."

Frankie looked at the sheriff, then at Rev. Youngun. "Michael went to Jamie's barn."

"Jamie's barn?" the sheriff said, perplexed. "Why?"

"Says he didn't set the fire or any of the fires," Rev. Youngun said.

"But she doesn't want to see him and . . ." the sheriff stopped and took Frankie by the arm. "Did you or Sutherland set fire to the Younguns' barn?

"Man with matches got hand bit," Frankie said.

"Bit by what?" Rev. Youngun asked. Frankie pointed to the badger hole.

"Looks like a badger hole," the sheriff said. "Who got bit? The man with matches?"

Rev. Youngun thought for a moment, then shook his head. "Sutherland's hand wasn't bit."

"That's what Frankie saw," Frankie said, not wanting to tell a secret.

"You saw what?" the sheriff asked.

"Frankie saw Michael go to Jamie's barn and then leave. Frankie watched Jamie and her daddy shout and . . . and . . ."

"What are you talkin' 'bout?" the sheriff said in frustration. "Man with matches got bit, and you saw somethin' at the Johnson place and . . . and what else?"

Frankie shook his head. "Frankie don't tell secrets."

"Tell me this," Sheriff Peterson said. "Do you think Sutherland's goin' up to see Jamie's pa? Is he goin' to burn somethin' on their property?"

Frankie thought for a moment. He didn't want to tell a secret. *Is the sheriff askin' a secret . . . or is he . . . ?*

Frankie couldn't decide. Touching the tip of his nose, he pinched his nostrils and held his breath.

"Frankie," the sheriff asked again. "Do you think Sutherland headed up to the Johnson place?"

Frankie exhaled loudly, then began nodding. "Yes. Yes. Yes!"

"Then let's go," the sheriff said, mounting up. "There's somethin' goin' on that still don't add up."

50

Final Truth

❖

When Sutherland got to Leonard Johnson's cabin, he banged on the door, forgetting that Jamie was inside too. All he wanted to do was catch the man who had destroyed his life and kept him from marrying Jamie.

"Come out!" Sutherland screamed. He had the locket clutched in his hand.

Johnson peered through the window. His hand was wrapped in a cloth. "Sheriff's comin' for you, Sutherland. They're gonna put you away for good this time. Hope they hang you like they did your barn burnin' father."

"You lied before, and you're a liar now, Johnson," Sutherland said. "You burned the Younguns' barn, and you burned Frankie's shed and the doctor's shed, didn't you?"

Jamie sat in the corner, rocking back and forth. *Michael is just outside the door. I can't let him see my face,* she thought, wrapping the scarf around her head. "What's he talkin' about?" she asked her father.

"Nothin'," Johnson snapped. "He's a crazy liar."

Her body quivered. She wanted to run out into Michael's arms and pretend nothing had changed between them. Then she glimpsed the mirror on the wall.

"You're the barn burner," Sutherland shouted, banging on the door.

"See what I'm tellin' you, Jamie," her father whispered. "He's crazy."

"Open the door," she said. "He won't hurt you."

"No. He's been burnin' half the town down. He probably wants to kill you."

"We gotta talk," Sutherland said from the other side of the door.

"We got nothin' to talk 'bout unless you're ready to turn yourself in," Johnson said.

"Open the door, Father," Jamie said louder.

Sutherland kicked at the door. "I didn't burn Jamie, and you know it. But I caught you burnin' the Younguns." He banged louder.

"If you don't want to die where you stand, you better get out of my way," Johnson growled, taking hold of the door handle.

"Don't hurt him," Jamie said.

Johnson looked up at the rack of guns. "He's dangerous," he mumbled, taking the shotgun down from the rack.

"No," Jamie said, "I said, he won't hurt you."

"I got to keep you safe from him," Johnson said, snapping open the barrel. He put in two shells. "He tried to kill you before."

Jamie shook her head. "You've been lying to me."

Johnson turned, his eyes and nostrils flaring. "Hush. You don't know what you're talkin' 'bout."

"You never sent my letters."

"I did," he said, feeling cornered.

"I saw where you burned them," she said, holding up the tattered, burned corner of her last letter. "And you've been lying about what happened that night to me, haven't you?" Johnson ignored her. "You can't hide from me any longer, Father."

Sutherland called out. "If you don't come out, I'm comin' in."

"Michael," Jamie shouted. "He's got a gun."

"Jamie! Jamie!" he shouted, his heart racing. "Is that you?"

"It's me," she said.

"Come out. Please. I love you. I've always loved you."

"It's too late, Michael. But run. My father wants to hurt you."

"Whose side are you on anyway?" her father snarled.

"Michael's," she said, walking toward the door.

"You're not goin' anywhere," her father said, grabbing her arm.

Rev. Youngun followed the sheriff on his horse named Lightnin'. Maurice rode behind him, leaving Sausage to play with Dangit.

Frankie looked at the Younguns. "Help Frankie."

"What do you want us to do?" Larry asked, putting his hand on his friend's shoulder.

"Help Frankie get to Michael Sutherland."

"Why?" Terry asked.

Frankie thought for a moment. "Frankie can't tell. It's a . . ."

Terry stopped him. "Yeah, yeah, yeah. It's a secret."

"Let's take the back trail," Larry said. "We can cut through the ridge and beat them there."

"But we're in our nightshirts," Terry said, looking down.

"So?" Larry said. "Just tuck 'em in and start runnin'."

Taking the back trail, they cut across the ridge and ravine. Terry stepped on a sharp rock. "Hope this ain't no wild goose chase."

"Come on," Larry yelled back.

"We look like four lunatics runnin' through the woods, tryin' to find our brains," Terry mumbled.

"Wanna hold hands?" Frankie said, reaching out.

"That'll be the day," Terry said, racing ahead.

They took the steep trail up the last ridge and came up to the Johnson place. They hid behind a fallen tree and watched. Larry picked up sticks and passed them around.

"What are these for?" Terry asked.

"They're rifles," Larry said.

"Count me out of any charge," Terry said, nodding toward Johnson. "He's got a real gun."

Down below, Johnson stepped through the doorway. Sutherland looked at the shotgun pointing at him. "You know I didn't set the fire that hurt Jamie."

"I don't know nothin' 'cept that you're a barn burner and you should be hanged," Johnson said coldly. "Or maybe I'll just shoot you where you stand."

The Younguns didn't know what to do. "No, no," Frankie moaned.

"What?" Larry whispered.

"Frankie knows. Frankie knows what happened."

"What happened? What do you know?" Larry asked.

"Frankie knows a bad secret."

"You gotta tell someone," Terry said. "Bad secrets aren't good to keep."

Larry heard the horses coming up the trail and waved to the sheriff and his father. "Sutherland's down there," he said to the sheriff.

Maurice and Rev. Youngun dismounted behind the sheriff.

"What are you kids doin' here?" Sheriff Peterson asked.

"We've been guardin' the place until you got here," Larry said.

"Okay, soldier," the sheriff said, "keep it up."

Sheriff Peterson started down toward the house, but Rev. Youngun held him back. "He's got a shotgun."

"So do I," said Maurice.

The sheriff nudged Rev. Youngun. "Johnson's hand is bandaged. 'Man with matches got bit.' That's what Frankie said."

Frankie came up and said, "Frankie saw it. Frankie saw it."

"Saw what?" Rev. Youngun asked.

"Frankie knows who told a lie," the man-boy said excitedly.

Below them, Johnson screamed, "You are a liar! You burned my daughter! That's why you went to jail!"

Jamie watched from the window, her heart wanting to explode. *Oh Michael, be careful,* she thought.

Sutherland waved his arms. "No! That night when Jamie and I were talking about gettin' married in the barn, she told me to leave, and I did. I went to the edge of your property, then decided to come back and try to talk sense into you and let us get married."

"That's when you did it," Johnson said bluntly. "That's when you burned my girl."

"I didn't set the fire. I loved her. We were going to get married," he said, holding up the locket. "Look at this picture. She loved me. She was the only good thing that ever happened to me."

He saw Jamie looking through the window. "Jamie. Come out. Don't marry no one else. I love you. Don't you know that?" Jamie nodded, tears filling her eyes. "Come out, Jamie. It's all right."

Jamie hesitated, then shook her head, hiding her face.

"I don't care what your face looks like. I love you for you," Sutherland exclaimed.

Johnson pushed the shotgun forward. "You were trash then, and you're trash now. I told her so."

Sutherland laughed. "You lied to the judge. Tried to blame me for what I didn't do. For what *you* did."

"You're crazy!" Sutherland exclaimed.

Frankie felt his heart pounding. He'd never told a secret before. *Grammie said to tell bad secrets,* he thought.

He touched the tip of his nose and pinched his nostrils. Then it came to him. "Do what Grammie says," he mumbled, running toward Johnson's house.

"Stop him!" the sheriff exclaimed.

"Oh, Lord," Rev. Youngun whispered.

Johnson raised his shotgun toward Frankie. "Don't come no further." Then he heard another sound.

"It's me, Sheriff Peterson." The sheriff stepped slowly down the hill.

Frankie ran up and stood in front of Sutherland. "Grammie said to tell bad secrets."

Johnson frowned. "Frankie, you best be quiet."

"Do what your Grammie said," Sutherland said gently.

"Grammie's dead," Frankie said. "Man with matches got bit," he said, pointing to Johnson's hand. He looked at the sheriff, who nodded.

Sutherland coughed. A wave of grief swept over him. A feeling he hadn't felt since his own mother died. "I'm . . . I'm sorry, Frankie," he said. "Your Grammie was a good, good woman."

"Get out of here, Frankie," Johnson growled. "And keep your mouth *shut.*"

"Grammie said to tell bad secrets," Frankie said.

Johnson spit. "Your Grammie's dead, so you listen to me now."

Frankie shook his head. "Grammie said to tell the bad secret Frankie knows."

"Tell what you know," Sutherland whispered. "It'll make you feel better."

"Shut up!" Johnson snapped.

"Johnson, did you burn the Younguns' barn?" the sheriff called out.

Johnson shook his head. "He's the barn burner," he said, pointing to Sutherland.

"Man with matches got bit," Frankie said, pointing to Johnson's hand.

"What happened to your hand?" Rev. Youngun called out.

Frankie started to talk again, but Johnson cut him off. "Don't open your mouth."

"Let him speak," Sheriff Peterson said. "And you best put that shotgun down. I got a posse of men with rifles aimed at you now."

Maurice stepped forward into the lantern light. "We got a lot of guns aimed at you."

Behind him, Terry looked at Larry. "That's a fib if I ever heard one."

"Adults call it stretching the truth." Larry shrugged, taking aim with his stick rifle.

Frankie looked at Johnson, who had not put down the gun. "Frankie saw you through the barn window. Saw you scream at Jamie."

Johnson panicked. "Frankie! You promised not to tell," he said in desperation.

"You said bad names to her. You pushed her. You hit her. Frankie saw you knock the lantern over. You ran and left Jamie in the fire. Frankie pulled her out. Frankie saw it all."

Johnson didn't say a word. It was as if he were in a trance.

Sutherland hugged his friend. "Did you save her life, Frankie?"

Frankie nodded. "He said he'd kill me if I told. Said it was a secret."

Sutherland spit at Johnson's feet. "That's the truth, isn't it Johnson?" Leonard Johnson didn't speak. "She was tellin' you that she was goin' to marry me, and you were callin' her names again. You were drunk again, weren't you? Left her in the burning barn."

"I did not!" Johnson said coldly. "I wasn't drunk. You're a murderin' liar."

Jamie stepped to the doorway. All eyes were on her face, wondering what was behind the scarf. They couldn't help themselves.

"Yes you were, Father. You were so drunk you could hardly stand up." She began crying. "And they called you a hero for saving my life. I'm so ashamed of you."

Jamie dropped the scarf from her face. Everyone stared. "I know now you didn't do it, Michael. Father said he saw it all and . . . and . . . he lied."

She broke down crying, then looked to Frankie. "And you saved my life . . . you did . . . not my father. You're the hero, aren't you?" Frankie blushed.

Sutherland stepped forward to take her in his arms, but Johnson pushed him back with the gun.

Frankie wagged his finger toward Johnson. "Frankie saw it! Saw you knock the lantern over and run."

"You're lyin'," Johnson moaned, feeling the memory of the night come over him.

"I've heard enough," the sheriff said. "I'm takin' you all down to my office."

"Tell the truth, *hero*," Sutherland said, pushing toward Johnson.

"Step back," Johnson warned.

"No. You blamed me for what I didn't do," Sutherland said, moving forward, the gold locket reflecting the lantern light. "Then you pretended to be a hero for what you didn't do."

"Stop right there!" the sheriff ordered. "Don't tempt him, Sutherland."

"What do I got to lose?" Sutherland said quietly. "I'm nothin' but trash. Nothin' but a barn burner's son."

"No you're not, Michael," Jamie whispered.

Johnson took a step backward. "Sheriff, if you don't shoot this murderer, then I will."

"Don't shoot, Johnson," Sheriff Peterson ordered.

Sutherland continued, inching forward. "It was you who hurt Jamie! Called yourself a hero when it was Frankie you should have been thankin'. You lied in court so you wouldn't have to say what your drinkin' had done!"

The Younguns tried to see what was happening, but their father pushed them down behind the ridge.

Sutherland took another step toward Johnson and reached for the gun. "No, Sutherland!" the sheriff shouted.

Frankie tried to get between them, but Sutherland pushed him aside, just at the moment that Johnson pulled the trigger. The impact of the blast knocked Sutherland off the porch into a crumpled heap. The locket fell into the dirt.

Johnson backed away and stepped off the porch. "He's the barn burner . . . not me," he yelled—and ran off into the woods.

"Stop!" the sheriff shouted. The Younguns looked up, not knowing what had happened to Sutherland.

Johnson raced up toward Terry and Larry. "Oh jeesh," Terry said, dropping down to a snake's view. "Where's she goin'?" Terry asked, watching Sherry run down the side of the hill.

"Hold the line," Larry whispered.

"This ain't no time for games," Terry whispered. "Let's skedaddle."

Larry planted his feet. He was cool on the outside, but inside, his guts were roasting. "Ready, aim . . ." He didn't know how pale his face was, but he was standing firm, and that's what counted.

"He's got a gun, and we got sticks," Terry whispered, wanting to chew his fingernails off.

"Stand up," Larry hissed.

Terry got back to his feet. *Feel like jumping out of my skin.*

"Hold the line," was all Larry could whisper.

Terry watched Johnson charge toward them. He looked at the stick in his hands. "Sometimes I think you got the brains of a pea in a boxcar," he said, looking at his brother.

When Johnson was fifteen feet away, Larry shouted out in his deepest voice, "Halt, or I'll shoot!" Johnson couldn't see they were just kids and froze.

Terry coughed and tried to drop his voice, but it came out like an owl imitating a bullfrog. "Drop your weapon, and put up your gumdrops." Larry nudged him. "I mean arms."

Johnson did as ordered, and the sheriff came up behind him. "Just keep your hands up, Johnson."

Larry stood there with his stick rifle pointed at Johnson. The sheriff nodded. "Good work, soldier. You got some sand in you, don't you?" All Larry could do was nod.

Terry came up with his stick rifle pointing toward Larry. "Watch it," Larry said, "that thing's loaded." Terry just looked at him like he'd gone crazy.

"You could have gotten your heads blown off," Rev. Youngun said to his boys.

At the bottom of the hill, Sutherland felt the blood pouring from the wound and looked up to see Jamie rush forward. "Michael! Michael!" she cried, cradling his head.

Frankie crept up and knelt beside him. "You're not a bad boy," Frankie whispered, holding his hand. "You were nice to me. I kept your secret."

Sutherland nodded, then looked at Jamie. "I never hurt you, Jamie. I loved you. Please don't marry anyone else."

"Just you, Michael," she whispered. "I'll only marry you."

Sherry came forward and picked the locket up. "Here's your locket," she whispered, placing it in Sutherland's hand.

He looked at her and smiled. "Thank you, Sherry," he whispered. He put the locket into Jamie's hand. "You're the only good thing that ever happened to me."

"Don't talk, Michael. Wait until the doctor gets here," Jamie said, pushing her scarf against the wound.

"Inside my pocket," he whispered, nodding down. Jamie reached in and found a crumpled Ozark orchid.

"You remembered," she said, tears spilling down.

"I got a memory like an elephant," he smiled, wincing at the pain.

"Don't die, Michael. Please don't die," Jamie whispered.

51

A Million Smiles Away

❖

Though the people of Mansfield were relieved that the Sutherland nightmare was finally over, the trial of Leonard Johnson for shooting Michael Sutherland was a time for self-reflection.

Johnson's drinking had caused the barn fire which burned Jamie five years ago, but the people of Mansfield had believed his accusations against Sutherland. So they made Johnson a hero and sent an innocent man to prison . . . because he was a barn burner's son.

It was a lot for the town to think about, and Johnson had the rest of his life in the Missouri State Prison to reflect on what his drinking had caused. He was jailed as a barn burner and for shooting Michael Sutherland.

Mansfield also learned a lesson about protecting children. What Jack Sutherland did to his son should have been stopped. That abuse should *never* be tolerated or ignored.

After Michael was cleared of all charges, he and Jamie had a lot of catching up to do. With Michael recuperating in bed for several months from the shotgun wound, they had the time.

When he was able to walk, they went up to the bluff beyond her house where they looked into the pool of water and exchanged vows of hope for the future. They even found another Ozark orchid.

The men of Mansfield did a house raising for Michael and Jamie. Rev. Youngun married them in the living room of his home, and Sherry was the flower girl. Frankie served as the ringbearer and blushed when the bride kissed him on the cheek.

"Till death do us part." Jamie whispered, kissing Michael on the lips.

Even with the scars, her inner beauty radiated through. Their true love showed the town that beauty is what's inside a person. What a person is made of. Not what a person looks like or what his father did or didn't do.

Missouri Poole spent the rest of the summer trying to kiss Larry. He managed to outrun and dodge her advances, until the day she found him sleeping on the bank of Willow Creek with a fishing pole in his hand.

Larry was convinced that Terry had a hand in helping her, but he couldn't prove it. The pocketful of candy that Terry had the next day looked mighty suspicious, but with his fingers crossed behind his back, Terry said he didn't help her at all. Honest.

Maurice finally got to go on his vacation, even though it was not what he expected. Eulla Mae and the Younguns fixed up a makeshift camp behind the barn, and they all spent the night in a tent they made from bedsheets.

Terry was excited when Eulla Mae told him she'd baked a fresh cake with lots of sugar in it. But when he found it was a carrot cake, he was upset for the whole night about the "waste of good sugar."

Maurice didn't sleep well with the three Younguns snuggled up around him, snoring and snorting like a litter of pups. Then when Dangit and Sausage crawled in, Maurice snuck back to his own bed and decided that no place was quite like home.

After Frankie's grammie was buried, folks felt bad for the way they'd been so quick to accuse Frankie of something he didn't do. Just because Frankie was different, he wasn't any better or worse than anyone else. He was just one of God's children.

So they gave him a long-overdue medal for saving Jamie Johnson's life and reelected him as honorary Mayor of Mansfield. Frankie wore the shiny medal everywhere he went.

Dr. George took Frankie in until he could work out a place for him to go. Except for Frankie wanting to hold hands with Cubby when they said prayers, the boys got along fairly well, but Frankie needed special love and attention, and Dr. George knew who could fill the order.

Mom and Hambone Higgens came around day after day. Frankie was on their mind, but they didn't know where to begin. Dr. George knew they were trying to say something that was inside their hearts. All it took was for Frankie to walk into the room and hug them both. They finally agreed to take Frankie and moved him into their home.

The Younguns felt bad for what happened to Frankie's grammie and asked their father what they could do. "Small kindnesses come from big hearts," was all Rev. Youngun would tell them. "Do what comes from your heart."

So Larry, Terry, and Sherry did odd jobs around Mansfield and saved up enough to buy Frankie the perfect present—a caged pair of bunnies. When they took them over to Frankie's new house, they found Frankie asleep in the tall, warm grass, with his medal pinned on his shirt.

Mom came out. "Want me to wake him, children?"

"No, ma'am," Larry said. "Just tell him that the Younguns gave him these," he said, leaving the bunnies as a surprise.

But Frankie wasn't just asleep. He was off on a trip to his own special world, dreaming his favorite dream where he could be anything he wanted.

A place where he could be a fireman, a postman, or a policeman. A place he could run, jump, and hide, just like any other boy.

It wasn't that there was anything wrong with the way Frankie was; it was that his special world was his alone. A place where he was just a regular boy who didn't have to be different. If only for a little while.

"Hey Frankie, come on, we've been waiting for you to come play ball with us," Larry Youngun shouted.

"Frankie's comin', Frankie's comin'!" he laughed, his strong, young legs running with the wind.

"Tell us a secret," Terry cried out.

Frankie laughed, jumping high to touch the tip of the branch in front of him. "Frankie's as fast as a cheetah and as brave as a tiger."

"Come on, Frankie, tell us a secret," Sherry echoed.

"God's Frankie's bestest friend!" Frankie shouted.

"Tell us a real secret," Cubby shouted.

Frankie shook his head and jumped up to touch another branch. "Frankie don't tell secrets!" he shouted, landing in their arms.

The children linked hands and ran up the hill. Racing like there was no tomorrow, trying to catch the sun. Frankie was leading the way.

He was in his happy place. The place where he was just a healthy, normal boy.

And it was only a million smiles away.

About the Author

Thomas L. Tedrow is a best-selling author, screenwriter, and film producer. He prides himself on stories that families can read together and pass on to friends. He is the author of the eight-book series, The Days of Laura Ingalls Wilder, the eight-book series, The Younguns, and such new classics as *Dorothy—Return to Oz, Grizzly Adams & Kodiak Jack,* and other books and stories. Tedrow lives with his wife Carla and their four children in Winter Park, Florida.

An excerpt from *The Circus Escape*
Book Three in The Younguns series:

Upstairs, Terry hid behind the clothes hanging from the wooden pole that was nailed to the walls and served as a closet. He'd stuffed the cookie in his mouth as fast as he could, then turned around, not wanting his brother or sister to see that he'd accidentally on purpose taken two.

Gotta eat 'em quick.

Nibbling up the cookie crumbs off his shirt as fast as they dropped, Terry took out the advertising flyer he'd found in town. *Can't wait for the circus,* he nodded, looking at the handbill for the Harvest Festival that was coming. *Can't wait to eat all that candy.*

The Harvest Festival, with its food, games, and sideshows, was Mansfield's biggest fall event. It marked the end of the harvest when women could display their canning and baked goods, farmers could show off their animals, and children could just have fun.

Terry licked a cookie crumb from his lips, wishing he had grabbed a couple more. Then he heard his brother and sister coming up the stairs and wedged into the corner. Quietly picking up the almost invisible crumbs with his spit-wet fingertip, Terry folded up the handbill. In his other pocket was another flyer for the strange sideshow and all its forbidden delights. One that his father had told him not to look at because of the hootchy-kootchy dancing girls on it.

Without a second thought, Terry took out the forbidden flyer and felt a shiver up his spine. It always happened when he did something he wasn't supposed to.

"Where's Terry?" Sherry asked, looking into the room.

"Up here somewhere," Larry said. "Terry, Pa wants you downstairs."

Terry crouched as small as he could to keep them from seeing where he was hidden. If Pa wanted him, it meant work, which was something that Terry hated to do. He also didn't want his sister to rat on him that he was looking at the sideshow flyer. He silently read the words to himself:

FIRST TIME TO MANSFIELD'S HARVEST FESTIVAL
WOLF'S SIDESHOW OF FORBIDDEN DELIGHTS

COME SEE THE LARGEST GALLERY OF HUMAN ODDITIES
EVER ASSEMBLED FROM THE FAR CORNERS OF THE
EARTH!

Larry pointed to the hanging clothes and gave Sherry a *he's over there* nod. Sherry crept over. "What you doin'?"

"Nothin'," Terry mumbled, hiding the flyer.

"Pa told you not to look at that. I'm tellin'."

"You do and I'll stick a spider in your mouth when you're asleep."

"You still eatin' your one cookie?" Larry asked. Terry opened his mouth, showing a sticky mess.

"How come you always take longer to eat one cookie than we do?" Sherry wondered, parting the clothes and seeing the pile of crumbs.

Terry didn't want to admit to sneaking two, so he shrugged and mumbled with a gooey open mouth, "CauseI'maslowereater."

"You better get downstairs and see what Pa wants," Larry said.

"Gotta go to the privy," Terry mumbled, which was his greatest get-away excuse when faced with actually having to do chores. He swallowed the sticky lump and crawled out. He smiled at his sister. "Made up a nice poem for you."

"Don't want to hear it," she grumped, turning away. She didn't like Terry's poems.

"You'll like it."

"Tell it to yourself."

Terry ignored her and told her anyway, skipping in a tight circle around the room:

"I wish you were a brother,
Or even an old doll.
Heck, I'd even trade you,
For one of Ratz' the cat's hairballs."

"I'm gonna tell Pa!" she cried.

"Just kiddin'," he said, quickly trying to calm her down. "I'd rather have you around than an ol' hairball."

"Why do you make up those silly poems?" Larry asked.

Terry chuckled, wishing he could say the one in the back of his mind. Sherry looked at Larry who shook his head.

"Say it," Larry sighed.

"Say what?" Terry grinned.

"Say the other poem you're thinkin' 'bout."

"No," Sherry said, putting her hands over her ears, "I won't listen."

"Okay," Terry shrugged. "Since you asked for it, here goes:

"You look like a worm
Cooked in bug stew
With pink possum eyes
And turtle lips too.
With ears like a buzzard,
And legs like a spider
If I were you
I'd find a rock to hide under."

Terry smiled, looking at them both like he'd written a poem that should be recited at school. Larry just shook his head. "You're ignorant, you know that?"

Sherry took her hands from her ears. "I didn't hear a word you said, and I don't have turtle lips."